"Elissa, meet Cole Stephenson."

"We've met," Elissa said, rising slowly to her feet.

She forced herself to smile as she turned toward the man standing in the doorway. Her insides churned, her thighs trembled and she sensed Cole could see the panic in her eyes.

Despite the passage of five long years, Cole hadn't changed. Too bad. She'd hoped to find him less appealing. But he was as tall and strong and handsome as she remembered—altogether a very dangerous package.

One that, years before, had attracted and frightened her in equal measures.

Telling herself she'd been young and foolish then didn't dim her reaction today, however.

Despite all that had—and hadn't—passed between them, it was all Elissa could do not to run to her husband...or run for cover....

* * * *

TRIPLE TROUBLE:
Kayla, Elissa and Fallon—
identical triplets ready to take on the world!

Dear Reader,

September celebrates the onset of fall with a refreshing Special Edition lineup!

We begin this month with our THAT SPECIAL WOMAN! title. *The Secret Wife* by bestselling author Susan Mallery is book two in her TRIPLE TROUBLE miniseries and tells an uplifting tale about an estranged couple who renew their love. Look for the final installment of this engaging series in October.

Travel to the mountains of Wyoming with *Pale Rider* by Myrna Temte—a story about a lonesome cowboy who must show the ropes to a beautiful city girl, who captures his heart. Can she convince this hardened recluse that she loves him inside and out?

The sweet scent of romance catches these next heroes off guard in stories by two of our extraspecial writers! First, veteran author Carole Halston spins a delightful tale about a dad who's in the market for marriage but not love in *Mrs. Right*—book three of our FROM BUD TO BLOSSOM promotion series. And look what happens when a hard-driven city slicker slows down long enough to be charmed by a headstrong country gal in *All It Takes Is Family,* the next installment in Sharon De Vita's SILVER CREEK COUNTY series.

Finally, we round off the month with a story about the extraordinary measures a devoted dad will take for his infant son in *Bride for Hire* by *New York Times* bestselling author Patricia Hagan. And keep an eye out for *Beauty and the Groom*—a passionate reunion story by Lorraine Carroll.

I hope you enjoy each and every story to come!

Sincerely,

Tara Gavin,
Senior Editor

Please address questions and book requests to:
Silhouette Reader Service
U.S.: 3010 Walden Ave., P.O. Box 1325, Buffalo, NY 14269
Canadian: P.O. Box 609, Fort Erie, Ont. L2A 5X3

SUSAN MALLERY

THE SECRET WIFE

Published by Silhouette Books
America's Publisher of Contemporary Romance

To Larry—again—because you are still one of the
brightest stars in my universe. I wish you great
happiness and success. No matter what, I'll be here
for you and I'll always love you.

 SILHOUETTE BOOKS

ISBN 0-373-24123-2

THE SECRET WIFE

Books by Susan Mallery

SUSAN MALLERY

lives in Southern California where the eccentricities of a writer are considered fairly normal. Her books are reader favorites and bestsellers, with recent titles appearing on the Waldenbooks bestseller list and the *USA Today* bestseller list. Her 1995 Special Edition novel, *Marriage on Demand,* was awarded "Best Special Edition" by *Romantic Times* magazine.

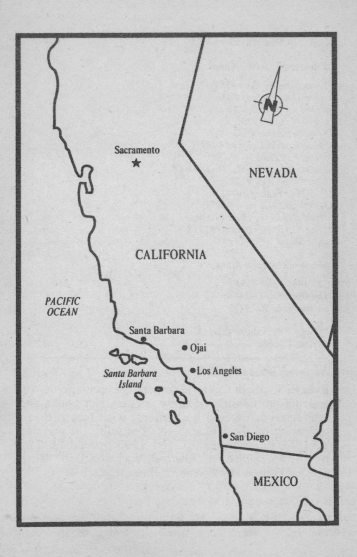

Chapter One

"Before I offer you the job I want to make sure you understand that, salarywise, we're talking about chicken feed."

Elissa Bedford glanced at the well-dressed older woman on the other side of the desk and laughed. "I noticed. Don't worry, Millie. I didn't apply because of the money. I'm a great admirer of what you're trying to do here, and I would like to help."

Elissa glanced around the office. The small administration building was nearly seventy years old. Despite the worn linoleum flooring and walls badly in need of paint, the charm of the original architecture showed through in rounded corners and molded ceilings. Between beat-up filing cabinets, where one might have expected inexpensive prints of famous paintings, original art covered the white spaces. Not the kind of art one found in museums, but creative masterpieces that came from the heart. They ranged from indistinguishable scribbles done in crayon to talented pen-and-ink drawings. A parade of children's contributions continuing a tradition that went back at least fifteen years.

The pictures themselves were different from those she remembered, as were the names of the young artists. Still, the familiar display reminded her of the pleasant times she'd spent here all those years ago. Some things hadn't changed. Had Cole?

Millie English, the woman conducting the interview, followed Elissa's gaze. "I see you've noticed our gallery. Those pictures are very special to us. They're chosen to be displayed for a number of reasons."

"I remember," Elissa said. "Talent has nothing to do with it. Having something put up on the office walls is a reward for good behavior, an improved grade or doing more than is expected."

Millie's pale eyebrows rose slightly. She glanced at the application in front of her. "You didn't say you were a former resident, so I'm going to have to assume you've done your research."

"Not really." Elissa leaned back in her chair. "My sisters and I used to visit the orphanage. It's been a long time, but I always remembered the gallery. I thought it was a wonderful idea. I still do."

"It's one of the reasons you want to help?"

"Yes," Elissa admitted, wondering if she was going to be forced to talk about all the others. Some of them were personal.

Millie studied her. The fifty-something office manager wore a stylish dress that might be off-the-rack, but only from the kind of department store that used the word *exclusive* to describe its clientele. Elegantly coiffured white-blond hair framed an attractive, well-made-up face. Millie used her half glasses both for reading and as a prop. Right now she stared over them, her expression kind. Yet Elissa had the feeling Millie English didn't suffer fools gladly.

"You don't know how tempted I am to pursue this line of questioning," Millie said, and tossed her glasses onto the worn desk. "However, we've been looking for help for nearly a month and you're only the second person to apply for the job." Her mouth twisted into a frown. "The other person had never worked in an office before."

Elissa motioned to her application. "You're welcome to call and check my references. I've had four years of experience in hospital administration. Although I enjoyed my work, I got tired of being tied up with paperwork. I want to work with people as well as computer keyboards. I thought this job would give me the chance to do both."

"You don't have to convince me," Millie said. "As I mentioned earlier, your salary includes room and board. You'll have several nights a week off, but you will be expected to be on duty some evenings. The orphanage is situated far enough from town to give us the room and privacy we need, yet it's close enough to be convenient for the schools. I think you'll like the area."

"I already do."

"Well, Elissa Bedford, I'm formally offering you the job. Would you like a chance to think about it?"

Elissa drew in a deep breath. As simple as that? Apparently Millie didn't have to check with anyone before making a final decision. "I wanted the job when I applied, and I still do."

"Great. When can you start?"

Before Elissa could answer the question, she heard footsteps in the outer office. Her throat tightened and the nervousness she'd been fighting returned full force.

Millie smiled and rose to her feet. "Ah, Cole's back.

Perfect timing. You can meet him. Now, don't let him scare you off. He's a little gruff and uncommunicative, but he's a brilliant director. If he hadn't stepped in to save the facility a couple of years ago, the Grace Orphanage would have gone under.'' Millie eyed Elissa speculatively. ''I suppose it would be too much to hope that you're single.''

''I'm—''

Millie cut her off with a wave. ''Forget I asked. Cole accuses me of wanting to run the world, and he's right. I swear, the man hasn't been on a date in over a year and for the life of me, I can't figure out why. It's not my business and I have to work at not meddling. I have four children, so I'm used to telling people what to do.'' She made an *X* on her chest. ''I promise not to play matchmaker.''

''I don't think Mr. Stephenson is going to be interested in me that way,'' Elissa said, knowing her comment qualified as the understatement of the year.

''Don't be so sure,'' Millie told her. ''In fact—'' The door to Millie's office opened. ''Cole. We were just talking about you. Look, I've finally found someone to help around the office. Elissa Bedford, meet Cole Stephenson.''

''We've met,'' Elissa said, rising slowly to her feet.

She forced herself to smile as she turned toward the man standing in the doorway. Her insides churned, her thighs trembled and she had a bad feeling he could see the panic in her face. But instead of running, she raised her chin slightly and met his hostile, disbelieving gaze.

Dark eyes fixed on her. Dark eyes filled with stormy emotions. Despite the passage of time, he hadn't changed much. Too bad. She was hoping to find him less appealing.

He was as tall and broad as she remembered. Thick hair fell to the collar of his short-sleeved shirt. Individually his facial features were faintly exotic—wide eyes that tilted down at the outside corners, a straight, broad nose, high cheekbones, wide jaw, firm mouth. Together they created a dangerous package. One that, years before, had drawn and frightened her in equal measures. Telling herself she'd been young and foolish then didn't lessen her reaction today. Despite all that had passed between them, despite the change in time and location, it was all she could do not to run toward him...or run for cover.

"Elissa."

His deep voice raised goose bumps on her skin. She waited for the inevitable questions, braced herself for his anger, but they never came. He simply looked at her. Was he comparing the woman to the girl he'd once known, or had it been so long, he couldn't remember much about her?

"So you *have* met," Millie said brightly. "How convenient."

Elissa spared the older woman a glance. There were enough undercurrents in the room that they were all at risk of drowning. Apparently Elissa was the only one to notice.

"It's been a while," Cole said. He leaned against the door frame. "What, five years?"

"Four years, eight months," she replied automatically, then bit down on her lower lip. She wanted to kick herself. Could she have sounded less mature? He was going to think she hadn't changed at all, and she had. Proving that was one of the reasons she was here.

"Five years. My, you were very young." Millie eyed them speculatively. "I'm sure the story is fascinating, but let's leave that for another time. Cole, if you'll excuse us, I want to show Elissa around the grounds and then let her get settled into her new quarters. You'll have plenty of time to renew your acquaintance in the next few days."

"Not so fast," he commanded.

Elissa hadn't known she'd been holding her breath until she let it out. Her sisters had warned her the plan wasn't going to work. After all this time, Cole would hardly welcome her with open arms. But what other choice did she have? She needed answers and he was the only one who had them. The job had been a perfect way in. Looked as if she was going to have to fall back to plan B…just as soon as she figured out what plan B was.

Millie walked around the desk and paused in front of Cole. "Don't you start anything," she said, poking his chest with each word. "We need help in this office and Elissa is the only decent applicant we've had in a month. I've been putting in extra hours, but I can't keep doing that indefinitely. If you're going to get all macho on me, then I'm out of here."

Cole straightened. "What does that mean?"

Millie didn't seem affected by his obvious irritation. She folded her arms over her chest. "Unless you can give me one good reason why Elissa shouldn't work here, I've already hired her. As the director, you can order me not to do that, but I'm warning you, if she goes, I go."

That got everyone's attention. "Millie, you don't have to do this for me," Elissa said quickly, wondering why the other woman was putting herself on the line.

"I'm not doing it for you," Millie told her, never taking her gaze off Cole. "And he knows it. What's it going to be?"

"You want one good reason why she shouldn't work here?" Cole asked.

"That's all."

He looked at Elissa. "You want to tell her, or should I?"

Elissa didn't know what to say. If Cole wanted to accuse her of something, there was nothing she could do to stop him.

"I'll do it, then," he said, returning his attention to Millie. "Elissa can't stay because she's my wife."

Millie deserved a lot of credit, Cole thought when his office manager didn't even blink. He didn't know if it was raising four kids, running her own business, or routinely entertaining groups of a hundred, but she was known for remaining unflappable. Just once he would like to see her speechless. Unfortunately, this wasn't the moment.

"Why should that matter? After all, aren't you the one always telling me your personal life is none of my business?" she asked without missing a beat. "Now, if you'll excuse us, I'd like to start the tour."

Cole didn't move, and Millie couldn't get around him to get out of the office. She glared, but he still refused to budge.

"I wasn't kidding," she said. "I give you and the kids as much as I can, but I'm about burned out here. We both know you can't manage this place without me."

"Why her?" he asked, wondering how much longer he would be able to pretend to ignore Elissa. Not looking at her didn't help. He sensed her, as if some homing beacon inside him had come to life as soon as she'd reentered his life.

"There's no one else here to hire," Millie said and glanced around the room. "At least give it a try. Three months."

After nearly five years of silence, Elissa walked back into his life. No explanation, nothing. And the one person who kept the orphanage running insisted he hire her. Even more amazing, he was considering it.

What the hell was wrong with him?

"Cole, it's not what you think," Elissa said.

He couldn't avoid looking at her forever. Her voice drew

him. Impressions formed. Gold-blond hair sitting high on her head. A few curls teasing her neck. Green eyes, pale skin, a wide mouth, usually smiling but now quivering at the corners. A soft white dress hiding curves. Curves he would recognize even after a lifetime of being away from her.

"Why are you here?" he asked. "If you need a job so badly, you could have found one in Los Angeles."

She stiffened. Did she know he'd kept track of her, or would she assume he was guessing? Of course he knew where she'd been living and working all these years. It was his job to know. She was his wife—or she had been once. Back before she'd left him.

"I want this one," she said.

"Why?"

"It doesn't matter why," Millie said. "I meant what I said, Cole. Decide. Give her a three-month trial. If she doesn't work out, we'll hire someone else. Assuming we can find anyone."

Millie was perfectly capable of following through on her threat to leave. In the past several months she'd worked nearly double her regular hours. Offering overtime or other incentives wasn't an option. Not only was the budget already stretched to breaking, Millie had always refused to accept a salary. Her presence at the orphanage was on a volunteer basis.

"You win." He moved into the room. "Three months." He fixed his gaze on Millie, but his words were for Elissa. "But if she makes one mistake, breaks one rule, she's out of here."

"Agreed," Millie said. "Come on, Elissa, let me show you around."

"That won't be necessary," Cole told his assistant. "It's

getting late. Why don't you head out and I'll show Elissa to her quarters?''

Millie's gaze narrowed. "Can you be trusted?"

"No," he said curtly. "But I won't hurt her."

"Or fire her?"

"That either."

At least not until he found out why she was back.

Millie turned to Elissa. "Is this all right with you? I'd insist on showing you around myself but I have a committee meeting for the art auction and—" She glanced at her watch, then shook her head. "He's really not so bad once you get to know him." She laughed. "Look who I'm telling. Of course you know that. Okay, kids, have fun. I'll be back tomorrow at the regular time."

She returned to her desk, pulled out a drawer and picked up a small handbag. "The application is filled out. We can do all those pesky government forms in the morning. Night."

With that, she sailed out of the room. Elissa looked a little shell-shocked. Cole was more used to Millie's ways. He knew when Millie was actually running late and when she was ducking out to avoid trouble. It wasn't tough to guess which she was doing this afternoon. He couldn't blame her. If he had an excuse, he would cut out, too.

"Have a seat," he said when they were alone.

As Elissa sank into the visitor's chair, he settled on a corner of the desk and stared at her. Stunned didn't begin to describe what he felt right now. His whole world had shifted, as if gravity had suddenly started working the other way, making things adhere to the ceiling instead of the floor.

He searched his heart, probing at emotions, trying to figure out what he was feeling. There was anger, a little disbelief, equal measures of desire for Elissa and disgust with himself. Maybe when the shock wore off he would feel more. Right now the dominant emotion was curiosity. Why had she come back? What did she want?

He answered that question himself, not wanting to think it was the truth, but knowing it must be. They could avoid the issue for days, or he could bring it out in the open right now.

"Are you here about a divorce?" he asked, telling himself he didn't care about the answer.

Her eyes widened. "No. I really just wanted the job."

The relief was instant, and annoying. He ignored it. "I don't believe you."

"That's okay. You don't have to." Her gaze slid away from his. "Do you want a divorce?"

Yes, his mind answered forcefully. Of course he did. They'd continued their farce of a marriage for far too long. It didn't make sense to stay connected legally when there was nothing between them emotionally or physically.

"That's not the point." He waited for her to call him on his evasive answer, but she didn't. Instead she studied the toes of her shoes as if they were fascinating. Her fingers twisted together on her lap and she shifted in her seat. Thank God he wasn't the only one feeling uneasy.

"You need to tell me—"

"I just wanted—"

They spoke at the same time. "Go ahead," he said.

She nodded. A loose curl jumped with the movement, caressing the back of her bare neck. Without wanting to, he remembered the feel of her skin against his fingers and his mouth. He recalled the taste of her, sweet and cool on the surface, hot and tempting just below.

Long-checked passion roared to life, searing him, leaving him nearly doubled over in pain and angling away from her so that she wouldn't see the instantaneous physical manifestation.

"I just want to let you know I didn't come here to cause trouble," she assured him, her voice low and quiet. "It's been a long time, Cole. Once, we meant something to each other. Now you ask me if I want a divorce and I can honestly answer that I don't know. I suppose I'm looking for closure. I thought spending some time together would allow me to do that."

She glanced up at him. Sincerity darkened her eyes to the color of summer grass. He didn't want to believe a word she said, yet she'd never been much of a liar. "There have been some changes in my life," she continued. "I don't want to work in an office forever. I've been thinking about going back to college and finishing my degree. Working here for a few months gives me the best of both worlds. I can get involved with some work that really makes a difference, and I have a chance to regroup."

Emotions shifted inside him, anger taking dominance over curiosity. She talked of recent changes in her life. He knew what that meant. A man.

The fact that neither of them had contacted the other in over four years didn't matter. The fact that *he'd* considered dating, had even thought about a divorce, was unimportant. Assumed betrayal fed rage.

"You played at your supposed acting career while you were growing up," he growled. "You played at being a wife, now you want to play at Lady Bountiful. We don't need you here. Get out!"

"No." Her low, calm voice was a contrast to his heated tones. She relaxed in her chair as if his outburst had eased her nervousness. "You agreed to let me work here for three months. You're many things, Cole Stephenson, but you're not a man who goes back on his word."

"If you're looking for a reconciliation—"

"I don't know what I'm looking for," she interrupted. "If you're so angry, why didn't you divorce *me?* You don't have an answer, do you? We were both young and we made a lot of mistakes."

"You walked out on me."

"You left first."

The unfair accusation drove him to his feet. "What the hell are you talking about? I never left you."

She leaned toward him. "You left me every day when you ate, slept and breathed work. I didn't exist for you except as a hostess and maid."

He noticed she didn't say bed partner. Just as well. In the end— He shook his head. He didn't want to think about that. He didn't want to think about any of it.

"Justify your actions any way you like," he said. "The bottom line is, I came home from work one day and you were gone."

He still remembered the shock of the quiet, the few words on the note, the stark emptiness of her half of the closet. She'd disappeared so completely, it was as if she'd never been there at all.

Elissa stood and looked at him. Late-afternoon light illuminated her pale skin. The last vestiges of childhood were gone, leaving her face hauntingly beautiful. He'd dreamed of her every night for a year, waking up aroused and alone. Then he'd forced himself to forget her. He'd nearly succeeded, too. He'd learned to live with the perpetual emptiness.

And now she was back.

"I'll accept half the blame," she said. "Maybe a little more. But not all of it."

"I'm not interested in reliving the past."

"Me, either." She gave him a faint smile. "Don't you

want a chance to put it all behind you? We used to be friends. Maybe we could be again.''

Yesterday if anyone had asked, he would have sworn his brief marriage was in the past. That he'd forgotten all about her. Now he wasn't so sure.

"We can't have changed that much," she said. "Look where we ended up. Right back where we started. At the orphanage.''

She had changed. She'd learned to stand up for herself. Five years ago his anger would have sent her sobbing to the bedroom. Afterward, she wouldn't have been able to look him in the eye for a week.

But despite the changes, he couldn't do what she wanted. He couldn't be friends. He'd never been her friend. He'd despised her until he'd known her, and then he'd loved her. In the past few years he'd grown to hate her. There was no middle ground.

"Three months," he said at last. "That's what I agreed to. Millie will explain your responsibilities. She's your boss, not me. Our first priority is the children. I don't want them confused or hurt. Therefore, as far as they're concerned, you're just Elissa Bedford. They don't have to know we're married.''

She squared her shoulders. "If that's how you want it. I meant what I said, Cole. I want answers, but I'm not here to make trouble.''

"Too late. You already have. And while we're reaffirming ourselves, let me remind you you're here on probation. One screwup, one false move and you're out. I wouldn't want to have to make this place work without Millie, but if that's my only option, I'm willing to risk it.''

"Fine.''

He forced himself to walk toward the door. "Your quarters are downstairs in the main building. Third door on the right. I'm sure you can find it yourself. Do you need help with your luggage?''

"I can manage."

"Good. Dinner is at five-thirty. Don't be late."

He made it into the hallway before she called him back. "Cole?"

He paused, but didn't turn toward her. "What?"

"Can't we *try* to be friends?"

He heard the plea in her voice, the tone that told him she didn't think her request was so awful. He thought about the weeks he'd tried to drink himself into forgetfulness, the endless nights he'd spent staring at the few pictures he had of her, tracing the flat, cold paper, wondering what he'd done that had made her leave. He recalled the gaping hole in his chest, the one left after she'd ripped out his heart.

He who had sworn never to love, never to trust, had loved and trusted only one. Elissa. And she had left him.

"No," he said quietly. "We can't be friends."

Chapter Two

Elissa placed her suitcase on the bed and glanced around the room. Even though she'd visited the orphanage several times in the past and knew better, she'd assumed her living quarters would consist of a narrow bed covered by a clean but worn bedspread, a single nightstand and maybe a bare bulb hanging from the ceiling. Obviously she'd been watching too many productions on Masterpiece Theatre. She might be the most recent resident at the Grace Orphanage, but this was the 1990s, not the 1890s, and she was a new employee, not a newly orphaned Sara Crewe.

She actually had two rooms, including a small but pleasant living area complete with a sofa, wing-back chair and a window that overlooked the rose garden. Her bedroom was spacious and airy, with light walls and drapes. A pale blue comforter covered the double bed. There was an oak dresser, two nightstands and a reading lamp. One door led to a good-sized closet, the other to a small private bath.

"I like it," she said aloud, then glanced at her suitcase. She'd left most of her belongings back in her apartment in Los Angeles. The odds of Cole actually letting her stay had been so remote, she hadn't bothered to pack much. "Rather bring too little than cart it all back."

The homey wisdom made her feel better. Although right now, it wouldn't take much. She opened the suitcase and pulled out the three dresses folded on top. After shaking them out, she walked over to the closet and hung them up.

As she smoothed the soft cotton fabric, she tried to tell herself it hadn't been so bad after all. At least he hadn't thrown her out.

But he hadn't wanted her here, either.

Elissa sighed and closed her eyes. Why was she surprised? In all the time they'd been apart, he'd never once tried to contact her, had never once tried to reconcile. The fact that he also hadn't bothered to ask for a divorce was a small comfort.

Maybe he'd forgotten all about her. Maybe coming back would remind him and he would want to end the marriage as quickly as possible.

That thought sent a flash of pain through her. Her breath lodged in her throat and she had to force herself to inhale slowly until the discomfort eased. She opened her eyes and squared her shoulders. For now, she was here. Unless something horrible happened, she had three months to figure out what she wanted from her life and from her husband. They'd kept things on hold for too long. One way or the other, by the time she left, she was going to have made a decision.

"You are," she told herself as she continued unpacking, "quite insane. Fallon and Kayla would be happy to tell you so."

She smiled at the thought of her sisters. Both women had

tried to talk her out of her plan to show up unannounced at the orphanage. They'd felt Cole would react better if he'd had some time to get used to the idea of seeing her again. What she hadn't explained—mostly because it was just too humiliating to admit—was the fact that if he was given notice, he might refuse to see her altogether. At least by arriving without warning, she had surprise on her side.

"You look nice. Millie must have hired you. Cole usually hires people who don't smile much."

Elissa turned toward the sound of the voice. A tall, slender girl stood in the doorway to her bedroom.

"I'm Tiffany," the girl said, and grinned. "I knocked but you didn't hear me." The grin faded. "Do you want me to go away?"

"Of course not." Elissa walked toward her. "I'm Elissa Bedford, and you're right. Millie did hire me."

"We can always tell." Tiffany was nearly as tall as Elissa's five feet five inches, with long, curly dark hair and almond-shaped brown eyes. Café-au-lait skin emphasized high cheekbones. A wide, mobile mouth curved up.

"I'm twelve," the preteen announced. "I'll be thirteen in less than four months. I'm a Christmas baby." Tiffany leaned against the door frame. She wore white shorts and a peach T-shirt. She had long arms and legs, smooth with a hint of muscle moving under perfect skin. She was already beautiful. In a couple of years Tiffany was going to cause traffic accidents just by walking down the street.

"Gee, my birthday's about as far from Christmas as you can get," Elissa said. "It's July first."

"Being a Christmas baby is special, of course, but I'd rather be born in the summer. At least then you get presents twice a year." The girl walked to the bed and sat down. Brown eyes fixed on Elissa's face. "I'm not really an orphan. My mother's a junkie. She's tried to kick it, but she can't. This is a more healthy environment for me. While I'd like her to straighten out, it's not likely. I'm dealing with that. Everyone thinks because I'm really smart and mature enough to understand I'm going to be a psychologist.'' She wrinkled her nose. ''I don't think so. I'd prefer one of the hard sciences. Where things are concrete. You know, like quantum physics.''

''Sounds great,'' Elissa said, realizing she didn't know enough about the difference between ''hard'' and ''soft'' sciences, let alone quantum physics, to have a comment on Tiffany's choice. And she wasn't sure she completely bought into Tiffany's claim of being so well-adjusted about being in an orphanage while her mother wrestled with a drug problem. ''How long have you been here?''

''A couple of years. I was in a foster home for a while, but that didn't work out. They thought my mother was dead, so I came here, but she wasn't. Cole said I could stay. So did the judge.''

Elissa returned to her open suitcase and pulled out several more dresses. Tiffany studied the floral prints. ''You have pretty stuff. But I don't see any jeans.''

''I don't wear jeans very much.''

''Shorts?''

''Sorry, no. I prefer skirts and dresses.''

''That's kinda weird.''

Elissa chuckled. ''Good weird or bad weird?''

The preteen grinned. ''Good weird. How'd you get your hair like that?''

Elissa touched the top of her head. ''I pulled it all up in a ponytail, then pinned it in place.'' She leaned forward and fingered Tiffany's curls. ''I could show you how to do it. You'd look great. Have you tried a French braid?''

Tiffany shook her head. ''I can't ever get it right.''

"It's not so hard. I'll show you. You can even learn to do it on yourself, although it takes a little patience."

Light filled dark eyes. "Really? That would be way cool."

"Way cool is my life," Elissa said solemnly.

Tiffany flopped back on the bed. "Did you meet Cole?"

"Sure."

"What'd you think of him?"

"He's changed," she said without thinking, then silently groaned.

Tiffany bounced to her feet. "How long have you known him?"

"Since I was your age. But we haven't seen each other in a long time."

"Wow. He's so old. So you've known him like forever."

"Sometimes it feels that way."

"What was he like?"

Elissa picked up a pair of loafers and placed them on the floor of the closet. "Pretty much a younger version of the way he is now. Very together, very determined."

Intense, she thought, remembering the way he'd stared at her when they'd first met. She'd had the distinct impression he'd disliked her for no reason other than what he thought her to be.

"Was he like other kids? Did he, you know, play games and stuff?"

"Sure."

Elissa realized five minutes too late that she was probably going to get in trouble for this conversation. Cole had warned her not to tell the children they were married. While he hadn't said anything about them admitting to a previous acquaintance, she had a feeling he assumed she would figure that one out on her own.

Excuse me for not getting it right, she thought to herself.

Frankly, some innocent chit-chat about their mutual past was nothing when compared with the deceptions she had planned for later. But if she didn't want to get fired on her first day, she was going to have to find a way to distract Tiffany.

She glanced at the clock and realized it was nearly 5:30. "What time is dinner?" she asked.

The girl followed her gaze. "Yikes. In a couple of minutes. We'd better get going." She grimaced. "If we get there too late, we have to sit with the little kids. They're okay and all, but sheesh, they really make a mess when they eat."

She grabbed Elissa's hand and tugged her into the hallway. "Come on. You can finish unpacking later." She barely paused long enough to let Elissa pull her suite door shut.

"I'm coming," Elissa said, laughing as she was dragged along. They stepped out of the building and into the early-evening breeze.

The Ojai valley was about two hours north and west of Los Angeles. In the summer the temperatures climbed well into the hundreds during the day. September might mean fall in other parts of the country, but here it was just another month of warm days with perfect blue skies and cool, star-filled nights.

Despite Tiffany's determined pace toward the dining hall, Elissa looked around at the grounds. It was much as she remembered, with lush lawns and tall, full trees. Bikes and basketballs sat in patches of shade. A couple of dozen children of various ages were all headed for the same low, one-story building at the end of the driveway.

She tried to superimpose the reality of what she was seeing onto the memories in her head. The trees were taller, the bushes thicker. Of course, the children's faces were different. But the orphanage itself seemed much the same. There was an air of quiet contentment around the place. Children might prefer a "normal" upbringing with natural parents, but if they had to survive on their own, the Grace Orphanage provided an admirable alternative.

"Oh, look!" Tiffany said, then waved her free hand. "Cole, Cole, over here. Look. I'm bringing Elissa to the dining room."

Cole spotted them. For a moment their eyes met. Elissa knew if they had been alone, he would have turned away and not acknowledged her presence. But with Tiffany and the other children around, he didn't have a choice. He gave her a tight smile that didn't come close to warming the chill in his dark eyes, then turned his attention to the pre-teen.

Instantly the cold heated to a welcoming warmth. "Are you acting as the official greeter?" he asked as he approached.

Tiffany nodded. "I like Elissa. Millie hired her, right?"

Cole touched a hand to his chest. "I made one mistake and you're never going to let me forget it. I fired the guy, didn't I?"

"Mr. Benjamin was mean and he had bad breath," Tiffany said, and shuddered. "None of the kids liked him. But Elissa's nice, so I forgive you." She looked around. "There's not gonna be any good seats left. I'll run ahead and save places, okay?"

She took off before either of them could respond. Elissa found herself watching the girl's long-legged stride, staring after her, knowing the only alternative was to look at Cole. And that would never do. Expecting him to be unfriendly was very different from actually experiencing the distance firsthand.

However, once Tiffany disappeared into the building,

Elissa had to focus on her companion. She risked glancing at him, only to find him staring at her.

She could get lost in his gaze. He'd always been intense, and that's what inevitably drew her in. Even as a child, she'd been curious about his soul-stirring thoughts. She'd wanted to understand the complex workings of his mind.

What was he thinking now? Did he wonder why she was there? Had he thought about her while they'd been apart? Did he remember, as she did, the good times they'd shared? Had he missed her even a little?

She wanted to know that he still cared, that some part of him had longed for her. But if that were true he would have come after her, or at least tried to get in touch with her. And he hadn't. Not even once.

"Tiffany is very interesting," she said when it became apparent he wasn't going to be the one to speak first.

"In what way?"

Elissa shrugged and turned toward the dining hall. Cole fell into step beside her. All the children had disappeared inside and they were the only ones left on the path. Sunlight shone through leafy branches, creating patches of light and dark. The moment had a surreal quality, as if she were living a dream.

"She told me about her mother," Elissa said. "That the woman is alive, but unable to take care of her."

"In polite circles we say that Tiffany's mom has a drug problem. For a while she was missing and presumed dead. That's how Tiffany ended up here. Her mother showed up in a hospital emergency room, half-dead from an overdose. Rehab hasn't helped in the past, so the judge said Tiffany could stay here."

"That's sad," Elissa said, thinking that she and her sisters might complain about their childhood, but at least they'd had parents and a home.

"What's important for Tiffany is that her mom is alive," Cole continued. "She can tell herself she still has one parent, so she's not a real orphan."

Cole had been a real orphan, Elissa remembered. And his dream of being adopted had never come true.

They walked in silence for a couple of seconds, then Cole asked, "How did you know I was here?"

"The orphanage newsletter. My sisters and I each get a copy. There was an article when you became the director."

He grunted in response. She wondered what he was thinking. Only people donating money received a copy of the newsletter. Did he think she was doing that out of concern, or maybe even out of guilt? She didn't have the courage to ask, so she searched for a question that would make *him* squirm.

"How did you know I was in Los Angeles?" she asked.

"You're my wife. It's my business to know where you are."

"But not your business to stay in touch?"

He ignored the question. "I don't know why you're here, Elissa, and I don't want to know. As far as I'm concerned, you're just another employee. I expect you to do whatever Millie tells you. You're to be here for the children and to stay out of trouble. Your social life takes a back seat to your work."

"My social life?" They'd reached the dining hall, but neither of them opened the door to step inside. "That's quite an assumption. If I had one that was that interesting, I would hardly be willing to bury myself up here. Believe me, you have nothing to worry about."

His forbidding expression said he didn't believe her.

"What's your point?" she asked. "Are you accusing me of seeing another man?" If only that were true. If only she *had* been able to forget Cole enough to date someone else.

But she hadn't. Even if she'd been interested, she wouldn't have allowed herself to pursue anything. Despite the nearly five-year separation, she considered herself a married woman.

"Whatever else has been between us," she said quietly, "I'm still your wife. I haven't betrayed you."

"Of course you have." He pulled open the door.

A burst of laughter surrounded them, effectively ending the conversation. Elissa clenched her hands into tight fists, then stepped into the building. Cole might have thought he'd won that round, but if he figured he'd defeated her, he was wrong. Many things had changed in the time they'd been apart. For one thing, she'd grown up.

"Over here!" Tiffany called. The preteen stood and waved.

Cole let out an audible groan. Tiffany had saved two seats together.

As they made their way across the room, Elissa glanced around. Children and employees ate together at round tables seating eight. Wide windows opened onto the grounds, letting in light and giving the room an open feel. A long buffet filled the far wall. A few children were in line, but most had already served themselves and found seats.

At the front of the room was a small platform. Cole headed toward it. Elissa didn't know if she should follow him or take her seat next to Tiffany.

"I'm going to introduce you," he said curtly. "You don't have to say anything. Just stand where the kids can see you."

Voices faded as soon as he took his place. He smiled, a genuine smile, like the one he'd given Tiffany. Elissa wondered if she was ever going to see one aimed in her direction.

"Evening, everyone," he said.

"Hi, Cole," the children and adults answered as one.

He made a couple of announcements about study hours and which movies would be rented for the weekend. Elissa used the time to glance around at the children.

They were an eclectic group, ranging in age from five to seventeen. There were fifty-seven children in all, and a staff of eighteen, including herself. Cole was the director, Millie the office manager. Two couples lived on the premises permanently and eleven college students worked part-time. Some came in on afternoons and weekends, others worked a night shift that allowed them to have free room and board while providing supervision in the sleeping quarters.

"Elissa is the newest member of our family," he said and nodded to her.

She smiled at the children.

"She's here to assist Millie in the office and to fill in anywhere she's needed. However, Elissa's only going to be with us for a couple of months."

She didn't hear the rest of what he was saying—she was too furious. Bad enough that he accused her of betraying him, now he was telling the children she wasn't going to be sticking around. She felt like the witch in Snow White. Why not just make her wear a sign. Warning—Do Not Take Apples From This Woman.

When Cole had finished his speech, the children clapped politely. Cole led her over to the seats Tiffany had saved. "Help yourself to the buffet," he said, and turned away.

"Aren't you eating with us?" Tiffany asked.

"Not tonight."

"But you *always* eat with us," she said, her voice close to a whine. "I saved you a seat."

He ruffled her bangs. "Next time, kid. I promise."

With that, he was gone.

As Tiffany took her through the buffet line and explained

which items were delicious and which should be avoided at all costs, Elissa couldn't help thinking about Cole. He'd been difficult and withdrawn when she'd known him before, and that hadn't changed. If anything, he'd gotten worse. But one thing was the same—he was a man of his word. He'd obviously meant what he said when he'd told her they would never be friends.

Three hours later Elissa closed the door to her two-room suite and breathed a sigh of relief. She'd enjoyed spending time getting to know the children, but it had been a long day. Her evening usually consisted of an occasional dinner out or some quality time with a good book. Trying to concentrate on a board game while being bombarded with questions from fifty curious children had sapped the last of her reserves. Still, she had one more thing she had to do before she could crawl into bed.

She found the blank pad of paper she'd left on her nightstand and returned to the living room. After clicking on a floor lamp, she settled into a corner of the sofa and nibbled on the end of her pen.

The kids' clothes were fine. Many were obviously hand-me-downs, but that happened in every family, not just at orphanages. Some of the buildings needed painting. That was one option, although not one that thrilled her.

She closed her eyes and thought about what she'd seen on her way into the dining room. Trees, grass, bushes, a couple of bikes, a basketball. She replayed the image and realized the basketball had looked flat, while the bikes were old and dented. Hmm, now that she thought about it, she didn't remember seeing any playground equipment. That's where she would start.

She opened her eyes and began writing. It didn't matter that Cole hated her, or that he would probably fire her if he knew what she was doing. This wasn't about him; it was about the children. Besides, she wouldn't be dissuaded from her plan. She could have everything in place with just a couple of phone calls. She couldn't wait to see the looks on the children's faces. Or the look on Cole's.

Chapter Three

Cole stepped into the administration building and heard the sound of female voices. Normally that wasn't enough to drive him back outside, but he recognized one of the voices as Elissa's. In the week she'd been working at the orphanage, he'd done his best to avoid her. He told himself he wasn't being cowardly; he was simply making the best of an awkward situation.

The excuse sounded feeble, even to himself, so instead of disappearing into the afternoon, he continued toward Millie's office.

Elissa's work space was in the reception area. He rounded the corner and braced himself for the impact of seeing her. No matter how many times he told himself it didn't matter, every time their eyes met, he felt the connection clear down to his soul. He hadn't known hatred and longing could coexist so easily.

But instead of finding Elissa working hard, he found her

sitting on the floor surrounded by boxes of photographs and three young girls.

They didn't notice him at first. Gina, the orphanage's ten-year-old resident genius, knelt next to Elissa, intently watching as Elissa braided Tiffany's hair. Shanna stood behind them, peering over Elissa's shoulder. As usual, the barely eight-year-old motormouth couldn't stop talking.

"How'd you learn how to do that?" Shanna asked, then reached up and touched her own bright red braid. "Could I learn? Can we learn to do our own? Maybe you could teach us and we could do each other before school. I like my braid. Do you like yours, Tiffany?"

Tiffany tried to turn to see what Elissa was doing. Elissa laughed. "Hold still. I can't braid if you're moving around."

"But I'm still not sure I understand how to do this."

"We'll practice for as long as it takes," Elissa told her.

Shanna leaned forward, resting one hand on Elissa's shoulder. The trust inherent in that gesture made Cole's gut tighten. Elissa had been at the orphanage only a few days, yet she'd already made a home for herself with the children. He supposed he should be pleased she fit in so easily. It was better for everyone. Yet he hated the fact that they liked and trusted her. Why couldn't they see what he saw? That she would leave them as easily as she'd left him? That none of this mattered to her? It was just an act, and as soon as he figured out what she wanted, he was going to throw her out of the orphanage and his life.

But not today. Today it was enough to stand in the doorway and watch her laugh and smile with the children.

In her summer dress, with her long blond hair spilling around her shoulders and the three girls gazing adoringly at her, she looked like a model in a photo shoot. The four of them were a study in contrasts. Elissa fair and blond,

Shanna with her freckles and red hair, and the other two girls adding the exotic elements. Tiffany's Eurasian and African-American heritage gave her a beauty seldom seen. No one knew about Gina's parents, but Cole figured she had a combination of Anglo and Asian features.

Four different females who looked so right together. It couldn't be chance. As he'd first thought—a photo shoot. But these kids hadn't been paid to act as if they liked her. They were doing it because their feelings were genuine. Weren't children supposed to be good judges of character?

Not in this case.

He leaned against the door frame and folded his arms over his chest. Gina was the first to glance up and notice him. Her shy smile broadened. She jumped up and ran to him. He picked her up and held her close.

"Hi, angel face," he said as she buried her face in the crook of his neck.

"Cole!" Tiffany tried to turn toward him, and giggled when she couldn't. "Look. Elissa's braiding our hair. Isn't it cool?"

"Very nice."

"I like my braid," Shanna said. "It's pretty. We're all gonna learn to braid like that, then we can do our hair every morning."

"Sounds like a great plan," he said, noticing Elissa offered him a tight smile and nothing else. He turned his attention to the child in his arms.

"What's new?" he asked softly.

"I want to learn French," Gina whispered.

He knew better than to laugh. "Why?"

"My teacher played a CD today that had some French words in it and I thought they were pretty."

"Did you ask her about learning another language?" Gina already spoke Spanish fluently.

Nod. "There's some cassettes I can listen to, and maybe she can find a tutor." She raised her head and stared intently at him. "I told her I didn't have any money."

Familiar frustration assaulted him. The budget at the orphanage had been stretched past the point of breaking. This was the price he paid for autonomy. There was never enough cash.

He shifted the slight weight in his arms. Gina might be two years older than Shanna, but she was nearly an inch shorter. However, the miniature package housed a brain that bordered on supergenius.

"You tell your teacher to get you the tapes and set up time with a tutor. We can afford it."

"Really?" Gratitude shone from her brown eyes.

"No problem." He set her on the ground.

Without wanting to, he glanced at Elissa. She gave him a brief smile.

"Despite how it looks, I'm really working," she said, finishing Tiffany's braid and securing the end with a rubber band. "Millie asked me to go through all the pictures and pick out the best ones. It's for the fortieth-anniversary issue of the newsletter. She said you were planning a special bound edition."

"That's right." They'd discussed it at the last board meeting. The book would be a pictorial history of the orphanage and sold to anyone interested at a small profit.

Tiffany stood and held out her hands. "Come on, girls. It's nearly study time. We don't want to be late. Thanks for doing our hair, Elissa." She grinned at Cole. "You should grow your hair long."

He tugged on her earlobe. "Not in this lifetime."

"You wouldn't look so old."

He stepped into the room and jerked his thumb in the direction of the door. "Don't you have to be somewhere?"

"Yes, sir." She grabbed each of the other girls and ushered them outside.

Elissa leaned back against her desk. "I hope you don't mind that I'm making friends with the children. You said not to tell them about our marriage, but you didn't say I couldn't get involved."

He shrugged. "Seems like a waste of time to me. You *are* leaving in a few months."

"I have a three-month trial," she said. "Not a death sentence. If you like my work and I like being here, I might just stay on."

He didn't dare think about that. He couldn't bear to have Elissa in his life. Not for any length of time. "I'm sure you'll find our world very boring."

"I don't know. There's a consistency that provides comfort. I can always count on you to think the worst of me."

Her quick response made him raise his eyebrows. He stepped closer, then crouched down beside her. Instead of flinching, she glared defiantly. He reached for the stack of photos on the floor beside her and picked them up.

"Were these already sorted?" he asked.

Her gaze narrowed. She seemed to be deciding if she was going to let him change the subject or not. In the end she did, leaning toward him to gaze at the black-and-white photo of twenty children standing in front of the administration building.

"There are boxes of photos by years," she said. "That helps. Some of them are identified, but others are blank on the back. We have school photos to cross-reference. I'm going to pick out a couple hundred of what I think are the best. Millie said you would take those to the planning meeting and make the final decision." She pointed to the boxes spread out around her. "The oldest are by the door, the newest over here."

He set down the pile he'd grabbed, then reached for a box by her left foot. After flipping through it, he put it back and took another one a couple of years earlier.

He settled on the floor and stretched his long legs out in front of him. The pictures were fifteen years old. He looked through them, finding familiar faces, snapshots of himself. But he didn't pause at any of those. Instead he searched until he found a picture of three girls.

Silently he handed it to Elissa. She took it and sighed. "Oh, my. Look at that. We're wearing the identical dresses Kayla and Fallon always hated."

She held the photo out so he could see it, too. Three girls, identical triplets of maybe ten or eleven, stood in front of a tree. The girls wore green dresses, with matching ribbons in their long, curly hair. They gazed at the camera solemnly, as if carrying out some sacred duty.

"We look a little smug," Elissa admitted. "It must have been our first visit here. I think 'adopting' an orphanage had been our manager's idea. We weren't really interested until we met everyone. I vaguely recall that first day being a disaster. Did everyone hate us?"

"Yup. You waltzed in here with your big car and fancy wrapped presents. Untouchable princesses."

She handed him the picture and shrugged. "That's hardly the truth. I think the whole visit was set up badly. It was better later when we just came out and played. I remember meeting you."

He didn't say anything, not wanting to encourage her to speak of those times. She didn't get the hint.

"You'd escaped for the day," she continued. "I found you out in the orange grove, reading. You were tall even then. Dark, with a stare that stopped me in my tracks."

He remembered everything about that moment. He'd been reading a textbook for school. Anything had been better than sticking around to entertain slumming celebrities. A snapping twig broke the silence of the afternoon. He'd looked up and seen a young girl walking toward him. She'd stepped from shadow into sunlight and it was as if she were an angel come from heaven.

He remembered the way the light had caught the gold in her hair. Her warm smile had slipped past his barriers and reached down to his hollow heart, filling him with a sense of belonging. Until then, he'd never been interested in girls, had never thought females had a purpose other than to be annoying. At fifteen, he hadn't known anything about love, nor had he fallen in love. That had come later. What he'd felt was the connection, the realization that this girl was going to be important to him for the rest of his life.

"Let's see," Elissa said. "I believe I walked up to you and said hello. And you told me to go away. Gee, Cole, it's been fifteen years and nothing has changed. One would think we could make a little progress."

The pain in her eyes belied her light tone.

He didn't want to think about her being hurt. "Maybe you should have listened," he said.

"And gone away?" she asked, then continued without waiting for him to answer. "I don't think so. We would never have talked, never have gotten to know each other." Her green eyes darkened with emotion. "Whatever might have happened between us, I don't regret the relationship. Or the marriage. I'm sorry if you regret either."

"A lot of things went wrong," he said, not willing to admit that his only regret was losing her. He took a deep breath and leaned back against the desk. If Elissa had never entered his life, could he feel more empty than he had when she'd left? He wasn't sure.

Silence filled the room. Elissa continued to flip through

pictures, but he sensed she wasn't really seeing them. While she was occupied, he had an opportunity to study her.

She wore her hair loose and it curled over her shoulders and down her back. He remembered the feel of those curls in his hands, the way the silky strands had slipped through his fingers. Light makeup accentuated her eyes and cheekbones. Her mouth was straight, not quite as mobile as it had been all those years ago, not so intent on giving away her secrets.

She hadn't changed the way she dressed, and he was glad. Feminine prints in soft fabric flowed over her body, merely hinting at concealed curves. Full skirts flirted with bare calves, tiny sleeves exposed smooth arms. In a world of jeans and T-shirts, she was an anachronism.

He feasted on the vision of her as if he'd been starving. In the past week he'd tried to convince himself that her return to his life meant nothing. He wouldn't let her matter. But all the telling in the world didn't change the fact that there was a part of him that had died when she'd left. Rebirth, however unexpected and unwanted, was still painful.

Elissa studied one photograph for a minute, then held it out to him. He leaned forward and saw himself eight years ago, standing proudly in his cap and gown at his graduation from UCLA. A young, shy Elissa stood at his side.

"Our first date," she said.

"You look about fifteen."

"I turned seventeen two weeks after this picture was taken. We were both still kids. You look so serious and determined. You always had a lot to prove." She set the picture down and glanced at him. "Right now you're a long way from that New York law firm, Cole. I thought you were going to make partner before you were thirty-five. What happened?"

"How'd I get here?"

"Why'd you give it all up?"

He shrugged. "I got tired of the rat race, and the rats winning. Like you and your sisters, I continued to receive the orphanage's newsletter. There were some financial problems, as well as a lack of administrative talent. I had money, I was looking for something different. This seemed an ideal opportunity."

"I remember you in suits and ties. The jeans are a change...a nice one."

"Jeans are more comfortable."

She angled toward him. "Millie says that you still practice law. You have a small office in Ojai and you do enough there so you don't take a salary out of the orphanage. She also said you do lots of pro bono work for a women's shelter."

Unwelcome embarrassment made him clear his throat. "Millie talks too much. I'm not any kind of hero, so don't go thinking I am. I do the law work because I like it and because it pays the bills. The shelter needs somebody and I'm convenient. Nothing more."

He wanted to ask her what other changes she'd noticed. How else had she been pleasantly surprised? How much of their life did she remember?

"You're more than convenient," she said. "But if the compliment bothers you, I won't repeat it."

Before he could lie and say that nothing about her bothered him, Millie walked in. If she thought there was anything odd about Cole and Elissa sitting on the floor together, looking at old photographs, she didn't say anything.

"Found anything we can use?" she asked, crouching down next to Elissa and picking up a handful of pictures.

"Quite a few. I'm separating them into different piles so that you can see an assortment from each decade. I thought you'd want to have a nice mix, and not a majority of pictures from any one year."

"Good thinking." Millie glanced at him and raised her eyebrows as if pointing out Elissa's efficiency. There was no point in explaining that he didn't object to his wife's work habits as much as he did to her presence.

"Who are those three girls?" Millie asked, holding out the picture of Elissa and her sisters. As the older woman asked the question, her gaze fell on the writing on the back. Her mouth opened but she didn't speak.

"My sisters and I are triplets," Elissa said. "We used to visit the orphanage." She shrugged self-consciously. "When we were younger we were on a television series called 'The Sally McGuire Show.' It was about an orphan. The three of us played Sally. The studio set up the first visit for publicity, but my sisters and I came back because we enjoyed visiting."

Millie stared at her. "I don't know what to say."

"Me, either," Cole added. "I've never seen Millie at a loss for words before."

His office manager made a rude gesture with her arm. "Quit trying to get the best of me," she said, and returned her attention to Elissa. "I've seen the show a few times. Isn't it still running on cable?"

Elissa moaned. "Far too often. Please don't make me watch it or tell anyone about this. My sisters and I did the best we could, but none of us were very good actors. After the first season, we didn't really like being on the show, but we didn't have much choice."

Millie studied the photograph, then Elissa. "You weren't interested in the fame and fortune?"

Elissa grimaced. "Fortunately there wasn't much of either. Seventeen years ago children weren't as big on television as they are now, especially girls. We had the occasional promotional appearance, but trust me, it was something we dreaded rather than looked forward to. We would have preferred meeting other kids one-on-one, but our mother never wanted that. She was more interested in the exposure possibilities.''

There hadn't been much money, either, Cole thought, remembering how a trust fund had paid for Elissa's college fees and board, but not anything else. All three sisters had had part-time jobs to cover spending money.

''You make it sound like it wasn't any fun at all,'' Millie complained. ''There had to be something you liked.''

''There was,'' Elissa said. ''Most of the time the actual work could be fun, although it got tiring and we really wanted our regular lives back. If the series did anything, it brought my sisters and myself even closer.''

''What is it like being a triplet?'' Millie asked.

Cole glanced at Elissa as she talked. Funny how despite knowing her sisters and having seen her with them so many times, he thought of her as a unique woman. In his mind, the sisters were as different as any three siblings. Physically, he could easily tell them apart, while their individual personalities only added to their separateness. Fallon was the oldest and the leader. She made decisions easily, took charge and expected to get her way. Kayla was the youngest, by how many minutes he couldn't remember. She took chances, had a charming air about her and generally saw life as an adventure.

Elissa was the middle child, the peacemaker. On more than one family gathering, he'd watched her mediate her sisters' spirited discussions. She'd subjugated her own wishes for theirs.

Now, watching her explain to Millie the intricacies of filming a series, he wondered how many times she'd wanted things done a different way but hadn't bothered to stand up for herself. In their marriage she'd usually been the one to bend to his desires. Usually, but not always.

Over the past years she'd changed. He wasn't sure if it was because she'd been on her own or if it was the result of growing up, but she didn't have a problem standing up to him anymore. Had her sisters noticed the difference, also?

Her sisters. He hadn't seen them in years. The last time had been a couple of months before Elissa had left him. From the time he'd slipped the engagement ring on Elissa's finger until he'd walked into the empty apartment and realized she'd left him, he'd been a part of her family. For the first time in his life he'd belonged. He hadn't realized how much he'd wanted a family—had needed the roots—until he'd had it all and lost it.

This time would be different. This time she wasn't going to suck him into her world. This time when she walked out of his life he wasn't going to miss her, because this time she wasn't going to get close enough to cause damage.

"How's it going?" Fallon asked.

Elissa leaned back on the bed and fluffed the pillows behind her head. "Great," she said enthusiastically into the phone.

"Liar." Fallon's soft voice took the sting from the word. "It's not going great or even well."

"You can't know that."

"Yeah, I can. For two reasons. First, I know Cole. There's no way he's going to let you walk back into his life without protesting, even just a little. And second, I know you. Seeing him has to be really tough. So I'll ask the question again. How's it going?"

Elissa closed her eyes and for a brief second wished she'd been born an only child. Then she wouldn't have to put up with this kind of well-meant meddling. Of course, the price of that would be loneliness and isolation. Meddling was a small price to pay for the knowledge that she was loved and cared about.

"Sometimes I think everything is going to be fine," Elissa said honestly. "Sometimes I think he's going to slip into my room in the middle of the night and strangle me."

"At least it's not boring."

Elissa smiled. "It's many things, but you're right. It's not boring."

"And if he does slip into your room to do away with you, you can always convince him to do something else with his time."

"Sure," Elissa said, trying not to think about the fact that she was the last woman Cole would be interested in sexually. "I wish he was more friendly. He barely talks to me, and when he does, I feel that he's judging me, or waiting for me to mess up."

"Are you surprised?"

"I guess not. This is where I admit I'd imagined him welcoming me back with open arms. Stupid, huh?"

"It's never stupid to dream, kiddo. We all do that. We can't help it. But Cole isn't exactly the forgiving kind. Even though he deserved what he got, you *were* the one to walk out on him."

"I know. Sometimes I think I acted hastily. Maybe I should have—" She shook her head. "I don't know. Who am I kidding? If he'd cared about me, he would have come after me, right?"

"Life isn't that simple." Fallon's voice deepened with concern. "I wish I was there to give you a hug."

"Thanks. But I have to do this one on my own."

"You never said why you went back. I know you're

there to see Cole, but is this about reconciliation or making sure the relationship is over?''

Elissa opened her eyes and stared at the ceiling. "I'm not sure. Either, I suppose. It's been long enough for us to figure it out. It's so strange. I thought seeing him would be enough to let me know what I'm supposed to do, but it isn't. There are still things about him I admire. And things that drive me crazy.''

"Be careful," Fallon warned. "Cole nearly destroyed you last time. Do you remember how you were when you came home from New York? I've never seen you that unhappy before or since.''

Her sisters had never asked for details about that time in her life, and Elissa hadn't volunteered the information. At first she'd been too hurt and humiliated. Later, she wasn't sure she would come out on the victorious side of the telling. What had seemed so cruel and insensitive at the time didn't seem quite so bad in hindsight. Had Cole been the ogre she'd always thought, had she been a child, or did reality lie somewhere in between?

"How's the brat?" Elissa asked, changing the subject.

"Kayla's still annoyingly blissful. She can barely mention her new husband's name without bursting into song. What I can't figure out is if he's so darn wonderful, why did she take so long to realize it? She'd worked for him for years.''

"Gee, Fallon, we can't all be as logical as you are when it comes to matters of the heart. Sometimes the rest of us just wing it.''

"That's pretty risky. Remember what happened the last time you did that. Maybe it would be better to be cautious.''

"Agreed," Elissa said, remembering a love so hot it had burned itself out. She knew; she had the burn scars to prove it.

Chapter Four

Cole left the administration building and headed for the main dormitory. Before he reached his destination, he heard a low rumble that shook the ground. He turned toward the sound and watched as an enclosed 18-wheeler slowed, then stopped in the driveway.

He stared at the vehicle. Millie kept him informed of deliveries, and she hadn't said anything that morning. It wasn't like her to forget.

He walked toward the truck, meeting the driver halfway. The long-haired young man smiled engagingly. "You Cole Stephenson?"

Cole nodded.

"Cool. Sign here and we'll start unloading."

Cole glanced at the computer printout detailing the delivery. It seemed to be a list of sports equipment. "I didn't order this."

The younger man shrugged. "Somebody did. Hey, it's

paid for. My job is to unload. I guess yours is going to be finding out who sent it to you. Maybe Christmas in September. So where do you want it?"

Even as he asked the question, a second deliveryman had already raised the truck's rear door. Several children had heard the truck and they dashed forward, wanting to see what was inside.

Cole returned his attention to the delivery sheet. There was a phone number on top. "Don't unload anything," he said firmly. "I'm going to call your office and find out what's going on. There must be some kind of mistake."

The truck driver shrugged. "Go ahead, but there's no mistake. We don't get many deliveries to an orphanage, if you know what I mean. I wouldn't confuse you with like a hospital or something. Besides, who else wants playground equipment?"

"It's not that I don't want it," Cole began, then shook his head. There was no point in explaining it to the driver. "Just wait. I'll be right back."

He jogged toward the administration building. Millie and Elissa were coming down the steps.

"What's going on?" Millie asked.

"Someone's trying to make a delivery. You didn't order any sports equipment, did you?"

"No. I couldn't. It's not in the budget. Even if it was, you would have to authorize that kind of purchase." She glanced at the truck. "A mystery. How wonderful. Come on, Elissa, let's see what this mystery looks like."

Cole allowed his gaze to settle on his wife. She glanced at him and gave a quick smile before Millie took her hand and pulled her along. He paused long enough to watch their progress, hating the fact that sometimes just being around Elissa was enough to make him feel that his world could be made right.

"Stick to what's important," he told himself, and stepped into the administration building. Unlike Millie, he didn't like mysteries and he was determined to get to the bottom of this one.

Fifteen minutes later he hung up the phone and admitted defeat. The order for the playground equipment had been received by mail, along with a cashier's check for the total amount, including shipping. The donor wished to remain anonymous, and the company would not give out the name.

He turned to glance out his office window and saw that his wishes had been ignored. Instead of leaving everything on the truck, the delivery guys had unloaded several boxes and were setting up what looked like a complicated jungle gym near a grove of trees.

As he watched, the children began opening packages. There were basketballs, soccer balls, baseballs, bats and mitts, goalposts, nets and hoops. Where the hell had it come from?

His gaze settled on Millie, who tossed a softball to Gina. Her husband was a successful executive in a Fortune 500 company. They regularly made large donations to several charitable institutions, including his. But she didn't give anonymously. As she put it, her husband enjoyed giving, but he wanted the tax deduction, too.

Elissa joined the duo. Elissa? He remembered their conversation from last week, when she'd told Millie about being on the television show. She'd been a child star. Could she be the donor?

He shook his head. She hadn't had any money when they'd gotten married. If there had been a fortune from that show, it was long gone. He might have complaints about her leaving, but she'd never been selfish or secretive. She wouldn't have kept that kind of information from him. So she couldn't be the one.

As he walked outside, he tried to figure out who had sent the equipment. Millie saw him approaching and waved him over.

"Isn't this wonderful?" she asked. "I know it's not as practical as a new restaurant-size stove, but the children love it."

"Any ideas about who sent it all?" he asked.

Millie frowned. In her designer silk summer dress and stylish low-heeled sandals, she looked as if she were attending a ladies' luncheon. Yet she threw a mean curveball during batting practice, and didn't mind sitting with sick kids, or helping anywhere she was needed. He didn't know what he'd done to deserve Millie in his life at the orphanage, but he was grateful.

"The Bayers often make a large donation about this time of year," Millie said.

"Agreed, but they always check with me first to see what we need. I was hoping they would buy the stove."

"Audrey Johnston?"

He shook his head. "She's going to have the buildings painted in the spring. We've already talked about it."

"Are anonymous donations that unusual?" Elissa asked.

"They are when they're this size," he answered. "It's one thing to get twenty dollars in an envelope, it's another for someone to spend several thousand dollars." He looked at the custom jungle gym taking shape on the green lawn.

"Millie, look!" Tiffany called. She pulled open a large box filled with baseball gloves. "Let's play."

"Okay." Millie put her arm around Elissa's shoulder. "I generally umpire behind home plate. How do you feel about taking first base?"

Elissa glanced down at her cotton dress. The feminine-style cap sleeves that left her arms bare and a bias-cut skirt that floated around her calves hinted at the curves below. At least she wore flat shoes instead of heels.

"I've never been an umpire," she said. "But I'm willing to try."

"It's not hard," Millie said. "Just check to see who makes the base first. The ball or the runner."

She called the children over and they quickly chose teams. Cole refused to be a captain. "I'll umpire if you want to pitch," he told Millie.

She shook her head. "I had a manicure yesterday. I'm not going to mess it up. We're having company for dinner." She fluttered her fingers at him. "Why don't you pitch?"

"Fine." Cole started for the center of the impromptu bases being set up around the lawn.

"Are you mad?" Elissa asked, trailing after him.

"About the donation?" He shook his head. "The kids love it. I wouldn't have thought about putting sports equipment on our yearly wish list, but it was a great idea."

"I'm glad."

He swung toward her, his gaze narrowing. "Why? You wouldn't happen to know anything about this, would you?"

She smiled. "Right. That's why I've been working in a hospital all these years. I have a secret fortune stashed away and finally decided to spend it on the orphanage."

Her gaze never wavered. He wanted to accuse her of several things, but none of them had anything to do with the unexpected donation. She was right. If there had been money from the series, the triplets wouldn't have had to work while attending college.

"Cole!"

He turned, and Millie tossed him the ball. He waited for the teams to decide who would be up to bat first.

"You used to play softball in New York," Elissa said, studying him. "I'd forgotten."

"Just a pickup game on the weekend," he said. "With some guys from the firm. I played more in college. There were several intramural teams."

"I'm sure that was fun. I was never much for sports. I think the hospital has a bowling team and touch football, but I didn't go."

"What about when you returned to college?"

Her green eyes darkened. "I didn't."

"Play sports?" he asked, even though he knew the real answer to the question.

"I never went back to school."

She made the statement almost defiantly. Cole turned away and watched the children still trying to decide who had to take to the outfield first.

"I thought you would know that," she said quietly. "After all, you knew where I worked."

"I didn't keep track of you that closely. I had a general idea about your life. That's all."

"I see."

There was a time when he'd known what she was thinking just by the inflection of her tone and the pauses between words. No longer. She'd become a stranger with whom he shared nothing but a past.

"I've been thinking about going back," she continued. "I would like to get my degree, although I'm not sure I want to stay in the same major."

"What's stopping you?"

"Myself," she answered honestly. When he looked at her, she shrugged. "It's been a few years. I'm not sure my brain remembers how to study. Plus, I would be the oldest student in all my classes. That's a little daunting. But I'm tossing the idea around."

"No one ever complained about having too much education," he said as an unfamiliar emotion flooded him. It took him a minute to identify it as guilt. Guilt because he'd finished his schooling and she hadn't.

"I'm sure I'll go back eventually. It's just that with the wisdom of hindsight, I know it would have been easier to keep going than to try to go back."

"That's not my fault," he said quickly. "I asked you to marry me, not quit college."

"I never said you did." Her quiet tone contrasted with his heated words.

"There are plenty of universities in New York," he went on. "You could have transferred. You're the one who wanted to leave it all behind."

"I'm not going to fight with you, Cole. I'm just saying that knowing what I know now, it would have been better to take that advice and transfer. However, at the time, neither of us thought of that. We wanted to be together and you had a job in New York. College wasn't important to me then."

You were.

She didn't say the words, but he heard them. Heard the demands of youth. He wanted to blame her for leaving school, but he knew in his heart the fault was his. He wouldn't have wanted her attending classes in New York. He would have been afraid of her wandering around a strange campus. Which was really stupid when he considered that she'd survived at UC Davis for two years. It wasn't the campus at all. In his heart he hadn't wanted her to get out and meet other people. Other men. Funny how he'd always expected her to leave him for someone else and in the end she'd left him for no one at all.

"I guess there's a lot we didn't think about," he said.

"We were both young. I loved you and wanted to be with you. That simplified all my decisions."

And now?

But he didn't ask that, either. Of course she didn't still love him. He didn't want her to. He'd already paid the price of her love, and it was too expensive for his tastes.

But for the first time he realized that she'd paid a price for marrying him. He'd taken her away from all she'd ever known and thrust her into a strange world. If someone had pointed that out to him at the time, he would have assured the person that being together would be enough for her. It hadn't been. Now, with the same hindsight she'd talked about, he realized it had been wrong to expect it to be. Elissa hadn't been just his wife. She had been, as she still was, her own person, with needs for a life of her own, separate from his. Just as he wouldn't have been able to exist just for her.

"Don't blame yourself for any of this," she said. "I don't blame you."

"Good, because it's not my fault," he said without thinking.

There was a combination moan and cheer from home plate. Millie had settled the question of who was batting first with the old game of Rock-Paper-Scissors. The losing team headed for the outfield.

"You need to stand on the other side of first base," he told her, pointing to the makeshift base near a large tree.

She nodded. "It must be great to always be so sure of everything," she said.

"What are you talking about?"

"Not taking blame. Knowing the failure of our marriage is completely my fault. You name it. You seem to go through life completely confident in your decisions and your frame of reference. I guess you sleep really well at night. Maybe you can teach me that before I leave.''

She turned and walked toward the base. He stared after her. He supposed he deserved what she'd said, even though she was wrong. He wasn't sure of anything, especially where she was concerned.

Elissa collected all the paid bills and stacked the envelopes. After sticking on stamps, she got the return address labels from her left-hand drawer and applied them.

In the past two weeks she'd settled into a routine of sorts. Her life at the orphanage was different from what she was used to, but she liked the changes.

In the morning she generally helped Millie in the office. The work was pretty basic. Filing, paying bills, setting up maintenance appointments, updating records. In the afternoon she sometimes continued her work in the office. Other days she spent with the children, supervising homework, answering questions, helping with play activities and generally just being around.

Millie strolled out of her office and stopped next to Elissa's desk. ''You're looking thoughtful.''

Elissa smiled. ''Not about anything earth-shattering. It's been two weeks. The time is going quickly. I was thinking about how different this job is from the one I had at the hospital.''

Millie sat in the visitor chair. ''I know I shouldn't ask, but is 'different' better or not?''

''Much better,'' Elissa assured her. ''I love all of it. Especially working with the children.''

''Good. I thought you might.''

''I find it satisfying, although I'll confess now that I had my doubts. I think I was afraid that the children might have gotten difficult over the years. These days, there's so much in the newspapers about problems with facilities like this one."

Millie nodded. "I know what you mean. I've done volunteer work all my life and I've found there's a real difference between orphaned children and those taken out of their homes for other reasons. Many children here had happy lives until their parents were taken from them. They are loving and basically normal. Children growing up in abusive homes or around violence are different. They are in pain and often lashing out. It's unfortunate." She crossed her legs, her normally pleasant expression changing to pensive. "Cole and I talked about opening a wing to help those abused children, but they require a level of expertise neither he nor the staff has. We have a child psychologist available, but she's not really on call except in emergencies. If our kids need to see her, it's by appointment. Also, the facility is too physically open. We couldn't keep anyone from running away, nor could we protect children from a battering or stalking parent."

"You can't solve all the world's problems," Elissa said. "I think what is being done here is very special."

"I agree. Sometimes I lose sight of that, as Jeff—my husband—keeps telling me."

Elissa thought about the photo on Millie's desk. It showed a handsome older man staring dotingly at Millie. Tiffany had mentioned that the photo was taken on their thirtieth wedding anniversary.

"He's very good-looking," Elissa said.

Millie grinned. "You bet. I was very careful before I got married. I checked out Jeff's dad and his grandfather. They were both very hot guys, even though I thought they were a little old. I was determined to stay married to the same man for my whole life, and even though love is about a lot more than looks, I figured I would have to wake up next to him for a long time. Why not make that a pleasant experience?'' She winked. ''About ten years ago Jeff admitted he'd done the same thing. By the time he proposed he had already decided my mom was a babe, for an old broad.''

''I don't think I believe you,'' Elissa said. ''You always talk about Jeff as if he's your whole world. You don't care about his looks.''

Millie laughed. ''You've caught me. It's true, I would love Jeff however he looked, but that handsome face, not to mention his body, are a plus.'' She fanned herself. ''I don't think we should talk about this much longer. He's in England for another ten days and with the time difference, not to mention the cost of calling overseas, phone calls only go so far. They're no substitute for being together.''

''I'm sure you're right.''

Millie sighed. ''I miss him so much. Despite what the media has led you to believe, sex is not just for the young. Jeff and I have thirty years together, and we've always had a passionate marriage.''

Elissa wished she could say the same. Maybe if she'd known how to please her husband in the bedroom, he wouldn't have spent so much time at work.

''I envy you,'' she said, then stared at her desk.

Millie leaned closer. ''If you don't want to talk about it, I completely understand. I am a meddling old woman. But I've been wondering about it since that first day when Cole said the two of you are married. Is that true?''

''Of course. Did you talk to him about it?''

''Mr. Iceberg? No way. Cole will do whatever he can to help the kids, even if that means talking about his past and his experiences here. But he doesn't open up to other people. It's just not his style. About all he said to me was that he didn't want word of your marriage getting out, so he would appreciate it if I didn't tell any of the children or the other staff members."

"I figured there was a reason no one knew," Elissa said. She picked up a pencil and turned it over in her hands. "Yes, it's true. Cole and I are married, although we haven't seen each other in nearly five years."

"Why?"

Elissa smiled. "Why are we married? Why aren't we together? Why aren't we divorced? Why am I here?"

"Feel free to answer any of those questions, in no particular order." Millie scooted her chair closer to the desk, placed her right elbow on the flat surface, leaned forward and put her chin in her hand. "I'm all ears."

Elissa wasn't sure what to say. She opened her mouth, then closed it.

Millie sighed. "Okay, I confess, I'm incredibly nosy. We'll still be friends, even if you don't answer any of the questions. Although if you don't, I'll probably die of curiosity and then you'll have that on your conscience."

The older woman meant well. She might claim to be nosy, but she was also kind, and for some reason, Elissa thought she might turn out to be an ally. While she wasn't ready to share all the deep, dark secrets of her soul, there were a few things she didn't mind the other woman knowing.

"Cole and I are still married because neither of us has asked the other for a divorce. We were together about six months, then I left him."

Millie straightened. "You left *him?*" She flushed slightly. "Oops. I didn't mean that exactly as it came out. It's just he's so..." Her voice trailed off.

"So Cole-like?" Elissa asked wryly.

"Exactly. We're talking major hunk, as my oldest granddaughter would say. I've worked with him for a couple of years, so I know he's a nice guy, too."

"Agreed," Elissa said. She wasn't offended by Millie's reaction. Elissa would have felt the same way if she hadn't known the whole story. "He's all that and more. But we were both very young. He expected a Stepford wife and I expected a knight in shining armor. Instead, we each got a flawed person, and love just wasn't enough."

"And now?"

Good question. "And now, who knows? I'm here because it's been a long time and Cole and I need to figure out what we want. We can't continue this limbo forever."

Millie nodded. "Thanks for trusting me enough to tell me that. I won't share what you've told me. Despite my big mouth, I'm pretty good with secrets. I wish I had a few to share, but my life is boring."

"I doubt that. I've heard that you travel a lot."

"Jeff and I used to. At first it was very exciting. Then when we started having children, we thought it would be good for them to see the world. I'm one of those people who needs to keep busy. Jeff has always insisted on a housekeeper, and even with four children I had way too much time on my hands. I was tired of volunteering all the time, so about ten years ago I opened a boutique. It's in Ojai. Seven years later I got tired of all the long hours. My oldest daughter runs it now. I decided I missed the volunteering, but I wanted to commit myself to one project and not just give a few hours here and a few hours there. So I came to work for the Grace Orphanage. Jeff had been on the board of directors for years. Actually, working here was his suggestion. For a while we thought the place wasn't going to make it, then Cole applied to be the director and the rest is history."

"I'm impressed," Elissa said, wondering how on earth

someone could raise four children and claim to have too much free time. Cole was right; Millie was a force of nature.

Millie smiled. "We've bonded. I'm so pleased. I knew the moment we met that we were going to be friends." There was a squeal of laughter from outside. She glanced in that direction. "The children are really enjoying all that sports equipment."

"I know. The jungle gym is great."

Millie made a great show of glancing at her perfectly groomed nails. "It was a lovely donation. Practical in a fun way. Not just anyone would have thought of it." She looked at Elissa. "Well done."

Elissa froze. Should she deny the truth? She'd never been a very good liar and wasn't positive she could bluff her way out of the situation. "I— When—?" She shook her head.

"It's interesting that the donor didn't want to be recognized. I wonder why that is."

"Some people prefer to give without all the fanfare."

"Maybe," Millie said. "Or maybe the person is afraid. Not of the giving, but of what the money represents."

"Some people don't like money," Elissa said, not sure what game she and Millie were playing.

"Do people who are afraid give it all away foolishly?"

"No. But it's nice to make a difference in people's lives."

"Is that why you're doing it?" Millie asked.

"Partly," Elissa admitted, realizing whatever the game, she wasn't going to win. "How did you guess?"

"It was easy. While our list of donors is long, only a few give in large amounts. I know most of them, so it was simple to eliminate names. The donor obviously had a connection with the children, which usually means they visit often or have lived here previously. I kept coming up blank. Then I remembered you and your television show. You didn't grow up with money—Cole told me that. Yet I'm not unfamiliar with the industry. There was money to be made. Is it in a trust?''

"Yes. It was released on our twenty-fifth birthday. This past July.''

"Cole doesn't know.''

It wasn't a question. "No, and I don't want him to. He's always had a chip on his shoulder about certain things, and that's one of them. Inheritances, I mean. I don't want to make him angrier," Elissa said, raising her hands and turning them palm up. "I just want to help.''

Millie smiled. "Good for you.'' She made an *X* over her heart. "I promise I won't be the one to tell your secret, although I think you're wrong about Cole and the chip on his shoulder. Oh, he has one, but it's not about money. I think if you told him the truth, he wouldn't mind at all.''

Elissa didn't believe her. If she told him the truth, it would give him an excuse to throw her out on her butt. As it was, they barely managed to speak without him getting angry at her. Even though he didn't yell, she could see the anger in the coldness in his eyes. If he hated her so much, why had he stayed married to her all these years?

She exhaled slowly. She hadn't found an answer to that one in all the time they'd been apart, nor had she found it in the two weeks she'd been here. Eventually the truth would come out—for both of them. Until then, she was content to wait.

"Do you have any more anonymous donations planned?'' Millie asked.

"I'm not sure. Why?''

"No reason.'' She glanced at her slim gold watch. "Oh, my, look at the time. I'd better head out. There's some mail on my desk. I'll take a look at that, then I'll be gone. You have a nice evening." The older woman rose to her feet.

"I will. Thanks, Millie."

"Thank *you*. You trust me, and that means so very much."

Elissa smiled. "I'm going to get something to drink, so I'll see you in the morning. Night."

When she returned to her desk twenty minutes later, Millie had already left. There were a few letters for her to type. She read the top one. It was to the director of a science camp in Santa Barbara. Millie had written that despite the generous discount, the orphanage couldn't afford to send the children to the program. There wasn't enough money to send everyone, and Cole refused to leave any child behind. Underneath the letter was a brochure for the camp.

Elissa looked it over. The camp ran four days, beginning the first weekend of next month. Although the children would miss two days of school, the program was recommended by their local school district as well as by the state's education office. It wasn't cheap, but with the discount offered to the orphanage, it was a bargain.

Elissa glanced toward Millie's office to make sure it was empty, then picked up the phone. What was that old saying? Better to be hunted as a wolf than live as a sheep. She laughed. No, that wasn't the old saying, but it worked. She'd lived too many years as a sheep, and while she wasn't exactly wolf material, she felt she'd made progress up the food chain.

If Cole wanted her gone, she would be gone, even if she did everything perfectly. Besides, she wasn't doing this for him, or even for herself. She was doing it for the children, and because it was the right thing to do.

Chapter Five

Cole sat in the dark auditorium and tried to concentrate on the performance. On stage, high school students delivered the lines from the Neil Simon play. When the audience burst into spontaneous laughter and Cole didn't get the joke, he realized he didn't have a prayer of focusing on anything but Elissa tonight.

He shifted on the hard wooden seat. How many times had he sat in this particular building? There were dozens of assemblies while he'd attended the high school and dozens more activities since taking over as director of the orphanage. By definition, the children he took care of had no one to show up to watch them perform. He made it a point to be at as many events as he could, as well as assigning different staff members. Some came, even when they weren't on duty. As Elissa had tonight.

He thought about moving his arm, but he didn't want her to know the soft pressure of her elbow against his was distracting. He refused to let her guess that the faint scent of her sweet perfume surrounded him in a cloud of arousal and memories. She might have grown up and become an independent, feisty temptress, but her perfume was the same. It made him think of pale skin and hot kisses. Elissa had many flaws, but her kissing ability wasn't one of them.

Without wanting to, he remembered the months they'd dated. He'd known she was a virgin and had tried hard to go slowly. Her request that they wait to make love until after they were married had made him grit his teeth, but he'd agreed. And because the need was so strong, he'd decided it was safer to do nothing at all. Nothing except kiss.

He fought against the memories, trying to force his attention back to the play. Mindy, one of his kids from the orphanage, was second lead and he was really enjoying her performance. But lines from a play, however witty, couldn't compete with the power of the past. Instead of high school students on a stage, he saw Elissa, her long curly hair tumbling loose over her shoulders as she laughed at him, bent forward and touched her lips to his.

He remembered reading once that a scent memory was a total sense memory. That it could invoke the past completely, engaging all the other senses. Maybe it was the night, his weakened condition after having dealt with her for over two weeks, or maybe it was her perfume. Whatever the reason, he found himself drowning in sensation as the past overwhelmed him.

Elissa kissing him, her hands on his shoulders, her mouth wet and warm against his. She rarely kissed back, preferring to let him invade. He hadn't minded. Not when she tasted so sweet and sighed so deeply. He remembered how after the first kiss, she'd often sagged against him, as if he'd stolen all her strength, as if the feel of him next to her was too much for her to handle.

Another burst of laughter recalled him to the present. He shifted again, this time because thinking about kissing Elissa had left him physically wanting to be with her. His arousal throbbed in time with his heartbeat and he was grateful for the darkness. His life was complicated enough without anyone knowing Millie's new assistant turned him on in a big way.

With a supreme force of will honed by years of wanting and not having, he studied the teenagers on the stage and forced himself to concentrate on the play.

Mindy, just sixteen and a gifted performer, delivered her line perfectly. The audience laughed again. Not even by the hint of a smile did she let on that she knew she was acting a part instead of living a real life. Fierce emotion burned in his chest. Pride. He'd felt it before.

At every parent-teacher conference, at every play, every recital, every spring concert, he sat and enjoyed a sense of pride for the children. They were the reason he wrestled with a never-big-enough budget, zoning, the state and an assortment of frustrations that made his days long. He'd been where they were and he knew how much they wanted to belong to something special. No matter the personal cost, he was determined to give that to them. In return, they grew up in ways that made him proud.

He wondered if he would feel the same if he had children of his own. If. Would he? Ever?

He shook his head. It was unlikely. He would never marry anyone again. He'd given Elissa his heart; he didn't have it to give a second time.

The play ended and the audience clapped loudly. Everyone rose to their feet as cheers erupted. Cole whistled, adding to the cacophony.

"Weren't they wonderful?" Elissa said, smiling at him. "Millie said the cast started rehearsals a month before school started because they wanted the play to be perfect. All that hard work paid off."

"They were great."

She wore her hair pulled back in a fancy braid with the end tucked under. Makeup accentuated her green eyes and full mouth. As usual, a soft, flowing dress whispered over curves and teased her calves and his imagination. Tonight the filmy fabric was pale peach. A slender chain rested at the base of her throat. He was torn between wanting to kiss that delicate hollow and ripping the necklace from her body. It fit too perfectly not to have been purchased by a lover.

"How do you stand it?" she asked.

He stiffened, wondering how the hell she'd read his mind.

She sniffed, then touched a finger to the corner of her eye. "I can't believe I'm nearly in tears over this. I've only been at the orphanage a short time, but I'm so proud of these kids. You must be overwhelmed by it every time you see one of them perform like this."

He relaxed. She hadn't known what he'd been thinking. If she stayed the full three months, she was going to be around several more weeks. He'd better learn to control his wayward thoughts. "The feeling never goes away," he said. "I'm always proud of them."

Overhead lights clicked on. The audience members started moving toward the rear doors. Elissa stayed in place, her gaze firmly fixed on his face.

"I envy you," she said. "You've created something very amazing here."

"Interesting. All this time, I've always envied you."

Her eyes widened in surprise, but he turned away before she could ask any more questions.

The next few minutes were a whirlwind of activity as he and the other staff members rounded up children from the audience and the cast and put them onto the bus. Twenty minutes later they pulled on to the private road that led to the orphanage.

As they rounded the corner he saw that all the lights were on in the dining hall. Millie's Mercedes was parked in front. As the bus pulled up, the older woman walked out and waved.

"I couldn't make the play, but I did want to help celebrate," Millie said as Cole stepped onto the driveway. "There's cake and ice cream for everyone."

He hugged her briefly. "I couldn't make this place work without you."

"I know," Millie said. "Don't you forget it, either." She turned her attention to the children. "Come on, come on. There's plenty for everyone."

She led the way inside. Cole stayed out in the cooling night air and made sure all the kids got off the bus. Elissa was last and she carried a sleepy Shanna in her arms.

"But I'm not tired," the eight-year-old insisted, then yawned. "There's cake 'n' stuff. I want some."

"I'll save you a piece," Elissa promised, giving Cole a quick smile. "I'm going to put this one in bed."

"I don't wanna go to bed," Shanna protested, leaning her head against Elissa's shoulder and closing her eyes. "I always miss the fun stuff."

He didn't want to think about how right she looked holding the young girl in her arms, or how much he wanted to walk with her to the dormitory and share the domestic scene. Before he could offer, Tiffany came over.

"I'll help you, Elissa," the preteen offered. "Don't

worry, Shanna. I'll make sure there's still cake for you in the morning."

"Can I have it for breakfast?"

Elissa rolled her eyes. "Don't even think something that gross. Come on. Bedtime."

"It's not your night to work," he said. "I can do it."

"Don't be silly. Go have fun with the other kids. I won't be a moment."

He ducked into the dining hall because the alternative was to watch her walk away. It didn't take long to get caught up in the celebration. After passing out cake and scoops of ice cream, he walked around the room, making sure everyone was having a good time. Before he could settle down himself and grab a piece of cake, Elissa was at his side.

"You've got to come quickly," she said, her eyes wide and dark with worry.

"What's wrong?" he asked as he signaled for one of the college students to take charge. He followed Elissa outside.

"It's Tiffany. She went into her room to get a sweater and when she didn't come out, I went to check on her." Elissa walked quickly, twisting her hands together as she talked. "She's curled up on her bed, sobbing. She won't tell me what's wrong. I don't think she's sick, but I'm not sure. She's crying as if her heart is broken." She pulled open the dorm door and headed for the stairs. "I know I probably should have been able to take care of it myself, but I didn't know what to do. I'm sorry."

He took the stairs two at a time. The orphanage had a doctor on call. If Tiffany was sick, Cole could call, or take the child directly to the emergency room. Had she eaten something bad? Was it the flu? Was it...

He paused at the entrance to the room. Four girls about the same age shared it, but Tiffany was the only one in there now. She lay as Elissa had described her, curled up on her bed, sobbing as if her world had been destroyed.

Each choking sob ripped through him, as did a wave of helplessness. What did he know about raising children? Who was he trying to kid? He was the last person who should be in charge.

He was about to ask Elissa to try to talk to Tiffany again when he spotted the crumpled envelope on the floor. He bent and retrieved it, then smoothed it flat. The feel of heavy paper told him it contained a greeting card.

A name and address were carefully written in Tiffany's handwriting. Stamped across that was the ink image of a hand with the index finger pointing to the left.

Moved and left no forwarding address.

Then he understood. He moved to the bed and pulled Tiffany into his arms. Her body shook with each sob. She clung to him as if she were in danger of falling and he was the only stable place in her world. He knew about that, too.

"It's all right," he said. "I know what you're thinking, but you're not alone. I'm right here."

Elissa checked the pot of coffee she'd made two hours before. It was at exactly the same level—full, less one cup. Should she toss it out and make fresh? Would Cole even bother coming to the kitchen when he had finished talking with Tiffany? Maybe he had gone straight to bed and she was waiting up for nothing.

Maybe, but a voice in her head said he would be coming here for coffee. She wanted to be waiting for him. Not only to find out what was wrong with Tiffany, but to once again try to make a connection with the man she'd married. They might have lived in the same location for nearly three weeks, but he was as much a stranger as he had been the day she arrived.

Footsteps in the hallway sent her hurrying to the door. Cole pushed it open before she could and stepped inside. She waited apprehensively, not sure what he would think when he saw her. But when his dark eyes met hers she saw nothing but exhaustion dilating his pupils. For once there was no anger, no suspicion.

"I've made coffee," she said, walking to the pot. "Let me pour you a cup."

"Thanks."

He pulled out a chair from the large table in the center and sat down. Elissa set the black coffee in front of him and took the seat on his right.

The large kitchen had been cleaned for the night. There were huge empty pots on the counter. The ancient stove gleamed with obvious care. The tile sparkled and the food in the pantry beyond had been neatly arranged by size and type. There might not be a lot of extra money at the Grace Orphanage, but there was plenty of caring. Obviously Cole set the example for that; if Elissa had had any doubts, tonight had eased them.

"How's Tiffany?" she asked.

Cole stared into his coffee mug. "Sleeping. It took nearly an hour for her to calm down. I guess I'm going to have to schedule her some time with the child psychologist."

"Is there anything I can do to help?"

He glanced at her, his expression hard. "Are you going to ask what's wrong?"

"No. If you want to tell me, I'm happy to listen, but if it's confidential, I don't need to know. Either way, I'd still like to help."

"The last of the good guys." There was a cynical edge to his voice.

So much for them connecting, she thought wearily. She'd been a fool to try. "Who did you fight with before I arrived?'' Elissa asked as she pushed to her feet. ''You win, Cole. I'll leave you alone. Good night.''

She got all the way to the door before he called her back. ''Elissa. Wait.''

She paused, but didn't turn around. Her stomach twisted painfully and she was way too close to tears. Why did he still have that kind of power over her? She hated it. Why couldn't she have come to the orphanage, met Cole and found out the sparks had long since extinguished themselves? But no. That would make life too easy.

''Tiffany's mother is a drug addict.''

''I know.''

''For the past year or so, her mother has been in a rehab program. She's had a few relapses, but she's always gone back to the program. She's been living in a halfway house on the premises of the rehab facility. Even though she knows better, Tiffany was starting to hope that her mom might kick the drugs. When she got home from the play, Tiffany found that the birthday card she'd sent her mother had been returned. She'd left the rehab center without telling anyone where she'd gone. Which means she's back on the streets.''

Elissa faced him. ''That's horrible. No wonder she's so upset. Her mother could be ill or dead. How can she stand not knowing?''

''It's worse than that.'' Cole returned his attention to the mug of coffee on the table in front of him. ''She hasn't just lost her mom, she's lost the dream.''

Without wanting to, knowing full well that he was going to bite her head off again, or find something to blame on her, Elissa returned to the table. This time, instead of sitting next to him, she took the seat across the table. Somehow the distance made her feel safer.

''I don't understand,'' she said. ''Isn't there a way to

find out what happened to her mother? Can't we call the police or something to trace her?''

''Sure, and I will. But that's not what Tiffany's upset about. You can't relate to this because you have family, but an orphan has no one. No parents, no family of any kind. Growing up that alone is very threatening, especially to a child. Everything they read or see on television is about mom, dad and kids.'' He gave her a brief smile. ''One exception is 'The Sally McGuire Show.' The children here watch it on cable all the time.''

''Although I'm thrilled they can relate, it's pretty humiliating to remember I used to do that. Go on.''

He leaned back in his chair. ''There's a hierarchy. How old were you when you lost your folks? How much do you remember? Do you have any photos or other memorabilia? That kind of stuff. The more, the better. Then there are the few special children. Those with a living relative who for some reason can't take care of the child. According to the rules of the orphanage, those are the lucky kids. They get the fantasy.''

Elissa nodded slowly. ''I understand. Everyone here has a dream about being adopted into a family, and the children with living relatives believe they have the best chance for making it come true. If only Tiffany's mother will stop taking drugs, Tiffany can be rescued. Her world made right.''

''Exactly.''

The night surrounded them. Although there were lights on in the kitchen, darkness invaded in the form of silence. Beyond these walls was the silence of sleeping children, dreaming dreams of families and homes in which they could belong.

She stared at the man across from her. Now, in the quiet,

he seemed to accept her. She didn't know how long that would last. Cole seemed so eager to find fault.

If only... If only she could get over him. If only the sight of him didn't make her heart beat fast. If only she didn't think he was the handsomest, smartest, most caring man she'd ever met—to everyone else, if not to her. If only his jokes didn't make her laugh. If only she could have fallen in love with someone else instead of him.

Dark hair fell across his forehead. The hint of stubble shadowed his jaw, making him look like a modern-day pirate. His firm mouth pulled straight and she wondered what he was thinking. About Tiffany or about his own broken dreams?

"Did you wait for your grandfather to come rescue you?" she asked.

He raised his gaze to hers. "You remembered?"

She remembered everything about their time together. "Of course. I was with you when you got the letter from him."

He laughed harshly. "The letter. Why does bad news always come through the mail? Can't anybody call it in?" He shook his head. "Don't answer that. Bad news isn't any better delivered on the phone. As for wanting my grandfather to come rescue me, sure I hoped he would. I never stopped hoping, until he informed me not to bother him again."

Elissa clenched her hands together tightly in her lap. She wished the old man was here so she could give him a piece of her mind. Cole would resent any sign of compassion from her, though, assuming—wrongly, of course—that it was nothing more than pity. Still, it was hard to sit still as she recalled the look on his face while he'd read the letter from his only living relative.

He'd been all of eighteen; she'd been a kid of thirteen.

Her visits to the orphanage had been erratic, but she'd come whenever she could. She'd had a huge crush on Cole and had assumed he merely tolerated her presence. It wasn't until later that she'd found out he'd had some feelings for her, too.

She'd begged her mother to let her come up to the orphanage to celebrate Cole's high school graduation, and the older woman had agreed.

Elissa and Cole had left the party and escaped to the orchard, which had been their special place. He'd pulled a letter out of his jeans pocket and waved it in front of her.

"I heard back from him," he'd said, his voice tight with anticipation. "My grandfather, I mean. I got the address of his company from the phone books at the library. I wrote him and told him who I was. Maybe he didn't know he had a grandson, right? It could happen."

Even at thirteen, Elissa had sensed the danger. She'd wanted to snatch the letter from his hands and destroy it. Not because if the old man wanted Cole in his life, then Cole would have to leave, but because she knew what the letter would say. Rich, powerful men didn't "lose track" of their children, or their grandchildren. If Cole's grandfather had wanted the boy with him, then that's where Cole would have been.

But she couldn't say anything or do anything. She could only be there as he read the harsh words aloud, his voice changing from eager to shocked and finally to ashamed.

"He doesn't want me," Cole had said, stunned, as the single piece of paper had fluttered to the ground. "He knew about me all the time and he doesn't want me."

It was the only time she'd ever seen him cry. It was the first time he'd taken her in his arms.

Elissa glanced around the kitchen, fighting memories and tears. She could still recall the awkwardness of his embrace, the rangy strength of his boy-man body. There had been nothing sexual about being in his arms; they'd shared pain as friends, perhaps as soul mates, although she'd been too young to realize that at the time.

In that single moment Cole had lost a lifetime of fantasy. All his dreams of home and family had been destroyed. She'd always known he carried a chip on his shoulder to avoid getting too close to anyone. After he'd read the letter, she'd understood how rare their friendship was to him. Now, with the hindsight of an adult, she was surprised he'd allowed her to get close. Maybe the difference in their ages had made her seem safe to him.

No wonder he had a fear of being abandoned. Yet he'd been willing to take a chance on her. He'd wanted to marry her.

And she'd left him.

Elissa stared at the table, but instead of clean Formica, she saw vignettes from her marriage. Cole coming home late at night, walking into the bedroom and holding her, even if she had been asleep. When she'd complained about him waking her, he'd told her he didn't mean to, but he had to know that she was there and okay.

She remembered holidays spent with her family, Cole watching almost enviously as she and her sisters joked together. She remembered presents he gave her, the big ones at her birthday and Christmas, the little ones for no reason. They were always beautifully wrapped, showing obvious care, but he'd often dismissed them as nearly meaningless.

It was, she realized now, fear. Fear of being left. It was what he'd dreaded most and the one thing she'd done to him.

No wonder he hated her.

"The irony in all this is that the old man invited me back," Cole said bitterly.

"What do you mean?" Elissa asked, forcing herself to let go of the past and give him her attention.

"About three years ago I received another letter from my grandfather. He'd been keeping track of me. I'd finished law school at the top of my class, been hired by a successful law firm and was doing well. To quote him, I'd 'earned' my way into the family and he was ready to welcome me with open arms."

No emotion flared in his dark eyes, but Elissa knew what he was feeling. Her skin prickled in response as waves of pain washed over him.

"You told him you weren't interested," she said.

"I wasn't that polite, but he got the message."

"I know that he acted like a jerk, but he *is* a relative. You always wanted to belong."

His mouth twisted down. "Not like that."

He leaned forward and rested his forearms on the table. Sometime while he'd been gone he'd rolled up his shirt-sleeves. The white cotton accentuated his tanned skin and muscled strength. He had great hands. Large with square palms and long fingers. His hands had made her feel safe, although she doubted he would believe that if she told him.

"Enough about my past," he said. "Let's talk about something else. How are your sisters?"

"They're fine. They asked me to tell you hello."

He raised his eyebrows as if to say he didn't believe her.

She reached up and nervously fingered the delicate chain at her neck. "I'm telling the truth. I didn't mention it before because you haven't exactly been friendly. I wasn't sure if your animosity extended just to me or to my entire family."

"I always liked your sisters," he said.

"Gee, thanks. They'll be thrilled." Too bad he hadn't liked her, too. Then they might have made the marriage work.

"How's your mom?"

She twisted the chain tighter. "About the same. We don't talk much. She's still angry at Fallon and me for refusing to do 'The Sally McGuire Show' without Kayla." She sighed. "I've never understood her anger. It's been years. I know the show was important, but our sister was in the hospital, for heaven's sake. No matter, she's not one to forgive. We exchange polite cards at the holidays and that's about it."

Cole's attention seemed to have drifted from the conversation. He stared at her with an intensity her words didn't require. "That must have great sentimental value," he said, motioning to her necklace.

She fingered the chain. "Not really. It's new and I'm not used to wearing it. I bought it for myself as a birthday present this year. A quarter of a century old and all that."

"I see."

The clipped statement confused her. Why would he care if someone had bought her jewelry? Unless he assumed it had come from a man. But there'd never been anyone but him in her life. Didn't he know that?

Silence surrounded them. She didn't know what to say. "I'll, um, check on Tiffany in the morning before school," she said.

"Good idea. If she's still upset, I don't want to send her to school. Either way, I'll get her an appointment with the psychologist right away."

"Fine."

They stared at each other. Elissa was the first to clear her throat and look away. Now what? She should probably make her excuses and go to bed. Only, she didn't want to leave. Not until he made her.

She smiled wryly. That statement applied to tonight as well as her stay at the orphanage. Despite everything, she was still drawn to Cole. The past might be far away, but she couldn't forget it. Or him.

Without wanting to, she returned her gaze to his. Something flared in his dark eyes. Something dangerous that drew her closer. She rested her hands flat on the table and leaned toward him.

Heat flared unexpectedly. Heat and a need that she barely remembered. He'd been the passionate one in their relationship. She'd usually been content to just be held. Sometimes, though, she'd wanted more. She'd never been sure what. The vague ache inside hadn't been for a specific relief—at least, not one she could figure out.

"Cole," she whispered, wishing he would…

What? Hold her? Kiss her?

Yes, she thought. She wanted him to kiss her.

His expression tightened. Fire flamed in his eyes as his jaw tensed. She recognized the desire; he wanted her, too.

Low in her belly an answering spark burst into life. But before it caught, cold, damp doubt snuffed it out. Doubt about what to do, doubt about how to please him. Doubt that he'd ever wanted her.

She straightened in her chair, her withdrawal breaking the connection.

As quickly as a spark turns to flame, his desire turned to anger. She saw it in his eyes, along with a darkness that looked very close to hatred. She recoiled from him.

His mouth twisted into a sneer. "Don't bother flinching," he said coldly. "I wouldn't waste my time. You've made your opinions on that subject very well known."

With that, he was gone.

She fought against the past and the present, against the pain and the tears. Their moment of connection had been only that—a moment. She'd managed to arouse her husband and make him hate her, all in the space of a minute.

Because she was afraid.

Because he thought she didn't want him in her bed.

Because he thought she had never wanted him there.

If only. If only things had been different between them. If only she'd known how to satisfy him. If only she'd had the confidence to tell him what she was thinking. If only she could be one of those women who actually enjoyed making love.

If only she knew what to do now.

She should be used to missing him, but she wasn't. While being with him wasn't as easy as she'd hoped it would be, she would rather be here with him than anywhere else.

Chapter Six

The fourth time Cole added the column and saw a different number flash on his adding machine display screen he swore softly and glanced at the open door. Laughter drifted in from the main television room. He kept an office in the main administration building and a smaller one here, in the largest dormitory, so that he could work in the evenings and still be close to the children.

He could just shut the door, he reminded himself. But he didn't. He always told the kids he was available to them anytime. Often troubled residents hovered outside in the hallway, waiting to be noticed and invited in. If he closed the door, he wouldn't know they were there and they wouldn't know he was really available.

Most nights the sound of approved television shows, childish conversation and laughter didn't bother him at all. Of course, most nights he couldn't hear the low undertones of Elissa's voice.

Without wanting to, even knowing it was a mistake that was going to cost him big-time, he rose to his feet and headed toward the sounds. He told himself he had to check on the children, but he recognized the lie even as he thought it. There was a staff quite able to check on the children. The person he *had* to see was Elissa.

The TV room was about forty feet square. Board games and beanbag chairs took up one corner. There was a pool table and card table by the door. At the far end stood a big-screen television, compliments of a car dealership raffle Cole had entered on a whim. He'd bought a ticket for a buck while waiting to hear on the financing for a new van for the orphanage. He'd walked with a great interest rate and a new big-screen TV.

Overstuffed sofas and chairs formed a viewing area. The lights were low as everyone focused their attention on the show. Cole ignored the actors at first, instead letting his gaze wander over the groups of kids.

The youngest ones were already in bed and a few were upstairs studying or reading, but at least a dozen of the residents had gathered around. Elissa sat on the middle sofa. Tiffany sat on one side of her, Gina on the other. Elissa had an arm around each girl.

Tiffany was still hurting, but she had started to recover. She'd had a few sessions with the child psychologist, which had helped. She'd been talking out her feelings. Cole wished there was something more he could do to help, but all that was left for Tiffany was the old cliché about time healing all wounds.

The characters on the screen changed as the show went to a commercial break. Instantly, the level of voices rose as the children started talking. Elissa answered a couple of questions and laughed at a teasing remark.

She was, he realized with a start, fitting in.

When had that happened? She'd been at the orphanage less than a month. She was young, pretty, smart and sexy as hell. What was she doing spending her life with a bunch of parentless children? Why was she back?

If she wanted a divorce, she was taking her time getting around to asking for it. When he'd hired her she'd said she wanted to figure out what she wanted in life. In the meantime, she wanted to do something useful. Could the answer be as simple as that? He didn't want it to be. He wanted to find out something terrible about her, something so awful he could get rid of her and not have to worry about Millie's wrath.

Or maybe he wanted to find a way to make her stay forever.

He pushed that thought aside. Elissa would leave. It was one of the things she did best. How long would she stay this time and how many hearts would she break when she left?

He studied Tiffany and Gina, noting the way they looked at Elissa as she spoke. They stayed in the circle of her arms, trusting her, eager to be with her, wanting to find in her the mothers they'd lost. They wouldn't find her in Elissa, but there was nothing he could say to warn them off. No one would believe him.

The image on the screen changed as the show resumed. Cole frowned as he realized it was a rerun of a Sally McGuire episode.

The young Sally walked into a long dormitory room and put her hands on her hips. "We've got three days until the costume party," she said seriously, her golden ringlets dancing with each movement of her head. "What are we going to do?"

Elissa groaned audibly. "I'm so awful, I can't stand it."

"Is that you?" Tiffany asked.

"Yup." Elissa shuddered.

Gina turned toward her. "How can you tell?"

"I just can. I know when it's my sisters and when it's me. Usually the work was split pretty equally, but there are a few shows when one of us was sick so the other two worked more."

"Was it fun?" Greg, an eleven-year-old asked, from a blue overstuffed chair next to the sofa.

"Sometimes. The hours could get long and it's really boring to wait between shots. But for the most part my sisters and I had fun."

"Why didn't you become a movie star?" Tiffany demanded.

Elissa turned toward her and leaned forward until their foreheads touched. "Because that takes talent and my sisters and I didn't have very much."

"How much?" Greg asked.

Elissa disentangled herself from the girls and held up one hand. With the other she measured about an inch on her little finger. "This much. You need a lot more to star in the movies."

"But you're good on the show," Tiffany said.

"Thanks, sweetie. It wasn't very demanding. The writers knew our limitations and made sure we weren't stretched too far. Besides, being a movie star isn't all glamour. There's lots of hard work. Traveling to different places, being away from people you care about. It's a difficult life."

Tiffany wrinkled her nose. "I've seen those magazines in the grocery store. Movie stars sure have a lot of trouble."

"Yes, they do," Elissa agreed. "Sometimes just getting through life can be challenging enough without having so much media attention focused on everything you do."

Cole wasn't sure whether or not to join the group watching television. As long as he could hear Elissa's voice, he wasn't going to get any work done. Maybe he should head back to his place, a small house on the edge of the property. At least there he wouldn't have to contend with his wife.

Before he could decide, he heard footsteps on the stairs. Mindy, the high schooler who had performed so well in the play, walked toward him. She held an algebra book in one hand and several sheets of paper in the other.

He nearly sighed in relief. He and Mindy could head over to the dining hall for their tutoring session. The complications of making x equal y should be enough to force Elissa from his mind.

But instead of stopping next to him, Mindy gave him a brief smile and stepped into the TV room.

"Don't you need help?" he asked as she moved past him.

"Not really." Her shrug was nearly apologetic. "Elissa explained some things to me a few days ago and now it all makes sense. I want to do my homework in here in case I have any questions." She cast a quick glance at the television. "Besides, I really like watching 'The Sally McGuire Show.' It's a hoot."

"Great." Cole's smile was automatic. He didn't want Mindy or anyone knowing that he resented Elissa's presence and her easy way with the children.

No, he thought grimly. Resented wasn't the right word. If he believed in his heart that she really planned to make a place for herself here, he would welcome her with open arms. For the children at least, if not for himself. But she wasn't here on a permanent basis. As soon as it suited her, regardless of the cost to anyone else, she would be gone.

Mindy settled on the floor in front of the center sofa and spread her papers around. Tiffany joined her. Gina leaned close to Elissa.

"I'm sorry you're not a movie star," the ten-year-old said.

"Why?" Elissa asked.

"If you were, you could marry a handsome prince. That's what movie stars do."

"They do not," Greg said, and frowned. "That's stupid."

"Greg, don't be a dork," Mindy said absently as she chewed on her mechanical pencil and stared at the book. "If anyone gets dibs on handsome princes, it would sure be movie stars."

Elissa smoothed Gina's straight bangs. "I knew a handsome prince once," she said quietly.

Gina's eyes widened. "Did you marry him?"

Elissa nodded.

Cole stiffened. As far as he knew, he was the only man she'd married. Somehow the phrase *handsome prince* didn't fit him. Was she mocking him?

"What happened?"

He forced himself to relax. What did he care about the answer?

Elissa tilted her head, as if deep in thought. "He decided he didn't want me anymore."

The hell he did, Cole thought furiously, refusing to acknowledge the sadness inherent in her words. *She'd* been the one to do the deciding in their relationship.

Familiar anger made his hands curl into fists. He had to get out of here before he said or did something he would regret. But before he could leave, Gina glanced up and saw him.

"Cole!" she called, her voice laced with delight. "We're watching 'Sally McGuire' with Elissa. Come watch with us."

At the child's words, Elissa turned. Her skin flushed as

her mouth dropped open. Obviously she hadn't known he was eavesdropping.

Oblivious to the tension between the adults, Gina pointed to the space on the other side of Elissa. "There's plenty of room."

If the request had come from anyone but Gina, he would have refused it. But shy Gina rarely asked for anything. He supposed he should be pleased that she and Elissa had connected. On some level he was; on another he was annoyed as hell.

As there was no way to gracefully escape, he made his way into the room and settled on the sofa. He made sure that there was as much distance between him and Elissa as possible. He didn't want to take a chance on touching her. Not when he hadn't learned to control his reaction to her.

"That's Kayla," Elissa said, pointing to the screen. Several children paraded around in pirate costumes, with a blond, green-eyed minx as their leader.

"She's the youngest?" Gina asked.

"Right. By several minutes. We never let her forget it, either. She always hated being the baby."

"Elissa, if I have an equation and I take the square root of one side, do I have to take the square root of the other?" Mindy asked.

"I don't know why you'd want to, but yes, you have to do the same thing on the other side. Don't forget to plug your solutions in to the original equation to make sure it balances."

Mindy wrinkled her nose. "I know. Sheesh, I hate algebra. Who thought it up?"

"I have no idea."

Cole noticed Elissa seemed to be avoiding him nearly as much as he was avoiding her. Was it for the same reason?

Did she recall that moment of almost-passion between them?

He'd read the desire in her eyes. At least, he told himself he had. Maybe all he'd seen was what he'd wanted to see. Nothing had changed. She hadn't wanted him in her bed five years ago, and she still didn't.

Her rejection of the physical side of their marriage had hurt almost as much as her leaving.

When would he learn? Why did she have to be the one? There were probably a couple dozen women who would find him reasonably appealing. They might not fall head over heels, but they could come to care about him. They might even find him sexually attractive.

Over the past few years a few women had indicated their interest. He'd wanted to respond. He'd wanted to take one of them into his arms and feel her tremble with desire for him. Just once.

But he never had. Not because they hadn't desired him, but because he'd never taken things that far. He couldn't; he was married. Even years of separation hadn't been enough to make him break his vows.

Tiffany stood and stretched. "I'm going to bed. Night," she said, and walked toward the sofa. She bent over and kissed Cole's cheek. "Thanks for everything," she said, her dark eyes bright with emotion.

"No problem, kid." He squeezed her upper arm.

She gave him a quick smile, then leaned toward Elissa and offered her a hug. From Elissa's surprised expression and awkward embrace, he figured it was the first time Tiffany had included her in the evening ritual.

He probed his emotions, expecting to feel anger or resentment but could find neither. Whether he liked it or not, Elissa was making friends and fitting in.

Friends. Isn't that what she'd wanted them to be?

Friends. He was never her friend. Maybe that's what had gone wrong between them.

As surely as the sun would rise in the morning, Elissa would leave. He knew that down to his soul. Yet he wasn't sure he could resist. If he couldn't have her in his life as his lover and his wife, would he want her as his friend?

A month ago he would have said no. Now, despite the pain, the resentment and the past, he wasn't so sure.

Mindy was the last of the kids to head off to bed. She closed her algebra book and grinned. "I'm done for the week. There isn't even a test until the end of the month. Now I can concentrate on important things."

"Like your acting?" Cole asked.

Her grin widened. "I was thinking more of figuring out a way to get Steve to ask me to the homecoming dance."

"Steve?"

Mindy rose to her feet, crossed the floor and patted his shoulder. "I love it when you go all protective on me. It's very sweet. Unnecessary, but sweet. Night."

With that, she left.

Elissa breathed a sigh of relief. She'd been terrified that Cole would leave before the children did, forcing her to hunt him down to explain. As it was, she could feel the heat of embarrassment staining her cheeks. What must he think of her?

She reached for the remote control and clicked off the TV. After briefly sorting out her thoughts, she cleared her throat and began speaking.

"It's not what you think," she said quietly, not quite able to meet his gaze. She angled toward him, staring at the center of his chest, at the faded sports logo on a field of dark blue. "I didn't tell the children about 'The Sally McGuire Show.' Millie brought it up a few days ago in front of Tiffany and Shanna. They're the ones who told everyone. Then tonight they insisted we watch a couple of episodes.''

She braced herself for his anger. He was so quick to find fault with her. But she hadn't done anything wrong. Scratch that, she thought, remembering the playground equipment and science camp application. She hadn't done anything *bad*.

Silence filled the room. If she hadn't been staring right at him, she would have sworn he'd left.

As he shifted in his seat, she realized the disadvantage of staring at the center of his chest—when he moved, the soft T-shirt clung to him, outlining the hard muscles of his midsection. Away from him, she could easily forget the raw power of his masculinity, telling herself it was just her overactive imagination. But in his presence she could be nothing but aware. His strength, his heat, his scent surrounded her until the world ceased to exist, except through him.

''I'm not mad,'' he said, his voice low.

''Really?''

She risked raising her gaze to his face. His dark eyes were unreadable tonight. No obvious emotion lurked there, or in the firm but pleasant set of his mouth.

''I know how Shanna found out. She ran to tell me the news as soon as she learned it. Shanna's a good kid, but she doesn't keep many secrets.''

''I noticed.'' Elissa leaned back in her seat. Thank goodness. The second he'd walked into the room, she'd been terrified he was going to blame her for the choice of television show. After what had happened—and not happened—the night of the school play, she wanted to avoid trouble.

Which didn't explain why she blurted out her next question. "If you're not mad about the show, what are you mad about?"

He stiffened slightly, then narrowed his gaze.

Elissa bit her lower lip, but didn't retract the words. Okay, maybe this wasn't the best way to avoid trouble, but she was tired of his attitude. It had been nearly a month and he hadn't loosened up at all.

"You're avoiding me," she continued when it became obvious he wasn't going to speak. "I hate that. I understand that we have a lot of things to deal with. There are unresolved issues from the past, our feelings, what we're going to do about the future. You can be angry about that if you want. I can't stop you. But at least have the grace to admit I'm doing a good job here. I know my way around the office paperwork and I connect with the kids."

He raised his eyebrows. "Angling for a raise?"

"Nothing so dramatic. It's just nice to be acknowledged."

"I'm sure Millie tells you you're doing a fine job."

Elissa almost smiled. He was good. She would bet money he'd been hell on wheels as an attorney. Millie telling her she was doing a good job wasn't the same as him saying it, nor did it mean she *was* doing a good job. After all, Millie might be biased.

Common sense and her previous experience with Cole told her this might be a good time to back off. She risked a lethal blow if she continued to toy with the tiger. Five years ago she would have gone running for cover. But she'd grown up while she'd been apart from him. She wasn't afraid of his temper or his intelligence. While his good opinion mattered, she'd learned she could get by without it. Maybe the tiger's tail needed a good tweaking.

"You're still mad," she said. "That's why you hold me at arm's length."

"I don't trust you," he admitted. "There's a difference."

His good opinion might not be necessary for survival, but his words still had the power to wound. The blow fell squarely on her chest, slicing at her confidence, bruising her pride.

A silence settled between them. Elissa refused to be the one to run away. She squared her shoulders and forced herself to take slow, deep breaths.

His gaze settled on her face. She felt his attention drift from feature to feature, as if he were comparing her to something. To the girl she'd been, perhaps? The ideal wife he'd always wanted? She hadn't compared favorably with the latter when they'd first been married. She would fall even further short of that elusive goal now.

How odd that she'd failed so completely at being his wife when all she'd wanted to do was please him. Despite the love that had burned so brightly between them, they hadn't made it work. If love wasn't enough, what was?

"Are you bored living here?" he asked.

His question was so at odds with what she was thinking, it took her a couple of minutes to process it in her brain. "Bored? Why would I be? If I'm not busy in the office, I'm helping with the children. There are a thousand things that need doing."

"I don't mean the work. I was referring to the life-style. You haven't been out since you arrived. Didn't Millie tell you which were your nights off?"

She shifted on the sofa, smoothing the skirt of her cotton sundress. "I'm not the disco type," she said. "Do they even still have disco?"

"Not really."

His mouth turned up slightly at the corners. Her heart skipped a beat. The man was good-looking enough to melt metal; what hope did she have of resisting him?

"I wasn't the one who wanted to move to New York," she reminded him. "Once we were there, I didn't much care for the pace of life in the city. I was always a homebody. Give me good friends or a good book and I'm happy."

He leaned against the back of the sofa and crossed one ankle over the opposite knee. "What about when you were on the show? You must have had a more glamorous existence then."

"I was a kid. Besides, it's not really glamorous. We had public appearances at local malls and stuff." Elissa shrugged. "It wasn't what you think, Cole. People imagine a star's life as perfect, but it's just like everyone else's."

"Everyone else doesn't have a poster that's now a collector's item."

She felt herself flush again. The triplets had posed for a Sally McGuire poster the second year of the show. It had sold very well and was now difficult to find. Fallon had told her a poster in mint condition could fetch as much as three hundred dollars. Too bad she and her sisters hadn't had a concession on that particular bit of merchandise.

"Some of the circumstances are different," she admitted. "But it's not perfect. The reality is we would drive to the public appearances, spend several hours signing autographs and talking to strangers, then we'd drive home. We were ten-year-old kids and that wasn't our favorite way to spend a weekend. Monday morning we were back on the set."

She shook her head, trying to banish the memories. "Kayla and Fallon get along now, but when we were younger, they were always fighting. It's so weird that we're only minutes apart in age, yet the three of us have very different personalities. Those two can really clash, while I'm the peacemaker. Sometimes it was a full-time job. I just wanted everyone to get along."

"But they didn't," he said.

"No. They fought. My parents fought. Then they broke up. All I ever wanted was a relationship that worked. I never had that."

"Not even with me."

She wasn't sure how he meant his comment. As an apology? A statement of fact? An admission of blame? Whatever his motivation, she didn't want to ignore the opportunity to talk about their relationship. There were things they needed to resolve.

"We both could have done better," she said.

"Yeah. Then this could have been ours." He raised his arm and motioned to the room.

She knew what he meant. Not the orphanage or the big-screen TV, but entwined lives, kids. A future.

"We really messed up, huh?"

He shrugged as if to say that sort of thing happened.

She leaned toward him. No way she was going to let him skate by this time. She wanted to know what he was thinking. "Doesn't that make you angry?" she asked. "We had so much and we blew it."

"Not angry." His mouth twisted down. "Sad. I thought it was going to be perfect and it wasn't. I thought you were going to stay."

And you didn't.

He didn't have to finish the statement. She heard the silent words.

"Don't lay that on me," she told him, irritated at the way he always brought the conversation back to her leaving. "You weren't home enough to notice I'd left."

"Then why did it hurt so bad to find you gone?"

The bitter words were his first admission of pain. They made her ache inside, for both their suffering. But she refused to be distracted from the point.

"You left before dawn every morning and you got back around midnight. If you weren't at work, you were attending parties put on by the law firm or by clients."

"They were business and I took you along."

"That's not the point, Cole. Your time was always about you and your career. It was never about us, let alone me. I had no life outside of you."

He glanced away. "I'll admit it was selfish to expect you to walk away from everything, then not consider that you could have continued your schooling in New York."

She brushed that off. "We've discussed that and we're equally at fault. I'm just saying that you were a hundred percent focused on the law firm. You had nothing left over for us. I spent my days and my nights waiting for you, wondering what you were doing or if you were even working."

His expression darkened. "What the hell are you talking about? Of course I was working. What else would I have been doing?"

Making love with another woman, she thought, amazed at how that image still had the power to haunt her. Even knowing that it was her fault if Cole had turned elsewhere didn't take away the pain.

"I don't know what else you would have been doing," she lied. "I just know you weren't with me."

"Maybe because you didn't want me there. After all, you slept best when you were alone."

Shame had a bitter flavor, almost as metallic as blood. If she could call back those words, she would. She still remembered that night. He'd stayed over at the office for three days, then had come home early the next afternoon, scruffy but elated that a case had gone well. The partner in charge had commended him, then given him a couple of hours off.

Cole had shown up with flowers and a bottle of champagne. In her mind they hadn't been enough to make up for the days of neglect. When he'd tried to kiss her, she'd turned away. When he'd suggested a nap together, she'd coldly informed him she slept better alone.

The words of rejection had hung between them, a line drawn in the sand. She'd wanted to take them back, to erase what had been said, but it was too late. His shuttered expression had told her all she'd needed to know. He wouldn't expose his pain to someone he couldn't trust.

He'd never tried to make love with her again.

Within the month, she'd left him.

"I'm sorry," she said simply, and forced herself to hold his hostile gaze. "I never meant to say that."

"What does it matter?" he asked wearily. "You thought it. That's enough."

"But I didn't. Not exactly."

"That's just semantics, Elissa." He shifted, placing both feet on the floor and facing front. He rested his elbows on his knees and clenched his hands tightly together.

She stared at the stiffness of his back, at the way the T-shirt stretched across his broad shoulders. To think this strong, handsome man had once loved her and she'd thrown it all away. There were no words left to describe her regret.

"We were both so young," she said at last. "We both made mistakes. Marriage requires flexibility and maturity. I didn't have either."

"You've become an expert?"

She flinched at his sarcasm. "I've grown up. I've taken the time to observe other couples. I'm willing to take a good part of the blame."

"I suppose I should be happy you don't want to hand it all to me."

His dark hair brushed against the back of his neck. She

remembered the silky feel of those short strands, the heat of him. She wanted to weep for all she'd lost.

"I wasn't ready for marriage," she said, confessing the truth out loud for the first time. "I loved you, but I didn't know how to be a wife. I was terrified, though I thought I could fake my way through it. Obviously, I was wrong."

He glanced at her over his shoulder. "Then why'd you marry me?"

"Because I loved you. I was afraid if I told you about my doubts, I would lose you. What if you weren't willing to wait for me? You were—" She closed her eyes against the memories, but they would not be denied. "I know you said you never noticed, but women everywhere wanted you. I saw it when we were dating while you were in law school and again when you joined the firm. I couldn't take the chance that one of them would get through to you."

Her eyes began to burn, but she blinked back the tears. Crying would accomplish nothing, except maybe making Cole despise her.

"You don't expect me to believe this, do you?" he asked.

She saw the annoyance in his eyes, the hurt, the ghosts of their past. But no compassion, no understanding.

"See, you don't get it even now. Of course you wouldn't have understood then. You would have thought I was rejecting you." She sucked in a breath. "Still, I should have tried. I didn't bother and I lost you anyway."

He turned his head, facing front again. "You didn't lose me," he said coldly. "You left. You walked out, just like everyone else in my life."

His words caught her like a slap.

If he'd lashed out at her, she could have defended herself. But the calm statement of fact as he saw it left her no recourse, no defense. What was she supposed to say? How could she explain that she might have physically left, but only because she believed he'd already emotionally moved on? It was only with the hindsight of an adult that she realized the mistakes they'd both made.

"If I'd known you cared that much, I wouldn't have left," she said.

"Yeah, right."

Familiar inadequacy flooded her. She sank into the sensation of never being enough. Once again she'd failed. Five years ago she'd had nothing to offer, and that hadn't changed. Even the money she planned to give to the orphanage was virtually meaningless. She couldn't buy meaning for her life. She couldn't buy being of value to another human being. She couldn't buy her way back into Cole's heart.

She reached out her hand toward his shoulder, wanting to touch him, needing to connect. If only he would take her in his arms.

But she could no more ask for that than she could ask for the moon. She let her hand drop to the sofa, then rose to her feet.

The pain of their physical and emotional separation made it difficult to breathe. Her heart wept for him—and for her. Had there ever been two more misguided souls? If only he had some use for her. If only she could turn back time. If only...

It was the story of her life.

"I'm sorry," she whispered, and quickly left the room.

Chapter Seven

"Here," Millie said, handing Elissa an oversize apron. "One of the perks of always having a housekeeper who is a wonderful cook is that I'm dynamite in the kitchen, but very messy."

Elissa eyed the older woman's designer dress. "Maybe you should change into something more casual."

Millie chuckled. "Haven't you guessed? I don't own very much that's casual. Jeff is a wonderful husband and a great provider. One of his few flaws is that he likes to see me dressed in nice clothes." She sighed dramatically. "It's a hardship, but one I'm willing to bear in silence."

"How noble of you." Elissa slipped on the apron, then wrapped the ties around her waist, securing them in front. "How big is this cake going to be?" she asked. "If a normal cake serves what, eight? Or is it ten? There's fifty-seven children, plus staff. Where's Mindy? I think we're going to have to use algebra to figure out this problem."

"Don't worry," Millie said. "We're making a normal cake using a regular-size mix. There will be a group celebration this Saturday night for Greg. This is private. Greg invites his closest friends. Kids only—no adults allowed. Get out the baking pans. They're over there."

Elissa moved to the far side of the cupboard and opened the right top door. Inside were dozens of different cake pans. "Round or square?"

Millie thought for a moment. "Round. It will be more fun to decorate."

"I don't understand," Elissa said. "Why is there a big celebration on Saturday if Greg's birthday is today, and why are we baking a little cake if there's going to be a big one later?"

Instead of answering, Millie glanced at the doorway. "I see you lurking there, Tiffany. Hurry up. You're late."

The twelve-year-old shuffled into the room. "I had homework," she said, her voice neutral but her expression haunted. Since getting the card returned and knowing she'd lost track of her mother, she had good days and bad ones. This was a bad one. "I still have some left to do. Maybe you should make the cake without me."

Without saying a word, Millie crossed the room and pulled Tiffany into a tight embrace. The girl hugged her back fiercely. Elissa swallowed against the tightness in her throat.

Cole had made some calls, but no one knew where Tiffany's mother was. Millie had told her that this sort of thing had happened before. Tiffany's mother made an attempt to get off drugs, then relapsed and disappeared. One of these days she was going to run out of second chances.

Elissa watched the elegantly coiffured woman and the exotically beautiful preteen. They clung to each other, held fast by a bond of affection that would survive through time.

A flash of envy cut through Elissa. She knew that the children liked her, but she hadn't been around long enough to make a difference in their lives. That's what she wanted, she realized. She wanted to have value to someone at least once.

As she watched them, she saw a single tear slip down Tiffany's cheek. Did the child cry for her mother or for herself? Elissa remembered Cole talking about the fantasy of an orphan finding a family. Of belonging. That dream had been ripped from Tiffany, leaving her with nothing but broken promises. The girl felt lost and unloved.

Elissa wished she had the right words to make it all better. Even knowing there probably weren't any words didn't make her feel any less inadequate. Of course, it was a feeling she was used to. Around Cole, she often felt inadequate. She had nothing to offer him, either. Growing up, her role in the family had been as the peacemaker. It was so passive, so without action. Kayla and Fallon were always going and doing. She was simply being.

She needed to be doing, she realized. And she was, for the first time in her life. Maybe she didn't know what to say now, but she would learn and she would get better at helping the children. They needed each other.

Millie set Tiffany at arm's length and studied her face. "It's Greg's birthday."

"I know," Tiffany mumbled. "It's just..." Her voice trailed off.

"It's just now that your mother's missing, you don't have anyone to make you feel special."

Tiffany's eyes widened. For the most part, the adults at the orphanage had been avoiding talking about what was bothering her.

"Greg considers you a good friend," Millie said. "If you take the time and effort to bake him a cake, he'll know that you think he's special. It's his birthday. Doesn't he deserve that?''

Fresh tears spilled down Tiffany's cheeks. She nodded once, then walked over to the drawer and pulled out an apron. "I want to help," she said, then wiped her cheeks and gave Millie a shaky smile.

"Good. Go get a couple of eggs from the refrigerator."

Elissa stared after the preteen as she walked across the large kitchen. "How'd you know what to say to her?" she asked Millie.

"I winged it. I've raised four children of my own, and I've worked here for a while. Sometimes it's just a matter of love, luck and common sense. I try to teach these children what I've taught my own. That doing something for someone else makes you feel good and makes that other person feel you care. You get to feel useful, they get to feel loved. It's a win-win situation. Jeff tells me I'm oversimplifying, but it works."

A few minutes later they were elbow-deep in cake mix. As Elissa adjusted the temperature on the industrial-size oven, Millie turned off the handmixer and pushed it toward Tiffany.

"You finish up. The mixing, I mean. You can lick the beaters when we're done."

Tiffany grinned. "I know."

She took the small appliance and turned it on. Holding the edge of the bowl, she carefully turned it, mixing the batter until all the lumps were gone. While Elissa poured the batter into the prepared pans, Millie and Tiffany split the beaters.

"Chocolate. My favorite," Millie said, then closed her eyes in enjoyment.

"Mine, too," Tiffany agreed, her good mood restored. "And Greg's." She rinsed the beater, then set it in the sink.

"I'm going to go play outside until the cake's done. Okay? Then I'll come back so we can frost it."

"Good idea," Millie told her.

Elissa set the timer above the oven. "I'm glad you insisted she help with the cake. She's obviously feeling better."

Millie rinsed her beater, then ran hot water into a dishpan. "A good deed, good friends and a little chocolate goes a long way to curing most of life's ills." She glanced out the window. "Those kids are really enjoying the sports equipment."

Elissa followed her gaze. She spotted Tiffany coming around from the rear of the dining hall. The preteen was hailed and invited to join an ongoing soccer game. She nodded her agreement and jumped into the action.

"I'm glad. That's why I bought it."

"The children aren't the only ones. Look." Millie pointed.

On the edge of the driveway, several younger girls stood patiently in line for their turn at double Dutch jump rope. Mindy held one end of the lines, with Cole at the other. He spoke as he turned, but Elissa couldn't hear what he was saying.

"He's great with kids," she murmured, for the thousandth time wondering what it would have been like to have stayed with him. If they could have made the marriage work, they would have a couple of kids of their own by now. Watching him with the children here had convinced her he would be a wonderful father. Did he feel the lack as keenly as she did? Was not having children of his own just one more thing he hated her for?

"There's a team of three girls who are really good jumpers," Millie said, adding dishwashing soap to the pan. She swished the water until it was bubbly, then turned off the taps. "I tease him that they're going to enter a competition and he's going to be drafted to go along as one of the turners." She shook her head, the movement causing sunlight to glint off her delicate diamond-and-pearl earrings. "Is that the right term? I can never remember. Anyway, I have this mental picture of all these teams of young girls, then Cole standing there looking out of place, but determined to win so his girls are happy."

Elissa dropped the rest of the dirty dishes into the pan. "I can see it, too," she said. "That's the kind of man he is."

Millie eyed her speculatively. "I know I'm an incredible busybody and it's none of my business, but..."

Elissa grinned. "What do you want to know?"

"I'll wash and you can dry," Millie said.

"Bribing me?"

"Maybe." The older woman reached for a dishcloth and began cleaning the mixing bowl. "Cole is very good-looking."

"Agreed."

"He's wonderful with the children, thoughtful, caring, but very masculine."

Elissa bit back a groan. Millie was going to ask why she, Elissa, had left him. While she considered Millie a friend, she wasn't sure she wanted to get into that. It had been a foolish mistake, one she would like to have the chance to go back in time and fix. But that wasn't an option. What was she going to say? Maybe the truth—that they'd both been young and foolish and that they'd acted hastily.

Millie handed her the bowl. Her blue eyes sparked with humor. "So, is he as amazing in bed as he looks?"

Elissa was pleased the bowl wasn't glass, because it slipped from her fingers and hit the counter. She caught it, wondering if her face was as bright red as it felt.

Millie didn't seem to notice. "He's hot," she went on, scrubbing the mixing blades. "The way he moves, those hands. I realize I have kids his age. It's not that I want him for myself or anything, it's just that I would have to be blind not to notice him. Also, he has that incredibly passionate nature."

"I, ah, well..." Elissa didn't know what to say. Millie had some firm views on the subject of Cole, and while they were accurate, the other woman was bound to be disappointed by the truth about what had happened in the marriage bed. Elissa was reluctant to confess all, mostly because she knew she was to blame for that failure.

"I was a virgin when we got married," she said at last. "So I really can't compare."

Millie waved a wet, soapy hand. "I understand. Cole's like Jeff. All that passion lurking behind gorgeous eyes. Even after all these years, I pinch myself and half expect to wake up from a dream. How did I get so lucky?" She lowered her voice to a confidential whisper. "The passion is important, that's for sure. When things are going badly, and in all marriages they do, if it stays hot in the bedroom, then you can ride out the storm. We've survived a lot of rough weather by locking our bedroom door and making love." She grinned. "Not that my children want to think about that. They're grown up with kids of their own and they still want to think they're the result of immaculate conception."

Elissa laughed with her, all the while wishing she had the courage to tell Millie the truth. Maybe the older woman could give her some advice. Or maybe it was too late for them.

The phone rang.

"I'll get it," Elissa said, putting down the bowl and crossing to the wall unit. She spoke into the receiver, then jotted a note on the pad stuck to the wall. When she hung up, she shrugged. "It was a message for Cole. About his legal practice. I'll put it in his office when I'm done here."

"That boy works too hard," Millie said.

"I know." Elissa was afraid the conversation would return to Cole's prowess in bed, so she changed the subject. "How's the boutique doing?" she asked.

Millie rinsed the beaters and set them on the drainer. "Wonderful. We have a new shipment coming in. You should come and look at the new clothes for fall. They're wonderful."

Twenty minutes later Elissa left the kitchen. The cake pans were cooling on the counter. She had the rest of the afternoon off. There were a couple of bills she had to pay, and a book she'd been looking forward to reading. She planned to take it easy.

Before heading to her suite, she detoured by Cole's office to leave his message. As she placed it on his desk, she noticed a stack of handwritten pages with a sheet across the front that said "Transcribe." There were several files, and they looked as if they'd needed transcribing for a while.

After casting a guilty glance over her shoulder, she thumbed through them. Cole had messy handwriting, but she'd always been able to read it. From the looks of things, he was working on a couple of cases. He probably couldn't find the time to transcribe anything.

She flipped on his computer and waited for it to boot. The bills could wait, as could her book. She would type for a couple of hours and then be out of his office before he even knew she'd been here. Cole might suspect who had helped him out, but he was unlikely to confront her about her extra work. At least she could feel that she was doing something to help him. It didn't make up for their past, but it might help straighten out their present.

* * *

It was nearly seven-thirty when Cole returned to his office. He could see light spilling out into the corridor. Hadn't he closed the door when he'd left that morning? Not that it mattered. Everything confidential was kept in locked files.

As he turned into the room, he heard the sound of someone typing on his computer keyboard. Just inside the office he came to a stop.

When Elissa hadn't shown up for dinner, he'd assumed she'd used her time off to go into town. He'd fought against the need to hunt her down and find out what she was doing. From the looks of things, she'd been here most of the afternoon.

He battled a rush of pleasure. He wasn't sure if it was from just looking at her, or from knowing she hadn't left the orphanage. Either reaction was a waste of time. Yet telling himself that didn't stop the contentment from soothing the ache inside.

"What are you doing?" he asked, his voice coming out more harshly than he would have liked.

She jumped and spun in the chair. At the sight of him, she touched a hand to her chest. "You scared me," she said, then laughed. "Uh-oh, you have that stern look, Cole. Don't be mad. I haven't done anything too horrible." She motioned to his desk and the few papers that had once been at the bottom of a very large pile of notes. "I came in here to deliver a message. When I saw all the notes you had to input, I just couldn't stand it. So I've been typing."

She stretched her fingers, then squeezed them into tight fists. "What time is it?"

"Seven-thirty."

"Oh, my. I guess I got lost in my work."

He walked to the desk and bent over her shoulder to read

the screen. Her typing was accurate, the formatting exactly what he would have done himself. He scanned the screen.

"You didn't have to do this," he said. "It's not part of your job description."

He was close enough to inhale the scent of her body. She wasn't wearing perfume tonight, although if he could have bottled the unique fragrance of her skin and sold it, he would have been wealthy beyond imagining. There wasn't a man in the world who would be able to resist that sweetness. He certainly couldn't.

"I wanted to help," she said. "It's my afternoon off, so I can spend it any way I like."

"I'll see that you're paid for your time."

She rolled her eyes. "Cole, don't be weird about this. I did something nice because I wanted to. Please don't take that away from me. Just smile and say thank-you."

He couldn't manage the smile, but he did say the words. "Thanks. I've been meaning to get to those notes for weeks."

Her grin was impish. "I could tell. Some of the pages are backdated to July. Look, I've only got a couple more to go. Give me ten minutes and I'll have them finished."

"I'd be an ungrateful beast to refuse. Have you eaten?"

She shook her head.

"I'll go fix you a sandwich and bring it back."

"That would be great. Thanks."

Fifteen minutes later he returned with a tray. In addition to the sandwich, he'd brought two cups of coffee and a slice of Greg's cake. He remembered chocolate was her favorite.

She was dusting his desk when he walked back in. She glanced up. "I couldn't resist."

All his papers had been neatly stacked. The laser printer hummed as it spat out transcribed pages. The trash was emptied, the dirty coffee mugs placed on the table by the door.

For a moment the past superimposed itself on the present. He remembered coming home to a sparkling apartment. His clothes had always been pressed and ready. He had memories of fresh flowers on their small kitchen table and heated-up dinners served on their wedding china. Even when things had started falling apart and she'd gone to bed instead of waiting up for him, she'd always left a note and something special by the plate in the refrigerator. Sometimes it was a perfect piece of fruit, or one of his favorite candy bars. Something that showed she'd been thinking about him during the day.

Had he ever returned the favor?

He set the tray in the center of the desk. "Eat," he commanded.

"Yes, sir." But instead of cowering, she gave him a grin, then reached for the sandwich.

He removed the second cup of coffee and took the seat next to his desk. He studied the dark liquid. "What did you do while I was at work?" he asked when she had finished chewing her first bite.

"When we were married?" she asked.

He nodded. "How did you fill your time?"

"I went for walks, cleaned the apartment, saw lots of exhibits at museums. I checked cookbooks out of the library, then practiced different dishes at home. I wrote letters. Nothing much." She took another bite of her sandwich and chewed slowly.

The overhead fluorescent light should have been harsh, but the bright glare only emphasized her clear skin and perfect features. Time had changed her, defining her face, erasing the last roundness of childhood. In the time they'd been apart, she'd grown up. He liked this new Elissa. Not just the physical changes, but the emotional ones. She'd become stronger, more sure of herself.

This new Elissa wouldn't be content to live her life through her husband. She would tell him to go to hell and do something on her own, whether it was to get a job or go back to college. He wished she'd been able to do that then. He didn't like realizing she'd lived her whole life for him, while he'd been living his whole life for his job.

"We were on different paths," he said.

"From the very beginning," she agreed.

"I should have been there more for you. I should have seen that you didn't have anything. I'm sorry."

Her green eyes darkened. She put down her sandwich and leaned toward him. "Thank you for saying that. You're probably not going to believe me, but those words mean a lot. We both made mistakes. Maybe we can learn from them and go forward."

"Yeah, sure."

But he didn't know what he was agreeing to. He doubted she meant giving their marriage another try. She'd walked away from it five years ago and had never made an attempt to reconcile.

"Cole, I need to go to San Diego for a few days next week. I'd like to leave on Thursday, then come back Sunday. Kayla and Patrick are back from their delayed honeymoon and Patrick's research center is opening. I'd like to be there for that."

"That's fine. Millie mentioned you haven't taken any time off, so you're due. Leave whenever you like." He desperately wanted to ask if she would bother coming back, but he didn't. He wouldn't believe her assurances, even if she gave them. If Elissa didn't leave on this trip, she would leave on another. Eventually he would walk into her room and find her gone. It was inevitable.

"You didn't meet Patrick, did you?"

He shook his head.

Elissa leaned back in her chair. "He's the vet at the clinic where Kayla worked through college. After graduation she stayed on. They became best friends. Then one day, things started to change between them." She smiled at the memory. "Kayla being Kayla, she refused to recognize she was crazy for the guy. She even had some bizarre notion that he was perfect for me. Can you imagine it? She invited me down to visit her so I could meet him."

Jealousy burned like acid in his gut. He set his coffee mug on the desk so he wouldn't hurl it against the opposite wall. "You're still married," he said, forcing himself not to grit his teeth.

"Oh, I know." She brushed off his comment with a wave. "I didn't go out with him, although I did drive down to see what all the fuss was about. From the second I saw them together, it was obvious they were madly in love and resisting the inevitable. I played Cupid."

Was that all she'd played?

He forced the question from his mind and swore silently. He refused to still care. If Elissa wanted to go with dozens of men, that wasn't his business. He was long through with her. He had to be. The alternative was to still care, which meant getting his heart ripped out when she left him again.

The printer's hum faded.

Elissa turned toward the machine and pulled out a handful of pages. "Here you are. Transcribed notes."

"Thanks," he said, taking the sheets.

"You're welcome. I was happy to do it. I want to help, Cole. I mean that. So if there are other things I can do, just let me know."

She rose to her feet. He did the same. They stood there awkwardly, staring at each other. He found himself studying her familiar features. She'd always been beautiful, but he would have loved her no matter what she looked like. He would have loved her forever, if she'd let him.

"Oh, Cole, don't look so sad. It's going to work out."

She took the papers from his hand and set them on his desk. Before he knew what she was going to do, she'd stepped close and wrapped her arms around his waist.

The unexpected hug left him defenseless. Even as he told himself to step away, he found himself hugging her back.

Without wanting to, he absorbed the feel of her next to him. Dear God, it had been so long. Familiar sensations assaulted him. Her cheek on his shoulder, her fingers pressing against his shoulders, lean lines and feminine curves taunting him. His own fingers touching her waist, his thighs brushing hers, his head bent so he could inhale the scent of her skin and hair.

His body trembled from the effort of holding back. He wanted to crush her against him, drawing her in so tightly that it would be impossible to tell where he ended and she began.

But through it all, the pleasure and the need, he remembered the pain. He could not endure that again; he couldn't take the risk. So he loosened his hold and lowered his arms to his sides.

She made a small murmur of protest. The sound ripped at him, demanding that he hold her again. Despite that, or maybe because of it, he curled his fingers into his palms and forced his arms to remain at his sides.

A few seconds later, reluctantly it seemed to him, although that could have been wishful thinking on his part, she released him.

Instead of stepping back, she looked at him. She had to raise her chin slightly for their gazes to lock. He read the questions there, and something that might have been desire.

Only, he knew better. Elissa had wanted many things from him, but sex wasn't one of them.

Then she did the most amazing thing. She rested one hand on his chest, palm flat, then raised herself up on her toes and kissed him.

Lips to lips, pressing softly. It wasn't seduction, although he was ready to be seduced. It wasn't comfort; he knew what mercy kisses felt like.

Every fiber of his being screamed at him to kiss her back. There was no reluctance in her caress. It would be so easy to tilt his head and deepen the contact. They hadn't done well together in bed, but they'd always excelled at making out. Maybe it had been all those years of practice while they'd been dating.

I want you.

For a moment his breath caught in his throat. Then he relaxed. Her lips wouldn't be lingering on his if he'd actually said the words aloud. She would have stiffened and turned away, repulsed by his animal nature.

He didn't want to think about that now. He didn't want to remember how her rejection of their lovemaking had been a personal rejection of him, of his body and his soul. He'd bared himself to her and she'd turned away in disgust.

Those memories battled with desire and won. So, despite the sweet pressure against his mouth, he did nothing. And when she broke the kiss and gave him a tentative smile, he found it easy not to smile back.

Her mouth straightened and the humor faded from her eyes. "I suppose I deserve that," she said. "I wish…"

She shrugged and left without saying what she wished.

He wished she would come back and kiss him again. Because the pain wasn't enough of a warning. If she'd kept it up a little longer, he would have given in. As it was, he was forced to spend the next half hour alone in his office, waiting for the proof of his desire to fade and the trembling in his body to still.

At least she was leaving for a few days. Maybe time apart would allow him to regain some distance.

But the thought of her being gone didn't please him. Instead he had the strong urge to call her back and ask her not to go.

Chapter Eight

Elissa pulled up in front of her sister's house. Before she had a chance to turn off the engine, Kayla and Fallon spilled out the front door and hurried toward her. Elissa quickly turned the key and opened her door. She found herself pulled into a group hug that left her breathless and laughing.

"We haven't been apart that long," she teased when Fallon and Kayla released her.

"It feels like forever," Kayla said. "Maybe because I'm married now."

"Uh-oh. It's only been a month and already days seem like months," Fallon teased. "See, getting married makes you old before your time."

"I'm ignoring you," Kayla said good-naturedly. "I know for a fact that you adore Patrick and that you're happy for both of us. Marriage is a fabulous invention. My only regret is that Patrick and I waited as long as we did to figure out we were in love."

"You're welcome," Elissa said.

Kayla kissed her cheek. "I believe I thanked you before, but I'm happy to do it again. Patrick is the best thing that ever happened to me. But let's not talk about that. What's going on in your life?"

"Nothing that exciting," Elissa said.

Fallon glanced at her white Honda. "Are you running away?"

Elissa waved at the luggage piled in her back seat. "No. I'm taking a few things back to the orphanage with me."

Kayla and Fallon exchanged knowing looks.

"It's not what you think," Elissa said quickly.

Faces that looked so much like hers that strangers couldn't tell them apart took on identical expressions of disbelief. Green eyes widened slightly and mouths turned up into teasing smiles.

"Uh-huh," Fallon said, linking her arm with Elissa's. Kayla took Elissa's other arm. "No problem. We believe you. We're even going to let you live with the illusion of privacy for a couple of hours. Then, when it gets late and we've lulled you into a false sense of security, we're going to pounce like rabid animals and wrestle your secrets from you."

Elissa turned to Kayla. "I think the kids are starting to get to her."

"She's always like this when the school year begins. She's nearly as hyper as her students. I'm sure that's why they adore her."

The three women started for the house.

"They adore me because I'm a good teacher." Fallon's teasing voice turned serious. "I'm going to miss it when I take my sabbatical."

Kayla shook her head. "I can't believe that I was the one with all the plans to see the world and you're going to be the one doing the traveling."

"Nothing turns out like we expect," Elissa said, thinking of her own odd relationship with Cole. She couldn't define it, nor could she explain her feelings.

Two nights before, she'd given in to impulsive feelings and hugged him. When he'd hugged her back, pressing his body to hers, she'd had a strong sense of homecoming. As if she'd only ever been alive in his arms. Odd, because the sex between them had been so strained.

She'd felt something else, too. Something like heat bubbling through her. As if her skin had suddenly grown too small. The achy sort of restlessness had followed her most of the night. She still couldn't explain it.

The front door of the house opened and Patrick stepped outside. Kayla's husband was a blond, blue-eyed hero type who could easily pose for the cover of *GQ*. "My three favorite women in the world," he said.

Elissa slipped free of her sisters and went to her brother-in-law. He took both her hands in his and smiled at her. "Elissa, welcome."

"You can still tell us apart," she said.

"Of course. Although I keep telling Kayla that the bonus is if we ever get bored with each other, one of you can trade places with her and I'll pretend not to notice. Three for the price of one, so to speak."

Elissa kissed Patrick on the cheek and grinned at him. "What do we get out of it?"

He winked. "I'm pretty amazing."

"Gee, and Kayla never thought to mention that."

Patrick released her and touched his chest. "I'm mortally wounded."

"You deserve to be. You're recently married and already talking about sister swapping?"

"Only in theory." His gaze lingered on his wife.

Elissa read the love there. As Kayla's sister and Patrick's friend, she was thrilled for the happiness they'd found together. As a person, she was willing to admit to a twinge of envy. Their relationship had been a little rocky at the beginning, but only because they were both so stubborn. It had been obvious to everyone else that they were wild about each other. They'd nearly had to lose each other in order to find where they needed to be.

She and Cole *had* lost each other—for years—and it hadn't helped at all. Is that what she wanted? To find her relationship with her husband? She shook her head. She didn't want that flawed relationship back; she wanted something stronger and more mature.

Patrick opened the front door and motioned for everyone to step inside.

"I hate to greet and run," he said, "but I have a few last-minute details to take care of for the opening of the research facility. Are you three going to be okay here by yourselves?"

The sisters looked at each other and laughed.

"We'll be fine," Kayla assured him, moving into her husband's embrace. "Amazingly enough, we're used to being alone together. We have fun."

"Okay. I'll be late. Don't wait up." He kissed her cheek, waved and left.

Kayla stared after him. "Did I get lucky, or what?"

"Very lucky," Fallon said, then turned to Elissa and added in a mock whisper, "This 'in love' stage is so gross. You think she'll get over it soon?"

"Probably not for another couple of months."

Kayla put her hands on her hips. "I can hear you guys."

"We know." Fallon grinned. "Come on, Elissa. You're bunking with me. Do you still snore?"

Elissa chuckled. "No, do you?"

"Never."

The easy banter reminded her of all the good times she and her sisters had spent together. They were a team against the rest of the world. With them, she belonged.

But even as the easy conversation continued while they collected her overnight case and showed her to the pleasant guest room she would share with Fallon, Elissa found herself wishing for more.

If only Cole were with her. Despite the distance between them and her confusion about her feelings, he was her husband and as much a part of her as the sisters with whom she'd been born.

Elissa dipped her spoon into the pint of strawberry ice cream. After a dinner of spaghetti with homemade garlic bread, the last thing she needed was a very rich, very fattening dessert.

"Heaven," she murmured, closing her eyes briefly as she let the treat melt on her tongue.

"That about describes it," Fallon said from her place on the sofa. "All we need is some well-oiled young man rubbing our feet."

Kayla shook her head. "I don't think so. I'd rather have my sugar-and-fat fix separate from any foot rubbing. I want to be able to fully concentrate on the experience."

"The foot rubbing or the eating?" Fallon asked.

Elissa chuckled. "The eating," she and Kayla said in unison.

Fallon nodded. "That's what I thought. Just checking."

"This is nice," Elissa said. "We were last together for our birthdays in July, but before that it had been close to a year. I like these get-togethers. Let's not let another year go by before we do it again."

"We'll be together at Christmas," Kayla reminded her. "That's not so far away."

"But it won't be the three of us," Fallon said. "You're bringing Patrick."

Kayla's green eyes darkened. "Do you mind? I know it was supposed to be just the three of us, but he is my husband and—"

"Stop it," Elissa said gently. "Fallon isn't suggesting you leave Patrick behind. We like him. The point was it won't be the same as just the three of us. I suggest we send him out on a fishing boat or something for the day and then make time to be alone together."

"That's great," Kayla said.

Fallon scooped up another spoonful of ice cream. "Little Elissa. Forever the peacemaker. I guess some things never change."

She was right, Elissa thought, glancing at her sisters. Kayla sat on the floor, her back against the sofa. She wore cutoff denim shorts and a tank top. Both had survived countless washings. There wasn't a lick of makeup on her face and her hair was pulled back in a messy ponytail.

Fallon claimed the other end of the sofa. Tailored trousers and a tucked-in short-sleeved silk blouse emphasized the slender feminine shape they'd all inherited. Fallon's hair was loose, but she'd blown it dry with a big round brush, taking the time to smooth out most of the curls. Conservative makeup emphasized wide green eyes and high cheekbones. If Kayla was the bratty one, then Fallon was the grown-up.

Elissa looked down at her floral print sundress. Long hours playing outdoors with the children had left her legs and arms faintly tanned, so she wasn't wearing panty hose.

Her minimal makeup was somewhere between Kayla's none and Fallon's professional appearance. She'd pulled her hair back into a French braid, then tucked the end under, securing it out of sight with pins.

They were a study in contrasts, as if a magazine editor had taken the same woman and given her three different looks. Their personalities were as different as their clothing choices.

She glanced at the remaining half carton of ice cream, leaned forward in the love seat and picked up the cover from the table. She firmly put it in place, then stood. Each of her sisters followed suit. She collected the cartons and took them to the freezer.

"You know they're not going to make it through the night," Kayla called after her.

"I know," Elissa said, "but let's at least pretend we have control." She returned to her seat and smiled. "So, what's new in your lives?"

Fallon and Kayla exchanged a look.

"No, you don't," Fallon said. She crossed her legs and raised her eyebrows. "You're the one suddenly living with her estranged husband. You go first."

Elissa resisted the urge to squirm. In the back of her mind she'd been expecting them to question her. It was one of the reasons she'd come to spend the weekend. Her sisters always helped her see things more clearly. Right now she was so confused about Cole and herself, about her feelings and what she was doing at the orphanage.

"We're not living together," she said. "At least, not how you guys mean it."

Kayla touched a hand to her chest. "Did I say anything about sex? Did you?" she asked, looking at Fallon. "I think not. Elissa, I'm deeply, deeply hurt you would assume that either of us would even stoop to consider that."

"Uh-huh." Elissa wasn't fooled.

"So *have* you done the wild thing?" Fallon asked with a straight face. "You don't have to go into a lot of detail. A simple 'Yes, but I haven't been on top yet' would be sufficient."

"You guys!" Elissa reached next to her for a small pillow and tossed it in their general direction.

Kayla nodded solemnly. "That would be a no, Fallon. Elissa and Cole have not done the wild thing yet."

Laughter exploded in the room. Elissa leaned back in the love seat and realized she was lucky to have two wonderful sisters who cared about her.

When the room was quiet, she drew in a deep breath. "I like being there. Our visits when we were kids were so fleeting we never really got a chance to understand the workings of the orphanage. I thought it would be a sad place, but it isn't. These children are warm and loving. All they want is to belong. While it isn't the same as a traditional family, they have something there, and it's quite wonderful."

"A new career choice?" Fallon asked.

"Maybe. I'm not sure. It's only been a few weeks, so I'm still at the 'in love' stage you get with any new job. Sometimes the work is hard and sometimes I don't know what to say to the kids. The office work is easy, but it's the children who give me a sense of purpose."

"Kids are great," Kayla agreed.

"Do you still stay in touch with that little girl you met earlier this year?" Fallon asked. "The one in the bad car accident?"

Kayla spent part of her day taking dogs to visit seniors at a nursing home. Earlier in the summer, she'd started visiting a young girl confined to bed in a body cast.

"Absolutely. Allison wasn't up to coming to our wedding, but Patrick and I visited her just before we left on our honeymoon, and showed her pictures." Kayla shifted on the floor and sat cross-legged. "So you like the kids at the orphanage. What else?"

"I also enjoy giving to them. I ordered a jungle gym and some sports equipment. They love playing with everything. It's very satisfying to watch."

"Elissa, tell me you're not being foolish with the money," Fallon said, obviously concerned.

"I know what you're thinking," Elissa said. "In the past I was very worried about our trust fund. The thought of having a lot of money was terrifying." She remembered the sleepless nights she'd spent as her twenty-fifth birthday had approached. While Fallon had devised a sensible plan for her money and Kayla had planned to travel the world, she, Elissa, had fretted.

"I never understood that," Kayla said. She rested her hands on her knees. "It's just money. It can't hurt you."

"It can if I turned out to be like our father."

Silence greeted Elissa's statement. She shrugged self-consciously. "I guess I never told you guys, but I was afraid of being just like him."

Fallon leaned forward. "Elissa, Dad was a drunk. He spent money on fast cars, expensive clothes and cheap women. You have nothing in common with him."

"I can be impulsive, just like him."

Kayla rolled her eyes. "Dating someone for over two years before getting married isn't impulsive. You're not self-destructive. He always was."

"I know. I see that now. But while we were growing up, Dad always told me I was the most like him."

"Wishful thinking on his part," Fallon said. "Elissa, you're a sensible, responsible woman. I applaud your desire to share your good fortune with others. I just want to make sure you don't give it all away in a fit of undeserved guilt.''

"You're right. I keep forgetting I'm not a scared little girl. I don't have to be perfect to be loved.''

Fallon grinned. "I've got news for you, kid. You were never perfect and we still loved you.''

Elissa smiled. A warm glow filled her chest. This is what she liked best about her sisters. The belonging. No matter what, she always had a place with them.

"I love you, too,'' she said. "Don't worry. I've hired a financial planner and she's investing the money for me. I've set aside a certain amount for charity. I think I'm going to be giving it to the orphanage. I want to make a difference there.''

"Oh, speaking of that, I made all the arrangements,'' Fallon told her.

"What arrangements?'' Kayla asked. "I swear, you two are always leaving me out of the good stuff.''

"Relax,'' Elissa said. "The children were invited to a special science camp offered at the local university. Even with the discount the state offered, they couldn't afford it. So I'm sending everyone.''

"She mailed me the application and a check,'' Fallon said. "I did the paperwork and sent it along. I also ordered a bunch of new clothes for the kids.'' The oldest of the three triplets cleared her throat. "I, ah, decided to order a few more things than you'd put on the list,'' she admitted. "I wanted to help, too.''

Kayla frowned. "See. I *was* left out. Just because I'm the youngest.''

"Ignore her,'' Fallon said.

Elissa looked at her triplet. "Thanks, Fallon. I appreciate it, and the kids will love it.''

"So Cole still doesn't know about the money?" Kayla asked.

Elissa shook her head. "I don't want to tell him. By having Fallon take care of the details, I can claim no knowledge and not actually be lying."

"Semantics," Fallon said.

"If it works, I'm not going to complain," Elissa said.

Kayla tilted her head. "So, how is Cole?"

"Grown up," Elissa said. "He probably was five years ago, but I never noticed. He's responsible, good with the children."

"Is he still angry because you left?" Kayla asked.

"Yes," Elissa answered, trying to keep her tone light. "He's not one to forgive and forget."

"Then he shouldn't have acted in a way that would force you to leave," Fallon said, bristling with temper. "That man was the most selfish, self-centered—"

"You're being redundant," Kayla said.

"I know, but I like it. Selfish, self-centered *toad*."

Elissa drew in a deep breath. "Fallon, I appreciate you taking my side, but I'm not entirely blameless. I could have tried harder, too. I should have talked to him, or tried to get a life of my own. I wanted Cole to be my entire world, and that's not realistic."

Fallon frowned. "So he's convinced you that everything is your fault? That's so typical of him. I don't know why I'm surprised."

"No, it's not like that," Elissa insisted. "He's a good man. If you could see him with the children." She thought for a moment, wondering how much of Cole's past she could share. Fallon had never really liked Cole, but she hadn't understood him the way Elissa had...and did.

"There's a wonderful girl at the orphanage. Her name is Tiffany and she's amazingly beautiful. Her mother is African-American and her father Eurasian, so she has stunning features and this gorgeous dark, curly hair. Anyway, her mother has a drug problem and has been in a rehabilitation facility. Recently Tiffany found out her mother had left the facility and no one knew where she was. Tiffany was crushed. I didn't know what to say to her, but Cole did. He took the time to hold her and dry her tears. He heard her out, made sure she got counseling. He was perfect. I could only stand by and wring my hands. I didn't like being that helpless."

"Fine," Fallon said. "He's great with kids, but a lousy husband."

"We were both too young," Elissa said. "He only gets half the blame."

"He broke your heart."

"I left him."

Fallon didn't look convinced. "So have you talked about getting a divorce?"

Elissa stiffened. "No. Of course not."

"Why wouldn't you? Isn't that why you went there? To start a civil dialogue so you could get divorced?"

Elissa glanced from Fallon to Kayla and back. "Why would you think that?"

Kayla smiled gently. "Why else would you want to see him after all this time?"

"Because—" She clamped her mouth shut. She didn't really have an answer to that one. "I wanted closure."

"On the marriage?" Fallon asked. "Wouldn't a divorce be the best kind of closure?"

"No. I don't want to divorce him."

"Are you still in love with him?"

"No, but—"

"Then what's the point? This is just a farce. It's been five years, Elissa. If he wanted you, he would have come after you. Maybe it's time for you to grow up and face the truth.''

Fallon wasn't saying anything Elissa hadn't told herself, but the badgering tone of the questions made her uncomfortable. She didn't confront people well.

"I'm not sure what Cole wants," she said.

"Have you asked him?"

"No, but—"

"Has he said he wants you around?"

"No. I think he wants me to leave. I—"

"Then the ball's in your court. If you don't love him, you should make a clean break. You both deserve that.''

"But, I—"

"Face it, Elissa. It's over for both of you.''

Elissa jumped to her feet. "Shut up," she said loudly. "Stop telling me what I feel. I might not still be in love with Cole, but I care about him. I'm not prepared to divorce him. I don't know if I'm willing to go the rest of my life without seeing him. I'm not ready to give up on my marriage.''

Instead of shouting back, Fallon smiled. "Is that what you came home to find out?'' she asked in a reasonable tone.

"Yes!'' Elissa yelled, then sank back onto the love seat. "I hate it when you do that to me.''

"Force you to say what you feel?'' Fallon asked.

"Exactly. Ignorance is easier to live with.'' She rubbed her temples. "Being with him makes me crazy. There's a part of me that wants to make it work, but I'm so afraid. Not so much of making mistakes, but of the fact that he doesn't need me. He's made this terrific life and there's no room for me.''

"He could think the same about you," Kayla said.

"Maybe." Elissa dropped her hands to her lap. "What if he doesn't love me anymore?"

"How does he treat you?" Fallon asked.

"He mostly tries to ignore me."

She thought about their kiss. She'd pressed her mouth to his and had waited for him to respond. He hadn't backed away, but he hadn't returned the embrace. Funny how in their marriage she'd always been so terrified to try anything because she was convinced she would do it wrong. With nothing to lose, it was easier to take the risk. Or maybe she was more mature now. Unfortunately she wasn't any more experienced.

The only thing that had kept her from being completely humiliated by his lack of response had been the bulge she'd seen in his jeans. He might have been able to keep his face impassive, but there were parts of him that reflected the turmoil he felt inside. He might not have wanted her to know, but their kiss had turned him on.

"If Cole didn't care about you, he would be able to treat you like one of the guys," Fallon said.

"It's true," Kayla said. "Remember how crazy I was at the thought of you and Patrick dating? I didn't know I loved him, but the jealousy nearly killed me." Her youngest sister shrugged. "I saw Cole's face when you were walking up the aisle at your wedding. I've never seen such raw emotion before. He loved you more than anything. I bet he still does."

Fallon nodded. "She's right, but that's not what's important. You have to figure out what you feel. Do you love him? Do you want to make it work again?"

"I don't know," Elissa said, wishing she could figure it out. "Even if I do, how do I get him to give me a second chance? He's never going to trust me again."

THE SILHOUETTE READER SERVICE™ - HERE'S HOW IT WORKS:

Accepting free books places you under no obligation to buy anything. You may keep the books and gift and return the shipping statement marked "cancel". If you do not cancel, about a month later we'll send you 6 additional novels, and bill you just $3.71 each plus 25¢ delivery per book and GST.* That's the complete price–and compared to cover prices of $4.50 each–quite a bargain! You may cancel at any time, but if you choose to continue, every month we'll send you 6 more books, which you may either purchase at the discount price…or return to us and cancel your subscription.

*Terms and prices subject to change without notice.
Canadian residents will be charged applicable provincial taxes and GST.

If offer card is missing, write to: Silhouette Reader Service, P.O. Box 609, Fort Erie, Ontario L2A 5X3

0195619199-L2A5X3-BR01

SILHOUETTE READER SERVICE
PO BOX 609
FORT ERIE ON   L2A 9Z9

CDMA Member

MAIL≫POSTE

Canada Post Corporation/Société canadienne des postes

Postage paid   Port payé
If mailed in Canada   si posté au Canada

Business   Réponse
Reply   d'affaires

0195619199   01

"That's easy," Kayla told her. "Men have one weakness. Exploit it."

"What would that be?" Elissa asked.

Kayla grinned. "Seduce him, honey. He won't know what hit him."

Seduce him. It was great advice for anyone but her. How was she supposed to seduce anyone? She didn't have the faintest idea where one started in a quest to seduce one's husband.

She'd almost asked her sisters. After all, they loved her and would be happy to give her advice. But she couldn't. Even though they shared nearly everything, the thought of them knowing she was a complete failure in bed was just too humiliating to think about. Not that they would have made fun of her or anything. She sighed. Did it matter who knew? After all, she was putting the cart in front of the horse.

Before she worried about the how, perhaps she'd better think about the why. Why should she bother seducing Cole...unless she was still in love with him?

What was love? At twenty, she could have defined it perfectly. Now she wasn't so sure. She admired and respected him. She wanted to spend time with him. Thoughts of him kept her awake at night. She wanted him to be happy in his work and in his life. She wanted to matter to him. Was that love?

As she drove north, she recalled their past and all the mistakes. She remembered the good times, too. The miles flew by. When she turned off the highway onto the road that would take her to the orphanage, she had the feeling of coming home. As if this was where she belonged.

It wasn't about the place, she realized as she parked her car. It was about being close to Cole.

She left her luggage in the trunk and hurried toward the main building. It was seven-fifteen. Most of the children would be in the TV room. Cole would be there, too.

Elissa stepped inside and followed the sound of voices and laughter. She found Cole sitting on the center sofa, with a pile of children all around him. Gina sat on his lap. They were, she realized with some dismay, watching an old Sally McGuire show.

She grimaced. That series was going to haunt her for the rest of her life.

Before Elissa could announce that she was back, Gina pointed to the screen. "Can you tell if that's Elissa or not?"

"Sure. It's one of her sisters."

Tiffany looked up from the jigsaw puzzle she'd spread on the floor. "How can you tell?"

"Elissa's the pretty one."

His simple compliment made her want to fly into his arms. He thought she was pretty. She clasped her hands together in thanksgiving.

"When is Elissa coming back?" Tiffany asked.

"Maybe later tonight. I'm not sure," Cole said. "She hasn't called. She might stay in San Diego awhile."

Elissa frowned. She'd told him she would be back this evening and here she was. Why was he saying that to the children?

"Remember, Elissa's stay here is just temporary," Cole said. "She's helping out Millie, but she's not part of the permanent staff."

Gina straightened on his lap. Her mouth formed a soundless *no*.

Tiffany tossed down a puzzle piece. "That's gross."

Elissa wanted to jump into the room and protest her innocence. She had no plans to leave. Then she remembered she had no plans to stay, either. She was here because Cole

he wanted to think about their marriage,
scussion had she considered the children.
to make a commitment to them, too? It
to make promises until she was sure.

ht to protect the kids. What choice did he
alked out on him.

out of the room and leaned against the hall
ruth slammed into her like an express train,
rough barriers, shattering pretense, leaving her
nd exposed.

she'd started to figure it out when Fallon had
er to admit she wasn't willing to discuss a divorce.
she'd known when she'd decided to come and see
. Maybe she'd always known.

Cole was her destiny. She hadn't come to the orphanage
do good deeds or give away her trust fund, or even to
find closure. She'd come because she loved her husband.
She'd never stopped loving him.

The trick was going to be getting him to give her a second chance.

Chapter Nine

Elissa wasn't sure how long she stood in the hallway, forcing herself to keep breathing in and out so that she didn't faint.

What now? She could hardly waltz into the TV room and announce her feelings. Aside from the fact that she wasn't the type to share those private thoughts publicly, she knew Cole wouldn't believe her. She needed a plan of action.

Voices from the other room carried out into the hall. The sound of the children made her smile. How simple life could be when one was young. Although it hadn't been for her or for Cole.

She forced away thoughts of the past and focused on the present. Her first step was to act normal. Until she figured out what else to do, Cole must never know about her change of heart. He would probably find an excuse to ge rid of her if he thought she was entertaining romantic thoughts about him. Better to play it safe...for now.

She straightened, smoothed the front of her dress, forced herself to smile broadly and sailed into the TV room.

"Hi, everyone," she said.

The children turned toward her. Gina, Shanna and Tiffany made a beeline for her. She dropped to her knees and hugged them. Warm, small bodies pressed against her. Young voices spoke in a cacophony of questions.

"When did you get back?"

"Did you have a good time?"

"Did you bring us anything?"

Elissa laughed. "This is the best welcome I've ever had. I had a wonderful time with my sisters and I'm very glad to be back. Oh, and yes, I did bring you guys something."

A couple of dozen pairs of eyes fixed on her. She glanced at Cole, who was still on the sofa but had turned to watch her. She shrugged apologetically. "There's this wonderful bakery near Kayla's house. I stopped on my way out of town and got brownies."

"Brownies!" Shanna stepped back and clapped her hands together. Her freckled nose wrinkled with delight. "They're my favorite. Can we have them tonight?"

Everyone turned to stare at Cole. Elissa tried to read his expression, but couldn't. He probably resented her for dropping in to his and the children's lives this way. Maybe the brownies hadn't been a good idea. But she'd wanted to bring them something, yet it couldn't be anything too expensive or Cole would suspect that she was the one who had bought the sports equipment.

He rose to his feet. "Are they in the car?" he asked.

"Yes. In four boxes."

"You'll need some help with them. Shanna, go tell the

kids upstairs there's a treat if they want one. The rest of you, stay here.''

A collective cheer rose in the room. Cole followed her into the hallway.

"Are you mad?'' she asked when they were out of ear-shot of the children.

"No, why?''

She shrugged. "Bringing back brownies like I did. I didn't mean it as a cheap trick or anything. I genuinely missed the kids. I was thinking about them as I packed to come back, and I thought about the brownies.''

As they stepped out of the main building and into the twilight, she felt his gaze on her. His unspoken disbelief was as loud as thunder.

"I really did miss them,'' she said defensively.

"I never said you didn't.''

"You didn't have to. You have the most eloquent silence of anyone I know.''

"If that was a compliment, thank you.''

She bit her lower lip. This was *not* the way to reconcile with her husband. But what was? Should she talk about the past? The future?

"How are your sisters?'' he asked as they walked toward her car.

"They're fine. They send their love.''

"I doubt that.''

She stopped and stared at him. He slowed, then turned to face her. In the semi-darkness he seemed to tower above her. His features were in shadow, and unreadable. His strength, the power of him, drew her. Despite everything, he made her feel safe. With him, she could find a place to belong.

"My sisters don't hate you,'' she said.

"Fallon does.''

"She's angry about a few things you did, but she actually likes you."

He smiled briefly. "I'd hate to see her behavior when she dislikes someone. Are they left beaten on the side of the road?"

"Cole!"

He shoved his hands into his jeans front pockets. "Did you have a good time?"

"Yes, I did. Patrick was busy with the opening for the research center. The entire structure wasn't finished, but the labs were, so they decided to christen it, or whatever it is you do to a building. Anyway, with him occupied, the three of us hung out together."

"Talking and eating ice cream."

She laughed. "Of course."

She looked at his face. He met her gaze. Instantly, thoughts of last week filled her mind. Her impulsive hug, her more impulsive kiss. Was he remembering it, too?

She felt herself sway toward him. She wanted him to kiss *her* this time. She wanted to feel his arms around her, his hard body pressing against hers.

Something hot sparked between them. She felt it singe her skin. Instead of causing her to step back and take cover, she moved closer. A single step. She breathed his name.

He pulled his hands out of his pockets and turned away. "Your car's over here, right?"

"Yes," she said, careful to keep the disappointment from her voice. "The white Honda. The bakery boxes are on the front seat."

If he noticed the clothes piled in the back, he didn't say anything. He grabbed all four boxes. "I'll see you inside," he said, heading back to the main building.

Elissa stood alone in the dark. Obviously realizing she was still in love with Cole wasn't going to be enough to win him back. She was going to have to find a way to win his trust. But how did a wife who had walked out on her husband—especially when that husband already had a problem with abandonment—go about rebuilding trust? How did she make him take a chance on her again?

Instinctively she knew there were no words that could convince him. It would take action. First she had to get his attention, then she had to keep it focused on them. He'd loved her once. Her sisters were right—he was acting too cautious for that love to be completely dead. There had to be some feelings left; otherwise, he wouldn't care if she was around or not. She had to find those feelings and bring them back to life. It wasn't going to be easy, but she refused to let the size of the task daunt her. Cole was her destiny and nothing was going to keep her from him.

Cole frowned as he opened the large box from the university. "Did we order any books?" he asked Millie.

"I'm on the phone," she called back. "Give me a sec and I'll be there."

He opened the container and stared inside. Under the welcoming letter was an inventory. According to that sheet there were fifty-seven name tags, fifty-seven notebooks, complete with itinerary adjusted to the age of the student, fifty-seven letters to be given to teachers explaining why the children would be missing school and what they would learn at the camp.

Camp? "The science camp?" he asked aloud. "There has to be a mistake."

He picked up the phone and punched the button for line two. Ten minutes later he hung up, no clearer on what had happened than when he'd first dialed the number.

Millie walked into his office. "What did you want?" she asked, then caught sight of the box. "What's that?"

"Our supplies for the university science camp."

Her eyebrows drew together. "I don't understand. Even with the discount offered, we couldn't find the money in the budget."

"My point exactly. Someone paid for the camp." Pleasure for the children warred with the sensation of being played for a fool. "Was it you?"

"Me?" Millie touched a hand to her chest. "Cole, we've been through this. Jeff is very specific about financial donations. You know he prefers to give money. Besides, I would have warned you."

Her blue eyes held his gaze. There was no reason for Millie to lie to him. She never had before. She preferred straightforward confrontations to subterfuge.

There was a knock on his open office door. Elissa entered the room. "Am I interrupting?"

"No," Millie said. "What's up?"

"I paid the bills. I've put everything on your desk. If you'll just sign the checks, I'll get them in today's mail."

Sunlight shone in through the window and highlighted the gold in Elissa's hair. She wore it up today, a pile of curls on the top of her head. A simple pink sundress left her arms bare and floated down nearly to her ankles. She could have posed for a cameo. Two parts innocence and one part temptation.

He wanted to ask Millie to leave, then lock the door behind her, sweep his desk clean and take Elissa right there, between the computer and the phone. Hard and hot, touching her, kissing her, tasting her until the rest of the world disappeared and all that was left was the fire burning between them.

As quickly as it had occurred, the image disappeared. There would be no moment of passion between them. That part of their relationship was long over. No matter how tempted, he wouldn't subject himself to that kind of humiliation again. Elissa had made her feelings on the subject very clear. She didn't like sex; she'd never once been swept away by passion; he didn't turn her on.

Elissa pointed to the box on Cole's desk. "What's that?"

"I was just about to ask you," he said.

"Me? But I haven't ordered anything." She crossed the floor and stared inside. "What is this?"

"Our letter of acceptance and the materials for the science fair next week. Someone paid for all the children to go."

Elissa smiled. "That's great. Who did it?"

"I don't know." His gaze narrowed. "I thought you could tell me."

Her smile broadened. "Don't look at me. I don't get paid that much."

He kept his expression hard, and her humor faded.

"Seriously, Cole, I never contacted the university about this science program. Now that you mention it, Millie and I did talk about it a couple of weeks ago. She said the university had offered a discount but it was still too expensive for you to send the kids. I'm glad someone else came through."

Like Millie, she had no reason to lie. On her pay, she could hardly afford something like this. So why didn't he want to believe her?

"So this is where the party is," a man said.

The three of them turned toward the door. Their UPS driver wheeled in several boxes on a dolly. "I've got a dozen more back in the truck," he said, and handed Millie a clipboard. "Here, darlin', why don't you sign this for me? And write something nice." He winked. "I don't suppose you're prepared to run off with me yet?"

The driver was all of twenty-six, a good-looking California surfer type.

Millie laughed. "Ronnie, one of these days I'm going to accept your flirtatious invitation and you're going to be left backpedaling so fast, they'll smell the burning rubber all the way to the Arizona border."

"No way, Mills. You know I have this thing for older ladies." He winked. "Hey, Elissa, Cole. I'll be back with the rest of the boxes."

The young man left. Cole stared at the new boxes. "Now what?"

Elissa grabbed the scissors from his desk and crossed to the stack. She opened the first one. "Clothes," she said. "For all the children." She looked at him. "I guess whoever is sending them to camp wants them to look good."

"Curiouser and curiouser," Millie said, and grinned.

"It's not amusing," Cole told her. A bad feeling nibbled at the back of his neck.

Thirty minutes later all the boxes had been opened and sorted. There were new jeans, T-shirts and sweats for all the residents. Millie had placed the clothes, along with the name tags and notebooks, into neat piles on the floor of his office.

"We'll tell the children at dinner tonight," she said. "They're going to be thrilled."

"I'm not happy with this," Cole said. "Something's wrong. The clothes are all the right sizes. How would anyone know that?" He stared at the two women. "Someone called to get that information. Who was it?"

Elissa and Millie, both kneeling on the floor, shared a look of confusion. "No one called me," his wife said.

"Ditto," Millie told him. "And before you go accusing anyone else, do you really think it's that important to find out who is being generous? Can't you just smile and say thank-you?''

''No.''

The older woman rose to her feet. ''Fine. You go ahead and waste time worrying about who dares to interfere in such a hideous way. In the meantime, you've got another problem.'' She picked up a letter from his desk and waved it in the air. ''The university rules require one adult per seven children attending. That means eight adults. We're going to be short three.''

Cole hadn't thought of that.

''Before you ask, Jeff and I would be happy to come along. We don't have plans for that weekend and Jeff's always been a science nut. But that still leaves you one short.''

''Okay.'' He thought about the college kids he had working for them. The science fair would interfere with their class schedules and he really hated to do that. Maybe one of them could juggle things and attend a different lecture.

''Elissa, would you like to go with us?'' Millie asked.

''Don't be ridiculous,'' Cole said. ''Elissa has no interest in that.''

Elissa smiled. ''Gee, Cole, don't feel you have to hold back what you're thinking. Just spit it out.''

He swallowed hard, fighting embarrassment. ''I didn't mean it like that. If you want to come with us, then you're certainly welcome. I didn't think you'd enjoy a science camp.''

He didn't think he would enjoy spending four days that close to her. At least at the orphanage he had his own office and lots of people around to act as a buffer. He'd chaperoned camps before. The adults were left to their own devices, and during the day that could mean plenty of time with nothing to do. The last thing he needed was hours spent in Elissa's presence. He didn't think he could stand it. Despite all his promises to himself that he would never be tempted by her again, he was only a man. There was no guarantee he would be able to resist the one thing he most desired.

"I think it would be interesting," she said. "Thanks for suggesting it, Millie. I'd love to go."

"Great," he said through gritted teeth.

He would just ignore her, he decided. That would be easy enough.

The science camp was held in an off-campus location just north and east of the city of Santa Barbara in the foothills. Botany students cared for the grounds, experimenting with different plants and fertilizers, creating lush growth and patches of exotic flora.

Cole stepped away from the sleeping cabin and told himself there was no reason for his grumpy mood. The camp was great, the weather perfect, the kids happy. What more did he want?

As if to prove that fate had a sense of humor, Elissa walked into view. Perhaps in deference to the outdoor activity, or perhaps to play havoc with his senses, she wore jeans. He'd never seen her in jeans before. Elissa was a soft and delicate woman, preferring gauzy cotton and whispering silk...and dresses. Always dresses.

He'd found it difficult to be around her at the orphanage, but at least there she was covered from shoulders to midcalves by loose clothing. Here, not only was she always underfoot, but the jeans and skimpy T-shirt left nothing to the imagination.

Tiffany ran up to Elissa and grabbed both her hands. The preteen spoke intently. When she finished her message, she ran off, toward one of the classroom buildings, obviously eager for her next lesson. Elissa shook her head in bewilderment.

Before he could stop himself, he approached her. "What was that all about?" he asked, trying not to notice that her green T-shirt not only exactly matched and brought out the color of her eyes, but also molded to the shape of her breasts. The sight of the full curves made him remember what it had been like to touch her there, gently tracing pale skin and sweetly puckered nipples.

Elissa laughed. "I'm not sure. Tiffany just announced she loves physics and for sure wants to study it in college. She said something about a signal traveling in the opposite direction from the movement."

"What?"

"That was my reaction. She described it as a signal light. The message that the light has turned green travels in one direction to the drivers, then they move forward, which is the opposite direction." She held out her hands, palms up. "I was never very good at science. Obviously this camp is doing a great job."

"For the kids. I'm beginning to feel as if they're talking in a foreign language."

"Me, too." She smiled at him.

Without wanting to, he smiled back.

"Let's go for a walk," she said, pointing to a gravel path that led between the cabins. "I went that way earlier this morning and it leads to a stream. There's even water in it. That surprised me. I mean, it's summer in Southern California."

"There's been some rain," he said, wondering if the conversation could be more inane.

He fell into step beside her. Even as his brain screamed out that spending time with her was a mistake, his soul took pleasure in her company.

"I don't think I've seen you in jeans before," he said as they ducked under a couple of low branches and entered a cool, leafy world. There were unfamiliar grasses, boulders with moss and up ahead, the distinct sound of water rushing west to the ocean.

Elissa brushed her hair over her shoulder. "You haven't," she admitted. "I don't think I've ever owned more than one pair at a time in my life. Mine generally go out of style before they wear out. You know, pleats when they shouldn't have any, or cuffs or something. So I went to a store that specializes in jeans and bought the most basic pair they had. As much as I prefer dresses, I thought they would be silly up here at the camp."

"You look great."

"Oh." At his compliment, she glanced up at him. Pleasure darkened her eyes to the color of the moss. Her mouth curved up. "Thank you."

Their steps slowed. It used to be like this, he remembered. Quiet times together, moments of connection so pure, they nearly transcended reality. He wanted to forget the anger and the pain. He wanted to forget her leaving five years ago and the fact that she would leave in the future. He wanted to believe in her again, to believe in *them*. He also wanted half a million dollars for building repairs and new programs for the orphanage. He had an equal chance of getting both.

Elissa blushed faintly and turned away. As she did so, her foot caught on the edge of a rock in the path and she lost her balance. He caught her before she could fall, his right arm going around her midsection, his left hand encircling her left upper arm.

His forearm pressed against the undersides of her breasts. He could feel the curves, her heat and her rapid heartbeat. His mouth went dry.

Elissa leaned against him for a second, then straightened and moved away. He released her reluctantly. "I can't believe I did that," she said. "Thanks for saving me." She glanced at her hands. "I would have scraped them for sure and I hate it when that happens."

"No problem. Watch where you're going."

"Yes, sir." She laughed. "You give orders well. It must be all these years with the children. Or maybe you're a natural leader."

He led the way down the path, walking a bit in front of her so she wouldn't be able to see the physical manifestation of his desire. In less than a second he was hard and ready. Blood throbbed, leaving him aroused and uncomfortable.

He hadn't made love since Elissa. Hadn't wanted to be with anyone else. He'd assumed that part of him was dead, and he'd barely thought to mourn its passing. Now he realized his desires had just been dormant, waiting for the only woman he'd ever loved. On a good day he let himself believe she'd once loved him back. On a bad day he figured he'd been nothing but a childish crush that had refused to die in time to avoid causing him pain. Regardless, he'd never been able to forget there was a side of their relationship, a side of marriage, she'd always hated.

"It's easy with the kids," he said. "I remember what it was like to be one of them."

"I'm sure that helps."

She was right behind him, but he didn't dare turn around. Not yet.

"But it's more than that," Elissa continued. "Some people are born with the gift of communication. Look at Millie. She was never in the orphanage and she's terrific with the children, too."

"She raised four of her own."

"She mentioned that. I must say, I really admire what she does here. She could easily spend her days going out to lunch with friends, or shopping, yet she puts in hours at the orphanage and doesn't expect anything in return."

"Millie's a special lady and we're damned lucky to have her." Cole had long ago realized the place would fall apart without his assistant. "She's touched a lot of lives. Last year she and Jeff celebrated their thirtieth wedding anniversary. The party was huge. Everyone who knows them wanted to help them celebrate."

His condition had subsided, so when the path widened, he slowed to let Elissa walk next to him. They meandered down to the edge of the stream. Water rushed over rocks and the claylike earth below. Leafy branches hung low and green bushes grew right to the edge of the water.

"I knew she'd been married for a long time," Elissa said, "but I didn't know it was thirty years. That's amazing. I remember when I worked on the series there was this woman who played the housekeeper. Her name was Mrs. Beecham. She used to tell us that love was like a tornado. Fast and powerful. That's what we were to look for in our lives. When Kayla and Patrick were trying to figure out what they felt for each other, Kayla kept worrying that it wasn't a tornado. There'd been no sudden storm of passion. Just a quiet love that grew out of years of knowing and caring about each other."

"If half of what Millie says about her and Jeff is true, and I suspect it is, they have both," Cole said. Sadness replaced his feeling of well-being. He and Elissa had experienced love as a tornado. It had destroyed everything in its path, leaving both of them lost and battered.

"I wish my parents had had either," Elissa said. "I never knew why they were together. They always fought. The divorce was almost a relief."

Almost, but not quite. Elissa stared at the stream and folded her arms over her chest. Cole stood next to her.

"Sometimes I imagine my parents would have been like Millie and Jeff," he admitted. "If they'd lived. It's just a kid's fantasy, but I figure there's no point in letting it go. They're gone and I might as well picture them happy."

Elissa glanced at him. "That's sound logic, Cole. They must have loved each other very much."

He shrugged. "I'll never know. I assume they did. My father walked away from a fortune to marry my mother."

"Sometimes I think people only appreciate things they've had to work to get. If it comes too easy, it's also too easy to let go."

Was she talking about them? About their marriage? Any sacrifice had come on her part, not his. She'd given up her family, the place where she'd grown up, her education. What had he surrendered in the name of love?

"You're right," he said.

"Really?" She spun toward him, obviously surprised. A strand of her hair caught in a tree branch. She tugged at it, trying to free herself.

"Let me," he said, moving closer. He unwound the curl. She smiled her thanks.

Around them, several birds sang to each other. Water continued to dance noisily over the rocks. The breeze rustled in the trees. A symphony of sound. They blocked out the real world...and the past. They allowed him to forget.

So instead of releasing the curl, he let it coil around his finger. Smooth, cool silk, just as he remembered.

In the shadows her eyes dilated. Her mouth trembled. She waited, as if the decision were his to make. An illusion of power.

The wanting, as strong as ever, swept through him. But this time was different. Dangerous. Because he couldn't keep on hating her. The anger didn't return on demand and when it did, some of the edge was gone.

Without wanting to, he'd started liking her. Was friendship far behind? He'd never been her friend, wasn't sure he was up to the task. Friendship required a permanence he wasn't sure he could accept. Feelings that transcended time. Friends forgave things lovers never could.

"And when you leave me this time?" he asked.

"What if I don't?"

His mouth curved up in a humorless smile as he released the curl and moved away. Friendship was a possibility. Trust was not.

Chapter Ten

"Left foot—green!" Alice, one of the camp counselors, called out.

Elissa laughed. "It's physically impossible," she said as she tried to slide her left foot across the sheet of plastic on the carpeted floor.

Tiffany beat her to the plate-sized spot of color closest to her. Elissa already had her right foot and right hand pressing against other colored spots. Cole, through circumstances she hadn't quite understood, was also a player on her mat, along with Greg.

"Try this," Cole said. "I'll move back one spot and you can slide under me to the corner one."

She glanced at him, then at the distance. "I don't think my legs are that long."

"Try it," Tiffany said happily. "Cole can put his arm around your waist and hold you up if you start to fall. He always does that with me."

Elissa did as her husband and the preteen suggested. Amid squeals and giggles, she found the green spot and balanced precariously.

Outside, rain from the unexpected storm pounded against the windows. According to the weather report, sunshine would greet them in the morning, but for tonight, everyone was playing inside the lodge.

Elissa was thrilled with the change in plans. She had a feeling that the original schedule for a cookout and campfire sing-along would have kept her apart from Cole. Since their walk that afternoon, he'd been avoiding her, going so far as to wait for her to seat herself at dinner, and then choosing a table on the opposite side of the room.

Had she upset him that much? If she had, was it a good thing or a bad thing?

Not that it mattered, she thought happily as Alice called, "Right hand—red!"

Elissa bent over and slid her right hand to a red spot.

"Great," Cole muttered, and stretched over her. "Can you move a little?" he asked.

"Sure." She leaned to her left, bringing her hip in contact with his stomach. A shiver rippled through her, nearly upsetting her balance.

Greg dived under Elissa and claimed a red disk for himself. On the mat next to them, Millie gave a shriek of laughter and collapsed to the floor, bringing the other three players with her. Jeff, her husband, pulled her close and kissed her soundly.

"You never were much good at this sort of thing, were you?"

Millie patted his face affectionately. "I'm unbeatable at board games, so I don't mind."

"I don't, either."

Elissa was so caught up in their display of love that she twisted a little too far. Her bare right foot slipped.

"No, you don't," Cole muttered, holding her around the waist. "If you go down, we all go down."

"Greg, look out," Elissa called as she started to wobble.

The boy rolled off the mat. As he did so, he bumped into Tiffany, who fell heavily against Cole, who released Elissa. They tumbled into a heap of arms and legs.

Somehow Elissa found herself lying against Cole's chest, her thighs nestled against his. Unfamiliar heat poured through her, making her want to squirm closer. The need was so powerful, only the crowd around them kept her from doing so. What on earth was wrong with her? She'd never felt anything like that when they were married.

She had read enough to realize that the hot, tingling in her breasts and between her thighs was a sign of sexual arousal. She wanted him—badly. She wanted Cole. She did! She who thought she would never feel anything but frightened by the thought of sex was actually entertaining sexual thoughts.

"You all right?" Cole asked.

"I'm fine."

"Let me get up first," he said, moving her off him, then rising to his feet. He held out a hand to assist her.

As their fingers brushed, sparks arced between them. She might not be able to see them, but she could sure feel them. Lightning strikes of fire on her bare skin. Was this what he'd felt all those times he'd touched her?

He pulled her to her feet, but didn't release her hand right away. "You're not hurt, are you?" he asked. "Did you hit your head?"

"Don't worry about it," she said. "Nothing happened." At least, not in the way he imagined. She pressed her free hand to her chest and felt the rapid beating of her heart.

Her knees were weak, her thighs trembled. She'd never experienced anything like this before. She was twenty-five years old and she felt as if she'd just figured out the secret to the world.

People stood around in small groups talking until the last team was left hunched over their slippery mat. The winners were congratulated, then Alice announced it was time for bed. There would be lots more science to be studied in the morning.

Elissa leaned against the sofa and watched Millie and her husband exchange a private smile. They murmured good-night to a few children and made their way to the long hallway that led to their section of the dorm.

Would the older couple make love tonight? There had been something in their exchange of glances that had made her think so. Elissa felt a sharp pang of envy. That's what she wanted for herself. A solid relationship built on trust and love. Time to establish patterns and rituals, silent communication and memories. She and Cole hadn't had that. Not the time or the trust. She wasn't sure they'd even had love. They'd had a flash so bright it had burned away everything in its path. The intensity had frightened her.

She crossed to the small library by the front door. The quiet offered her a place to think. The drapes were open at the window and she walked over to stare out into the night. An outside light illuminated the rain and a few bushes just beyond the building. But she didn't see the well-tended grounds. Instead she remembered being with Cole while they were still engaged. She remembered long hours at his apartment when he would hold her and kiss her. She'd enjoyed that a lot, although she'd always sensed he kept himself under tight control. A part of her had feared what would happen when he took what he wanted.

She pressed her forehead against the cool glass. He'd

honored her request to remain a virgin until they were married. Their wedding night had been a nightmare. Preparing for the day had left her exhausted and tearful. Cole had prowled their honeymoon suite with the restless energy of a caged leopard. She'd known what he wanted, what he had every right to claim. She'd wanted only to be held.

But she'd believed it was wrong to ask for that, after she'd denied him for so long. So she'd changed into the beautiful white nightgown her sisters had bought her, and she'd stood by the bed.

She'd asked that he turn out the lights, so in her mind there were only unexpected movements in the dark. He'd entered her gently, but she'd been tight and it had hurt even before he'd broken through the barrier of her innocence. She'd cried then, silently while he'd thrust into her and hoarsely called her name, then later, alone in the bathroom, using a thick towel to muffle her sobs.

The rest of their honeymoon had been a blur of lush tropical sights and couplings in the dark. She remembered Cole trying to go slowly, wanting to touch her and kiss her as he had before they'd been married. She'd been the one encouraging him to just enter her and get it over with. The sooner he started, the sooner it would be finished.

She thought about the sensations she'd felt tonight while they were playing the game and Cole had stood so close to her. For a long time she'd assumed there was something wrong with her. She saw couples in movies and on television, she read books in which characters fell in love. The women all seemed to feel something, to want their mate as much as he wanted her. The moans of pleasure had always made her uncomfortable. What on earth were they going on about?

Occasionally, not often but sometimes when she and Cole had made love, it had been pleasant. She remembered a Saturday morning when he hadn't had to go to work. He'd brought her breakfast in bed, then they'd talked together. He'd brushed her hair, then had spent the longest time kissing her neck and back. When he'd entered her that time, there hadn't been any pain at all. She vaguely recalled a sense of anticipation. But she hadn't "exploded" into anything, the way they talked about it in books.

Elissa understood instinctively that her rejection of Cole in bed had been the breaking point of their marriage. She didn't know how or why, but by refusing him sexually, she'd refused the essence of the man.

Was there a way to make up for that? Was there a way to take back her words and actions? Was she sure things would be different this time? After all, why would the love-making be any better?

"It doesn't matter," she told herself. She wanted a second chance with Cole, and if that meant putting up with a little pain and some awkward touching in the dark, she would.

And when you leave me this time?

Her breath caught in her throat as she remembered his words. No matter what, he would always believe she would leave him. She couldn't blame him for that. She had abandoned him, first sexually, then physically. Gaining his trust was going to be difficult.

"Elissa?"

She turned and saw Cole standing in the doorway of the library. "Is something wrong?" she asked.

"No. I wanted to make sure you're all right. You got very quiet at the end of the game. Are you sure you're not hurt?"

She stared at his familiar face. The dark eyes, the high cheekbones, the shape of his mouth. His perfection gave her pause. How could this man ever have loved someone like her? What had she done to deserve him? How could she have been so stupid as to let him go?

A small fire crackled at the far end of the room. Fighting the fear that he would reject her, or worse, say something so scathing she would be scarred for life, she took his hand and led him to the sofa in front of the fire.

"Have a seat," she said lightly, releasing his fingers and waiting to see if he would join her.

Several expressions darted across his face. Concern, curiosity, mistrust, acceptance.

"What's going on?" he asked as he settled on the far end of the sofa.

She took the corner opposite. The couch was small and they weren't that far apart. If he stretched his fingers out along the back and she did the same, they could easily hold hands. Not that that particular piece of information was going to be useful tonight. It was unlikely that Cole was feeling that friendly toward her.

Beyond the snap of the fire and the silence of the room she heard nothing. "Have the others gone to bed?" she asked.

"For the most part. A couple of the older kids are still up reading, but they're in their rooms."

So they were alone. She took a deep breath. She had no planned speech, nothing beyond a need to connect.

"I've been thinking about us," she said. "Being with you reminds me of the past. We've both changed. I know I've grown up in the past five years and now I can see things more clearly."

He didn't respond. Except for a slight tightening around his mouth, he might not have heard her at all.

Fear made her shudder, but she forced herself to continue. This was important—for both of them.

"I can see the mistakes I made in the marriage. The

biggest one was leaving. I'm sorry I did that. It seemed so right at the time. I thought we'd both already given up on the marriage and there was no point in hanging on to something that was dead. But it wasn't dead. I think we gave up on our marriage too soon. What do you think?''

Cole stared at her, at the light and shadow from the firelight playing on her face. He'd always thought she was beautiful; tonight even more so. She had an otherworldly quality about her, as if she was some mystical creature more part of a dream than of the waking world.

Did he think they'd given up on their marriage too soon? He couldn't answer that question—he didn't dare ask it of himself. If he did, he might unleash a need so powerful, he would be swept away forever. He wouldn't allow himself to get that lost again. What if he didn't find his way back?

"Cole?"

She bit her lower lip. Her agony was obvious. She'd put herself on the line and was hoping for some response from him. A word, an action, anything.

He couldn't speak; the risk was too great. He might say something dangerous to himself. He might admit to a feeling he'd long since buried. So he chose action instead.

He slid across the sofa until their knees pressed together. Moving slowly, so she would understand what he was going to do and have ample time to pull away, he drew her into his arms. But instead of leaning back, she melted against him. Instead of protesting, her mouth parted as if she anticipated his kiss. Instead of pushing to escape, her hands rested on his shoulders and urged him closer.

His lips touched hers. In the back of his mind he waited for the rejection, but it never came. Instead, her mouth clung to his, almost seeking, as if this was what she'd wanted all along.

She smelled sweet and womanly, the scent of her skin

as tempting as he remembered. Even knowing she was going to reject him, he angled his head and deepened the kiss.

He pressed his lips against hers, wanting to feel all of her. He brushed back and forth, discovering sensitive skin he'd only been able to dream about. The reality was better than what he'd remembered. While his hands still spanned her back, she was more relaxed than he recalled, her muscles seeming to respond to his touch with quivering awareness.

She slipped one hand up his scalp, moving her fingers through his hair, letting the short strands fall back. With her other hand she squeezed his shoulder, as if anchoring herself to him.

Passion grew. His arousal throbbed in aching counterpoint to his heart. His chest tightened. Blood roared in his ears.

He moved one hand to her neck and touched the soft skin there. She moaned. At the sound, her lips parted slightly and he crept inside.

The moist warmth beckoned. Her tongue met his, brushing gently against him, welcoming. Powerful need flooded him. He held back, not wanting to plunge too quickly, not wanting to frighten her.

As he swept across the sensitive skin of her inner lip, she arched against him. The hand at his shoulder tightened. She tilted her head more, opened her mouth wider, urging him on. He felt himself falling deeper into mindlessness. He knew the danger of going there, but how was he to resist her?

As their tongues circled and explored, as hot, fiery sensations shot through him, he found himself wanting her more than he ever had before.

He moved his hand up to her ear and traced the shell-like shape. She pulled back slightly as a soft giggle escaped her throat.

They broke the kiss and stared at each other. Passion dilated her eyes. With her lips parted and damp from his kisses, she was the most amazing woman he'd ever seen. For reasons he would never understand, the only woman he'd ever loved had returned to his life.

Slowly, tentatively, she pressed her mouth to his. He let her, holding back the need to plunge and claim. Instinctively he understood she needed to find her own pace. When her tongue tested the seam of his mouth, he parted for her. She darted inside, touching tip to tip, before retreating. A shudder rippled through him.

"Cole," she murmured, then pressed her mouth to his neck. She licked his skin. Every muscle in his body went rock hard. His groin flexed painfully. He forced himself to lower his hands to his sides and not respond.

She discovered him. Like a cat sniffing out a new room, she touched, kissed and even nibbled her way across his neck and up to his face, pausing at some places, returning a second time to others. Cool fingers traced his eyebrows, his cheekbones and his nose. She leaned close and took his earlobe in her mouth. Her sucking motion nearly drove him to his knees. Every cell in his body cried out for release. He wanted to rip the clothes from her and find rest between her silken thighs. Yet he continued to do nothing. The joy of her touching him was better than release. He'd always wanted her to touch him, had always hungered for that kind of contact.

She shifted until she was kneeling on the sofa. Dropping her hands to his shoulders, she urged him to lean back, then she straddled him, settling her hot feminine center against his thighs. He wanted to touch her there. Not sexually, although he wouldn't mind doing that, but to find out if she was aroused. In the long nights after she'd left, he'd had time to think about what had gone wrong between them. Some of it, he'd admitted, had been his fault. At times he'd taken her when she wasn't ready. He'd wanted to hold back, but he'd been young and horny, and she'd insisted. With the hindsight of years of loneliness, he realized that he'd been a less than perfect lover.

His excuses were pitiful at best—youthful impatience and fear. Fear that he was going to lose her anyway, but if he claimed her often enough, she might not go. Perhaps he'd secretly wanted to get her pregnant, hoping that a child could make her love him in a way he could not accomplish on his own.

Her mouth against his drew him back to the present. As she bent down, her hair swung forward, concealing them in a private world of golden curls. Her hands rested on his shoulders and her lips parted, drawing him inside.

He couldn't resist her. He plunged into her mouth, seeking solace and passion in equal measures. She took all of him, caressing him, moving her hips slightly as if to urge him on.

He took her at her word. He placed his hands on her thighs, then moved them higher up her hips to her waist. There he paused, absorbing the heat of her kiss until his blood boiled and his muscles began to tremble. Only then did he move higher still, slipping around to her rib cage before finally reaching her breasts.

As his fingers gently touched the undersides of her curves, he felt the unmistakable coolness of withdrawal. Her back stiffened and her thighs tightened around his, but not in desire. Her hands pressed against his shoulders and she pushed away.

"Cole, I..."

He dropped his hands to her waist and moved her off

him. "Don't bother," he said harshly, need reduced to ashes, and anger taking its place. "I remember the message. Look but don't touch, right?"

He stood and walked to the window. Humiliation tightened his chest. How many times had she done this to him? How many times had he done it to himself? He couldn't believe his needs and desires were different from any other man's, yet Elissa had the unique ability to make him feel like a rutting animal.

He heard her speak, yet the images from the past blotted out her voice. He recalled all the times they'd made love because he wanted to. How, despite his requests, she'd never once initiated anything, had never once touched him. He remembered her lying in bed, unresponsive, urging him to "get it over with." He remembered her turning away. Eventually she'd gotten tired of pretending.

"To answer your question," he said bitterly. "No, we didn't give up on our marriage too soon. The mistake was getting married in the first place."

She had moved up behind him. He saw her reflection in the window. "You can't mean that," she said, her eyes dark with pain. "I won't believe it."

"Believe what you want, it's true. You never wanted me. Not from the beginning. It would have been a hell of a lot easier on both of us if you'd had the courage to tell me the truth."

Pain twisted her mouth. "I did want you. In my way."

He spun to face her. "What does that mean? You wanted to hold hands and pass notes after class? I'm a man, Elissa. Not some adolescent you can toy with."

"You don't understand."

"You're right about that. I'm a man, with a man's needs. I'm not a boy. I thought you were grown up before, and I was wrong. Obviously that hasn't changed."

She flinched as if he'd slapped her. "That's not true."

"Isn't it?" He glared at her. "Can you honestly tell me you didn't hate making love with me?"

"Yes," she said earnestly. "Hate is the wrong word. I was scared and confused. Sometimes you frightened me. I wanted to take things at a slower pace. I wanted to figure out what was going on and not have to worry about losing control."

Defeat tasted bitter. Elissa didn't want him and he hadn't been able to find it in himself to want anyone else. "We haven't made love in five years," he said. "It doesn't get much slower than that. As for not wanting to lose control, you've got it all wrong. Losing control is the point."

Elissa watched him go. It took her a moment to figure out he looked odd because she was watching him through a film of tears. She brushed at her eyes, refusing to give in to that particular weakness.

Everything had gone wrong, she thought grimly. For a moment she'd thought she'd gotten through to him. Then she'd messed everything up.

Old feelings of inadequacy flared up, leaving her feeling small and stupid. What was wrong with her? Why was she incapable of getting even one thing right? She loved Cole and she wanted him back. So the first thing she did was alienate him.

She returned to the sofa and sank onto the cushions. The kissing had been incredible. She'd felt things she'd never experienced before. Her body had glowed as if touched by fire. She'd wanted his hands everywhere. Yet when he'd touched her breasts, she'd reacted badly. Why? He'd never mistreated her or hurt her. Sometimes lovemaking had been uncomfortable, not truly painful. What was she so afraid of?

She closed her eyes and remembered the past. Remembered being with Cole in bed. Her face flushed as she recalled his intensity. Despite the dark, she could feel how he focused on her. The sensation of inadequacy returned. She'd never known what to do and always felt that every move was wrong. She hadn't liked being naked. How much time did he spend analyzing her physical flaws? Cole had wanted her to touch him, but that had been difficult, too. Touch him where? How? What if she did it wrong? What if she disgusted him? In the end it had been easier to turn away.

"You're a fool," Elissa said, covering her face with her hands.

How could she fix what she was doing wrong when she wasn't even sure what the problem was? She loved him, but she'd loved him before and it hadn't been enough.

She raised her head and frowned. Last time, love had fought with fear and the fear had won. This time she was determined to change the outcome. She might not know much about sex, but she knew enough to know that Cole had wanted her and for a while she'd wanted him back. What she had to do was figure out a way to capitalize on the desire and keep her fear in check. She was going to have to find a way to get back in his bed. Once there, she would have a fighting chance of finding her way back into his heart.

Chapter Eleven

For the third time in as many hours, Cole left his bed, crossed to the open window and stared out into the darkness. The storm had passed, leaving behind cool air and bright stars. He gazed at the heavens as if God would provide him with answers.

He shook his head. No point in praying for miracles at this point. His life, along with his marriage, was long past saving. Now he would have to learn how to endure without her. He would have to find a way to exorcise Elissa from his being and exist in a gray and hollow world. How hard could it be? He'd managed the task five years ago. By now he should be an expert.

Perhaps those lessons would return to him in time, but for now there was only the hurt and the shame.

You frightened me.

His hands clenched into fists. He who had only wanted to love her and please her had instead invoked fear. He was a monster. The worst kind of man—one who terrifies women.

Self-hatred swept through him as powerfully as the passion had just a few hours before. He tasted the acrid flavor, wondered how long it would be until he could look himself in the eye.

What had gone wrong? Had he been so eager to have her in his bed that he'd misread the signals? He felt like some emotionally deformed creature who should be locked away from polite society, left alone to pay the price for crimes, both imagined and real.

A logical part of his brain reminded him that he hadn't done anything wrong. Elissa had kissed him back. She'd touched him and had encouraged him to touch her. At no time had he forced her. When he'd put his hands on her breasts and she'd wanted him to stop, he had. He'd behaved like a gentleman.

The logic should have worked. In his head he believed the words. But in his gut he knew they were false. If his wife, if the woman who had sworn before God to love and honor him for the rest of their lives, found him so abhorrent, he must be a monster.

He closed his eyes against the beauty of the stars and remembered a night long ago. Their wedding night, when Elissa had walked into the bedroom in a beautiful, sheer white gown. She'd looked as pure as the virgin she was, as otherworldly as an angel. Yet glimpses of her barely concealed flesh had reminded him she was very much a woman.

She'd been exhausted from the preparations for the wedding and the day itself. At the time he'd thought about telling her they could wait, but when she came and stood before him, rational thought had fled.

He remembered taking her in his arms and kissing her.

She'd kissed him back, but not with her usual passion. Still, when he'd hesitated, she'd urged him on. It *was* their wedding night. It was right that they make love.

Even now he could remember the exquisite pleasure of entering her. How perfect she'd been, how tight. He recalled the barrier of her innocence, her slight cry of pain when he'd broken it, her tears and her blood.

Now he realized he should have waited until the next morning. He should simply have held her all night, letting her get accustomed to their newfound intimacy. When they were both rested, he should have kissed her until she was mindless with passion, then he should have pleased her in other ways before entering her.

But he hadn't. That one night had set the pattern for the rest of their marriage. A marriage where Elissa "offered" and he took. No matter how he tried to give back, she refused to let him please her. The more she withdrew from him, the more desperately he needed her, until they were caught in a cycle that had only one escape.

He leaned against the windowsill. Nothing had changed. He would be a fool to let himself think it had. All he could do now was make sure he didn't repeat the same mistakes he had tonight. He would avoid her both physically and emotionally. He would distance himself until she was gone, then once again he would learn to live without her.

At least he'd protected himself in one area. This time he'd managed to keep from falling in love with her again.

Saturday morning Elissa and Millie lingered over breakfast. "We should really start our day," the older woman said cheerfully, but made no move to leave the table.

"Agreed." Elissa's response wasn't quite as perky, but then she wasn't glowing the same way Millie was. Obviously her friend had enjoyed the night in her husband's arms. Her eyes were bright, her expression a combination of contentment and self-satisfaction.

"Or we could have another cup of coffee."

"That sounds great."

Millie chuckled and reached for the pot. They were the last two people in the dining room. The children had eaten quickly, then rushed out to begin their last full day of the program. The adults had followed more slowly.

Millie looked around at the groupings of tables. "This is a wonderful facility. The children have enjoyed their time here. As no one else is going to know to say it, I will. Thank you for paying for this."

Elissa shrugged. "I'm happy to do it. I get so much pleasure out of watching them here, I almost feel selfish. I'm really giving them things because it makes me feel good."

"That's a fine reason to be charitable. Most of us do find joy in helping others."

Elissa sipped her coffee, then cupped her hands around the mug. "I didn't expect to," she confessed. "The joke in my family is that my sisters and I are like the three bears. One too hard, one too soft and one just right. When the money we'd earned from the show was first put in trust, I was terrified. My parents were divorced and my mother was already thinking of remarrying. My father lived an extravagant life-style that eventually killed him. He'd always said I was his favorite, the one most like him, and I knew when I inherited the money I was going to die, too." She looked at Millie. "Pretty silly, huh?"

The older woman leaned forward and touched Elissa's arm. "No, it's not. It's very sad. From what you've said about your mother, you were never close to her. So you never discussed your fears with her, did you?"

Elissa shook her head.

Millie's blue eyes darkened with compassion. She made a *tsk* of concern. "Then your reaction is perfectly understandable. How old were you? Thirteen, fourteen?"

"About that."

"Cause and effect make sense to children. They don't always understand that life is more complex than that."

"Thank you," Elissa said, grasping Millie's hand and squeezing. "My sisters have teased me about my fear of money, and I've outgrown most of it, but no one has ever made me feel my reaction was normal."

"You forget I have four children of my own. I'm an expert." Millie smiled. "So you're not as terrified as you were?"

"Not at all. Originally, I thought when I inherited the money I would simply give it all away. Fallon is the 'just right' sister and she had a sensible plan. Keep some, use some to travel, give some to charity. Kayla wanted to live it up until the money ran out. She's come to her senses, too. So while I plan to help the orphanage, I'm also investing a portion of the money."

Millie leaned close and lowered her voice. "Why do you keep it a secret from Cole?"

"For a lot of reasons. I didn't tell him when we were dating because I thought he'd resent it. Then after we were married, I felt guilty for keeping the information to myself. I never found a good time to tell him. Now I'm afraid if he knows he'll keep me around for what I can give the children, instead of keeping me around because I can make a difference with what I do and who I am. Or he'll hate me for being 'Lady Bountiful' and toss me out on my butt."

Of course, after last night she would be lucky to last the week. No doubt he would fire her as soon as they returned to the orphanage.

Elissa nearly groaned in frustration. She'd so wanted things to go right. If only…

She shook her head. She was finished with if onlys. Now was the time for action. Just as soon as she figured out what that action was supposed to be, she was going to do it.

Millie released Elissa's hand and leaned back in her chair. "It's really none of my business, and you must feel free to tell me so if the question makes you uncomfortable, but is there any chance of a reconciliation?"

Elissa resisted the urge to bury her face in her hands. Instead she offered her friend a shaky smile. "You don't know how much I wish I could tell you yes, but I don't think so. I was never a very good wife, and time away from Cole hasn't seemed to have improved my skills." She stared into her mug of coffee. "I still love him, but that's not enough. It never has been. No matter how I try not to, I continue to fail him."

"I don't understand, Elissa. Fail him how?"

"I, um…" She could feel a blush climbing her cheeks. If this were anyone but Millie, she wouldn't be having the conversation at all. But Millie could be trusted. Even more, Millie had years of experience, not to mention four children, three of whom were married. No doubt the older woman had some excellent advice to give. Elissa knew she had to do something. If she didn't figure out a way to change, she and Cole were destined to keep repeating the mistakes of the past.

"Is there another man?" Millie asked quietly.

Elissa jerked her head up and stared. "Of course not. There never has been." She laughed low in her throat. "No, having an affair isn't the problem. Quite the opposite. You see, I can't figure out how to please my husband in bed."

The words hung between them. Much to her credit, Millie's only reaction was to sip her coffee.

"Please him how?" Millie asked after a moment. "Cole is a very passionate man. I've caught him looking at you a time or two, which is what promoted my question about a reconciliation. I know he still feels desire for you, if that's what you're worried about."

Elissa shook her head. "It's not that," she whispered miserably. "I don't know what to do. I never knew what to do. I was a virgin, and while the kissing part had been nice, I never cared for the rest of it." Her face was on fire, her voice trembling, but she forced herself to continue. "He always wanted me to participate, to initiate lovemaking and to touch him. I never knew what to do. So it was easier to let him just do it and get it over with. Sometimes it was easier to turn away."

"And now?" Millie prompted.

Elissa traced small circles on the Formica table. "Now I want things to be different. But I'm still afraid. Last night we were kissing and everything was great. Then he touched me and I sort of froze. Before I could relax, he reacted to the rejection and said a lot of horrible things. I tried to explain, but how can I when I don't understand it myself?"

"Elissa, it's so easy. I promise you can make this work, but first I have a couple of questions."

"All right."

"Do you want Cole back in your bed?"

"Yes. Though I'm not sure what to do with him when I get him there."

Millie smiled. "We'll figure that one out later. My second question is do you find Cole physically appealing? Can you close your eyes and imagine yourself being with him, both of you naked and touching? Does that picture bring you pleasure or make you uncomfortable?"

Talking about it made Elissa want to squirm, but she dutifully closed her eyes. She remembered kissing him last night, how her body had tingled and heated until she ached with an unfamiliar need. She remembered straddling his thighs and wanting to press her center against him, rubbing back and forth. It wasn't difficult to shift those memories, changing the images until they were both naked.

She thought about his hand on her breast. Last night she'd gotten scared and had withdrawn because she'd started thinking too much. She'd worried about the door being open and someone walking in on them. She'd wondered what he would want her to do back. All her old fears had risen to the surface, blocking out everything she'd tried to do to create that moment with him.

She looked at Millie. "I want to make love with my husband. I want to not be afraid and I want to know what on earth I'm supposed to do."

"Good. I suspect you don't have anything wrong with you that can't be cured by a little information and some practice. I assume you've never climaxed during sex?"

Elissa resisted the urge to dive under the table, curl into the fetal position and whimper. "No, I haven't," she said through lips numb with humiliation.

"Then we have a place to start. When we get back to Ojai, we're going to go to the library together and we're going to find you several books on sex. It sounds to me as if you and Cole had the classic problem of a terrified female virgin and an overeager male partner. Most couples manage to work out their differences, but you two got caught in a cycle that left both of you feeling inadequate."

"That sounds right."

Millie glanced around the room to make sure they were still alone, then leaned close. "Men are, for the most part, physical creatures. They don't have our years of training that suppresses that part of our nature. Also, when you think about it, their sexuality is out there. If they're turned on, it's tough to hide. Sometimes they get embarrassed because they think they want us too much. With a little support, we can teach them that this desire is a good thing.'' Millie's blue eyes twinkled. ''Right now you're going to have to take my word on that. My point is most men need a woman to assure him that his base nature is acceptable. As I've told my daughters, accept the penis and you accept the man.''

Elissa swallowed hard. ''Gee, there's something I can cross-stitch on a pillow.''

Millie grinned. ''It's true. When a man feels accepted, he'll do anything for his woman. The thing he most wants to do is please her. By pleasing her, he feels he has value in the relationship. He feels special when she wants him. For now, you have to work on making Cole think you want him. You need to get his attention.''

Elissa remembered how they'd parted last night. ''He's going to run in the opposite direction when he sees me.''

''We can break him of that. Your first homework assignment is to touch him.''

Elissa shook her head. ''I'm not very good at that.''

''It's easy,'' Millie assured her. ''Men love to be touched. Their favorite place is, well, you can imagine, but it's not a good place to start. Aside from sending a rather interesting message, it's hard to do in public.''

''What would the neighbors say?'' Elissa murmured, stunned by all the information.

''Touch his arm, his shoulder, his back. Anywhere. Brush against him. Be close. You want to do two things. First, you want to be comfortable with him physically. Second, you want to get his attention in a positive way. This should accomplish both.''

Elissa nodded. "I can try that."

The older woman grinned. "Don't worry about opportunity. I'll have a little chat with Jeff and we'll organize a football game this afternoon. You can start there."

Elissa felt overwhelmed by her task, yet revived, as if this just might be possible. "Thank you for telling me all this. I appreciate you taking the time."

"Don't thank me. I'm helping because I like to, and because over the past couple of years I've grown to care about Cole. He deserves a little happiness in his life. I always wondered why he never went out or seemed interested in anyone. Now I know why. You can win him back, if you truly love him."

Elissa said a quick prayer that her friend was right.

"Jeff and I will be team captains," Millie said.

Cole grinned at his assistant. "If you're on opposite teams, then this is going to be touch football instead of tag, right?"

Millie winked. "You know me so well. I think you'll be my first choice."

Cole obediently stood behind her. Jeff called one of the children and so it went. Elissa waited nervously. As she'd expected, Cole had been avoiding her. She hadn't had a single chance to put Millie's plan into action. But the morning hadn't been spent in vain. She'd taken a couple of hours to go for a walk on her own and really think about why she'd found it so easy to reject the physical side of her marriage.

What she'd learned hadn't pleased her. She was starting to suspect she'd been secretly punishing Cole, using sex to make him as unhappy as she was. While she'd been willing to go to New York with him, once there, she'd missed her friends and family. She hadn't had a life and had expected him to provide her with one. When he hadn't, she'd wanted revenge. Sex was a powerful weapon. Unfortunately, she'd ended up punishing both of them and had, in the process, ruined something quite wonderful. Now those patterns and fears were second nature. She was going to have to learn new ones. But first she had to figure out how to touch her husband.

"I want Elissa on my team," Jeff said.

As she moved to the right side of the field, she passed close to Cole. "We're gonna kick butt," she said, lightly placing her hand on his upper arm. She felt his muscles tense, then he pulled away. It was a start, she told herself, refusing to get discouraged. She had a lot to make up for. They couldn't heal in a single afternoon.

A half hour later Millie's plan became clear. By putting Elissa and Cole on opposite teams, they had the chance to tackle each other. Unfortunately, every time Elissa got the ball, Cole let the children run her down.

Elissa met Millie's frustrated gaze and shrugged. They couldn't *make* Cole tackle her.

Millie snapped her fingers as if she'd just had a great idea. In the huddle she gestured with her hands, then, acting as quarterback, threw the ball to Cole. As circumstances, or in this case Millie, would have it, he caught the ball about three feet from Elissa. There were no kids around, and no one else between Cole and their makeshift goal.

"Don't even think about it," she told her husband, and dived for him.

He paused in obvious indecision, then took a half step back. Her shoulder connected with his midsection. He was off balance and tumbled to the ground.

The football went flying. Elissa heard Shanna scream with excitement as she scooped it up and ran for the touchdown. For a second she couldn't remember if Shanna was on her team or Cole's. Then her body connected with his, all the air rushed out of her and she didn't care.

She clutched her chest and gasped. Nothing happened. Her body convulsed. Cole twisted quickly, rolling into a sitting position and helping her sit up, too.

"It's okay," he told her, supporting her back with one arm. "You got the wind knocked out of you. You'll be fine in a second. I know it's scary, but you can breathe. Just relax."

Easy for him to say, she thought, trying not to panic. She opened her mouth and finally sucked in a breath. Her lungs filled with air. She inhaled again and again.

Cole stroked her cheek. "Don't go overboard or you'll hyperventilate. Slowly, now. Are you hurt?"

He was so close she could see the line on his neck where smooth skin gave way to the first hint of stubble. His mouth twisted with concern. She stared up at him, feigning more weakness than she actually felt.

"I feel a little woozy," Elissa lied, and rested her head against his chest. "Sorry, Cole. I shouldn't have tackled you like that."

"Hey, it's part of the game. I'm worried about you." A couple of the kids headed their way. Cole waved them off. "She's fine," he called. "Just got the wind knocked out of her. Keep on playing."

The hand on her back stroked her from shoulders to waist. His free hand grasped hers. "Do you think you can stand?"

Ignoring the guilt and telling herself this was for a good cause, Elissa bit her lower lip and nodded tentatively. "I think so. It's sorta hard to tell. At least I can breathe now."

"We'll go slow," he promised.

He kept one arm around her and assisted her into a standing position. She allowed herself to sway toward him and was instantly caught against his hard body. This playacting would set the women's movement back fifteen years. She sent a silent apology out into the cosmos.

"There's a bench under that tree," he said, motioning to a wooden seat by the edge of a path. "Can you make it?"

"If you don't mind giving me a little support." She tilted her head slightly. "I'm sorry, Cole. Maybe you'd rather Jeff helped me."

He scowled. "You're my wife, Elissa. I'll take care of you."

It had been a long time since anyone had wanted to take care of her. Cole had always been protective of her. Why had she forgotten that?

He assisted her to the bench and helped her sit down. Then he settled next to her, his body angled toward hers, her hand clasped in his.

"Everything feel all right?" he asked. "Nothing sprained or broken?"

"I'm just a little shaken," she said, and tightened her fingers around his. With her other hand she squeezed his forearm. He looked surprised, but didn't pull back. Out of the corner of her eye she saw Millie give her a thumbs-up. Obviously the older woman approved of her tactics.

A shiver caught her attention. It shot up her arm and settled in her belly. She realized his thumb was brushing back and forth across her palm. As he was watching the football game, Elissa doubted he even noticed what he was doing. Her breath caught in her throat, but this time it came from a rush of affection, not from a body blow. The impact was just as startling. At that moment if Cole were to ask her if she could stand, she could honestly tell him no, because her knees were too weak.

The trembling had nothing to do with any injury and everything to do with awakening desire...for her husband.

Chapter Twelve

Elissa adjusted the pillows behind her and stared at the book resting on her lap. Who would have thought there was a whole world out there that she'd never known about? Especially considering she'd been married and living with a man.

She glanced at the other books stacked next to her. As promised, Millie had come with her to the library and helped her pick out several books to study. Humiliatingly, one of them was written for teenagers, complete with detailed sketches and photographs, and was all about the basics of sex. When she'd protested, Millie had informed her that until Elissa knew what Cole's and her anatomy looked like there was no way she was going to figure out where it all went.

Until she'd opened the book and stared openmouthed, she hadn't realized how little she'd seen her husband naked. At her request, they'd always made love in the dark. He'd convinced her to shower with him a couple of times, but she'd been too embarrassed to enjoy the experience and had spent most of her time trying *not* to look at him.

Now, as she read the books and added to her list of questions for Millie, she felt a sense of regret. According to what the experts said, looking was half the fun. She had to admit, that thinking about it now was sort of exciting. She'd always enjoyed watching Cole move around a room, taking pleasure in his strength and grace. She liked the breadth of his shoulders, his well-formed hands, his legs. Why wouldn't she have liked the rest of him? She refused to believe she could take a marking pen and draw a line across his body, naming one part of him beautiful and another part of him hideous. She loved every bit of him, inside and out. His soul, his heart, even his anatomy made him the man who had stolen her heart.

She remembered what Millie had said about loving the "maleness" as much as the man himself. One of the books from the library had said the same thing. That a man's sense of self-worth was influenced by a woman's acceptance or lack of acceptance of that most intimate part of him.

Elissa smiled as she realized that even alone in the privacy of her bedroom she wouldn't allow herself to think the P word, let alone say it.

"It's just a word," she said aloud. "It describes something. How on earth do you expect to touch it if you can't even say it?"

She sucked in a breath. "Penis," she whispered, then shot a guilty look around the room. When lightning didn't strike her dead, she laughed.

If she hadn't been blushing, she might have pronounced herself cured.

She flipped through the book on her lap. She finally had

a reasonable understanding of her body and its workings. Unlike a male body, it was more difficult to tell when she was interested in sex. There was no obvious display of arousal, although according to these authors there were distinct signs. She'd never noticed any of them, but then, she'd never known what to look for before.

Thinking back to the kiss she and Cole had shared last week, she realized she had been aroused. If he'd touched her between her legs he would have felt the telltale wetness.

A shiver rippled through her at the thought of him stroking her there. She closed her eyes and grimaced. All those years before, she'd urged Cole to hurry. When he'd wanted to linger over the very things that would have made her enjoy their sexual relationship, she'd told him to get on with it. No wonder she'd occasionally found penetration painful. No wonder she'd never felt the tingling or tension of approaching release. She'd been so determined to disconnect herself from what was going on, she hadn't given either of them a chance.

Was it too late? She was determined to make sure it wasn't. She and Cole deserved happiness and she believed with all her heart that they belonged together. Therefore, they were going to have to make it work.

She picked up another book and turned to the first chapter. She was going to learn all she could so that when the opportunity showed itself, she would be ready.

Just like school, she told herself. Only this time, while the reading material might make her uncomfortable, the homework was going to be heaven.

Cole couldn't concentrate. It was a common condition these days, he reminded himself, and he might as well get used to it. Unfortunately, there was still work to be done, whether he could focus on it or not. Maybe he should think

about spending more time at his office in Ojai. He usually
hated to do that because it kept him away from the kids,
but he was beginning to think he didn't have a choice. It
was either be away from them or not get any work done at
all.

Or he could fire Elissa.

Most days, she *was* the source of his problems. Even
today, when he had other things on his mind, she haunted
him. If he got her out of his life, then he might have a
fighting chance. It was the solution that made the most
sense. But he knew he wouldn't…couldn't let her go. Not
yet.

She was everywhere. Even as he told himself he was
courting the most lethal kind of trouble, he found himself
seeking her out. It was insane. Hadn't her physical rejection
been enough to remind him of the pain of their marriage?
Did he need her turning away from him in bed again?
Couldn't he recall the intense pain he'd felt, as if he'd bared
his very soul and she'd found him disgusting?

Yet time and again he returned to her. He sat near her
at dinner, he listened as she spoke to the children, he made
excuses to go into the office.

Something had happened at the science camp. Something
other than her rejection of him. While that bitter memory
was foremost in his mind, so was the image of her gasping
for air after falling while playing football. In that split second, before he knew she hadn't been seriously hurt, he'd
thought he might lose her. He'd realized then that it was
better to risk pain and be around her than to live in a world
without her.

He would continue to keep his distance, he told himself.
This didn't mean he trusted her or even cared about her.
She was just a part of his life. A freckle or a mole he wasn't
fond of but was willing to keep around.

"Tell that to a doctor and they'll lock you up," he muttered. "Rightfully so."

It wasn't his fault, he reminded himself. He couldn't ignore Elissa, because she was everywhere. He couldn't turn around without finding her near him, next to him, touching him.

The touching. A brief pressure on his arm as she asked him to pass the salt at dinner. Fingers on his shoulders as she leaned over him to read what was on his computer screen. Soft, sweet breasts burning into his upper arm as she moved around him in a crowded hall. He spent his days aroused. Amazingly enough, he was getting used to it. Worse, he was starting to like it.

As if conjured by his thoughts, Elissa walked into his office. He didn't need to turn around to confirm her presence. Not only could he inhale the sweet scent of her perfume, he could see her reflected in his computer screen.

"Am I interrupting?" she asked, coming up to stand behind him. "Uh-oh. Your screen saver is on." She pointed at the small squares of light meant to represent stars moving across his black screen. "Either you've finished for the day or you don't know what to write next. Should I ask which?"

"You can guess."

"A difficult point of law?" she asked, resting her hands lightly on his shoulders.

He told himself to move away, to slide the chair either to the left or the right and she would get the message. But he didn't. And when her fingers tightened on tense muscles, he couldn't suppress a groan of pleasure.

"I'm drafting an agreement in a divorce settlement," he said, letting his head fall forward as her thumbs swept up his neck.

"From the women's shelter?" she asked.

"Yeah." He closed his eyes. "That's great. Thanks."

She dug in deeper, finding the source of his tension and kneading it into submission.

"But there's something else, isn't there?"

"Yeah." He was only half-aware of the conversation. "I hate that it bothers me, but it does. That's the hell of it."

"What bothers you?"

"I got a letter from my grandfather."

As soon as he spoke the words, he realized what he'd said. He swore under his breath.

Elissa barely paused in her ministrations. "What did he have to say?"

He shrugged off her hands and turned the swivel chair toward her. She leaned against the corner of his desk. Despite her calm voice she was obviously shocked.

He stared at her as if he'd never seen her before. Perhaps he never had. This wasn't the woman he'd married. Time and maturity had transformed Elissa into someone different. Someone he didn't know.

He liked the new Elissa. In some ways she'd gotten tougher. She no longer feared him or his moods. He appreciated not having to monitor everything he said. In other ways, she was softer, more open. Life had taught them both meaningful lessons.

Five years ago he wouldn't have wanted to discuss this letter with her. Not only would she not have understood, but he would have known instinctively that she would have resented any show of weakness on his part. She'd needed him to always be strong.

Today that was less important. While it wasn't his style to be a wimp, he no longer felt he had to conceal his worries from her. Odd that in some ways he didn't trust her at all, and in others he trusted her implicitly.

"You look as stunned as I felt," he told her. "It's not as bad this time, though."

"This time?" She folded her arms over her chest. "He's written you before?"

"About a month ago. He wants me to fly to New York and meet with him. He says we're family." The word tasted bitter. "After all this time, he wants to be family. Where was he when I was growing up?"

"Being a foolish, lonely man," Elissa said. "I don't think you should welcome him back into your life with open arms, but—" She broke off and gave him a tight smile. "Sorry. You didn't ask my opinion, did you?"

"I'd still like to hear it."

She nodded her thanks. "I think family is important, however annoying they can be."

"Maybe. I don't know." He leaned back in his chair and scowled. "These damn letters annoy me. There's something imperious about them, as if he's the Russian czar writing to one of his peasants."

"I doubt that's how he means it."

"See for yourself." He reached into the mess on his desk and pulled out a business-size envelope.

She took it from him and removed a single typed sheet of paper. He'd read it enough times to be able to follow along as she scanned the page.

Dermott William Stephenson III regretted that he'd missed so many years with his only living relative and wished to make amends. If Cole would be so kind as to call Dermott's secretary, a flight to New York could be arranged. The visit would cover many issues, including Cole's future.

He closed his mind against the rest of it. He didn't want to remember that.

As he looked at Elissa, at the way the waning sunlight

slipped into the room to illuminate her gold-blond hair, he thought about how much he wanted her. While they'd both grown up, he hadn't stopped needing her. But he wasn't going to push anything. Ever. He'd learned that lesson when he'd kissed her last week at the science camp. He refused to put himself through another rejection like that.

And yet... He rubbed his eyes. He'd frightened her. He understood that now. He'd taken things too quickly. He hadn't taught her that physical love should include pleasure. Guilt made him squirm. With the hindsight of time, he realized she'd never experienced climax. At least, not with him.

The thought of her with another man made him want to lash out in rage, so he pushed that thought away, too.

It was too late to fix the past, yet he felt he needed to apologize. The problem was, he wasn't sure for what. Would she even understand?

Elissa put down the letter. "He is a little regal in his tone. I'm sure he's used to having things done his way. You're probably the first person to defy him in years."

"All that talk about my future. I feel as if he wants to offer me a job as stock boy in one of his retail firms."

She smiled. "I'm sure you would at least be a management trainee." Her smile faded. "He's still your grandfather. My guess is that if you don't make some kind of effort, you'll regret it for the rest of your life."

"Maybe." He fingered the expensive, thick letterhead. "He's not exactly what I'd hoped for when I imagined a family. I wanted something more like you had."

"Me?" She touched a hand to her chest. "We were far from perfect."

"That was the point. Three sisters who adored each other. What could be better?"

"Parents who got along," she said, then shook her head.

"Never mind. That's a silly thing to wish for here. There are several dozen children in the next building who would gladly take any one or two parents, however imperfect. I've no right to complain."

"Sure you do," he said gently. "We always want something better."

"Fine. You envy me my sisters and I'll envy you your purpose." She settled on the edge of the desk, resting her behind to the right of the blotter. Her sandal-clad feet bumped into the built-in file drawers. "I'm twenty-five years old and I have no idea what I want to do with my life. Isn't that awful?"

"No. It's pretty common. The people who have already chosen a career that they like are the lucky ones, but I don't think they're the norm."

She nodded. "I want to do something with the children. I've been thinking about going back to college and getting my degree in administration. I would..."

She continued talking, but he no longer heard the words. There was something hypnotic about the sound of her voice. Something that drew him in.

He liked her.

The realization startled him so much, he nearly slipped out of the chair. Elissa stopped talking in midsentence.

"What is it?" she asked. "You've got the oddest expression on your face."

He stared at her intently. When had it happened? How had she slipped past his defenses? "I like you," he said, still shocked by the information. "We're friends."

"I'm glad I'm not the only one who thinks so."

She smiled at him. She'd smiled at him a thousand times before, but this time was different. This time her obvious pleasure reached down and touched the cold darkness of his soul.

"I've never liked you before," he said. "I've either loved you or hated you. There's been no middle ground."

"How do you like it out here?"

He thought for a minute. "It's not too bad."

For now. He acknowledged the voice inside that whispered she would leave him and that liking her might prove to be as dangerous as loving her once had been.

She nodded toward the letter. "What are you going to do about your grandfather?"

"I've written a reply agreeing to accept his high-handed invitation, but I don't know if I'll send it."

"I wish you would. Life is too short to avoid people who want to care about you. I know that now. He's an old man. He won't be around to ignore forever. I don't want you to have regrets."

The obvious implication being that she had regrets. He wanted to believe they were about him, about them and their marriage. He wanted to know that she wished with all her heart to have those days and weeks back again, to replay every moment and this time get it right. God knows that was his wish.

But neither of them was going to get that second chance. Life was a one-way street and U-turns weren't allowed. They couldn't go back; they could only go forward.

"It's not just about you," she continued, as if she could read his mind. "I also regret my relationship with my father. After the divorce I was so angry with him. Not only for leaving me, but for the drinking and the parties. He was never around. On the days he was supposed to visit with us, he was either drunk or hungover. So I punished him as only a teenager can. I refused to see him again, or even to speak to him. And then he was dead."

Her green eyes darkened with unshed tears. She blinked away the moisture. "That's what hurts the most," she said softly, her voice raw with emotion. "I never got to tell him I loved him. The last time I saw him before the accident, he asked me to and I said no."

"He knew."

"Did he? I'm not convinced." She drew in a deep breath. "The sad part is that I'd already forgiven him for everything. I loved him—how could I not forgive him?"

"You always were a generous sort."

"Not me," she said intently. "Never me, Cole. You. You were the one who forgave me a thousand times. No matter how I treated you, you always said you understood. When I think of what I did, what I said..." She shook her head. "I'm so sorry."

"Don't be," he told her gruffly. "I deserved everything you said."

"Never."

She slipped off the desk and took a step toward him. Before she bent down, before her hand rested on his forearm to steady herself, before he felt the heat and sweetness of her mouth on his, he knew she was going to kiss him.

He wasn't sure he could stand it. Not again. Not after what had happened last time.

Yet as she moved closer, her intent clearly exposed in her eyes, he found he couldn't move away. All his promises of avoiding rejection, of not putting himself in that position again, faded in the reality of being close to her. Nothing else mattered.

Her lips brushed against his.

Passion exploded and he wanted to haul her against him. But he'd learned that lesson well. Instead he did nothing.

She kept her mouth pressed to his, their breath mingling. He felt her mouth shift and she was smiling as she straightened.

"Nice," she murmured.

Instead of taking comfort from her single word, he felt as if he'd been sucker punched.

"It should always have been nice," he said, turning his head away and clutching the arms of his chair. If she hadn't been standing in front of him, he would already have walked out of the room. But he didn't want to risk touching her, and there was no way to get past her without physical contact.

She pressed her fingertips against his cheek, forcing him to look at her. "It *was* nice," she said.

At his grimace of disbelief she added, "Often it was very nice."

Humiliation filled him. "I never meant to frighten you," he said quickly, wanting to get it over with. "I just want you so much. I can't apologize for that, because I don't regret wanting you, but I'm sorry it scared you. I should have gone slower or been better or—"

"Shh." She slid her fingers around until they touched his mouth. "No more apologies. From either of us. We both messed up. We were young and ignorant. I understand a lot more now."

She might as well have slit him open with a knife and left him on the ground to die. It would have been more humane.

She jumped back as if she'd seen a snake. "What is it? Why do you look like that? What's wrong?"

Wasn't it obvious? "Who is he?" he asked, knowing it was self-mutilation to want to know.

"Who is who? What are you— Oh." Her expression softened into compassion. "No, Cole. There hasn't been anyone but you. What I meant is that I've been growing up while we've been apart. I understand some things more. At least, I understand them in theory." She blushed faintly. "There are some things you can't learn from a book."

Relief blossomed into desire. Focusing on the latter was easier than thinking about why he would care about her being with another man. "You've been studying the subject?"

She nodded. "A little. Want to hear what I've learned?"

He would rather she showed him, but he was willing to accept a good telling instead.

She took his hands and tugged him to his feet, then turned them until he was leaning against the desk and she was standing in the V of his thighs. They didn't touch anywhere except their hands, but the knowledge that they *could* aroused him.

"Men," she said. "All men need to feel desired as well as loved."

Somehow that didn't make him feel a whole lot better. If she'd said she desired him, that would be another story. But she hadn't.

"Women need to feel loved as well as desired. We spend a lot of time telling the other sex information they aren't looking for. At least, not while making love. Yet both sexes can learn from the other. Men can learn it's a turn-on to hear words of love and women can learn to appreciate and be aroused by their man's desire."

Speaking of arousals, Cole thought, trying not to shift, despite the uncomfortable pressure in his groin.

"I never got that," Elissa said. "I know now that when your eyes are bright, like they are now, that you're showing a vulnerability to me. You're trusting me."

"Great," Cole muttered, turning away, wondering if she could also read the humiliation. A couple more minutes of this and he wouldn't have to worry about her seeing his arousal. It would be emotionally beaten into a distant memory.

"I like it," she whispered.

Three small words. They whipped through him like a firestorm, leaving him hard and raw, every cell in his body ready for her and therefore exposed.

She bit her lower lip. "It's a little scary, but in a good way."

She rose on tiptoe and pressed her lips to his. This time when he didn't respond, she moved her mouth back and forth.

He held himself still, moving only his fingers, and that was to clench his hands into tight fists. He recognized her actions for what they were—a genuine effort to overcome her fears. Yet those fears had been a real part of her life for years. They would not be overcome in a single night.

She put her hands flat on his shoulders and pushed down. It took him a second to realize she wanted him to shift lower on the desk. He did so, spreading his legs and sliding forward until they were nearly the same height.

"Better," she said. "Now open your mouth."

"Why?" he blurted out without thinking. He knew why, but he wanted to hear her say it.

Color stained her face. Would she like the new rules or would she run? He held his breath.

She used her thumb and forefinger to squeeze his cheeks together. "Open your mouth or I'll be very crabby."

He shook his head. "Not good enough, Elissa. You have to be vulnerable, too."

She considered for a moment. "Fair enough." She sucked in a deep breath. Her fingers slipped from his face to his neck. She stroked his skin. He clenched his fists tighter and prayed for control.

"Open your mouth," she said. "I want to really kiss." She held up her free hand. "I know. I'm still cheating. I want to touch you with my tongue. I want our tongues to—"

He didn't let her finish. He bent forward and kissed her hard, parting his lips and letting her slip inside. It was that, or embarrass himself right there. Jeez, he'd never known words to be so damned arousing.

She took back control quickly, angling her head and plunging deeper. She clutched at his shoulders, then slipped her fingers through his hair.

He raised his hands to embrace her, then dropped them to his sides. He would hold on to the desk, something, anything to keep from frightening her.

She surged against him, her body pushing against his as her tongue circled his. She squirmed and rubbed, her breasts hot points of pressure that made him weak with longing. Her hips rocked back and forth, the apex of her thighs stroking his arousal to the point of madness.

Still he didn't touch her.

She broke the kiss and stared at him. "You're not going to do anything but kiss me, are you?"

He shook his head.

"Even if I ask you to?"

"Not yet." God, if she knew what this cost him. "Not tonight."

Her brilliant smile nearly blinded him. It was as if his words had given her the permission she needed.

She attacked him. Flirty little kisses dampened his jaw. Openmouthed kisses tormented his neck. She suckled his earlobe, then traced the outside of his ear.

With her hands she touched his shoulders, his arms, down to his hands clamped to the front of the desk. From there she trailed across his belly, making him groan audibly and his muscles tense with painful need. Then she returned her attention to his mouth.

This kiss touched his heart. He couldn't say why. As far as he could tell there was no sudden change in technique, nothing new learned. Maybe it was the honesty in her touch, the desire he felt in her hot, wet mouth and rapid heartbeat.

She clung to him as if he were her only point of reference in a rapidly spinning world. Her body was limp against his, her breathing coming in short gasps.

When at last she stepped back, her mouth was swollen, her eyes glazed with a wanting he'd never seen before. If he touched her most secret place, he would find it damp and ready.

He'd never wanted her so much in his life.

She gave him a shaky smile. "Wow," she managed, then licked her lower lip. "I don't know what to say."

"How about good-night?"

She blinked, obviously surprised. "What if I don't want to go?"

"It's still good-night."

It was too soon. He wanted her to think about what had happened between them. He wanted her to be hungry for a while. Not to punish her, but so that she could anticipate what would happen the next time.

She nodded slowly, then walked to the door. Once there, she looked back. "That was just chapter one," she said.

He grinned. "How many chapters are there?"

"Nine."

"I can't wait."

Chapter Thirteen

Elissa looked at the small pedestal table she'd borrowed from the storeroom. The round, antique lace tablecloth Millie had loaned her added a level of elegance to the setting, as did the simple white plates. There was an arrangement of cut flowers, white wine chilling in an ice bucket and a chicken-and-mushroom casserole on the heating plate in the corner.

She'd planned a dinner that was easy to keep warm, easy to serve and one of Cole's favorites. At least, it used to be. Surely a man's tastes didn't change that much in five years.

She glanced at the candles sitting in the center of the table. She could light them now or she could wait until Cole arrived. When she reached for the matches, she realized her hands were trembling. Okay, she would leave that for him to do. It might be more romantic, anyway.

"How much longer?" she asked out loud, and checked her watch. Five forty-seven. One minute later than the last time she'd looked. Was it possible to be this nervous and live? Her heart thundered in her chest, while the fluttering in her stomach had increased from the delicate sensation of butterflies to something that more closely resembled elephants line-dancing.

She forced herself to close her eyes and draw in a deep breath. Cole was coming to her room for dinner. That was all.

"Oh, but that's not all," she moaned, covering her face with her hands. Since late last week, when he'd told her about the letter from his grandfather and they'd shared those few intimate moments together, something had changed. Maybe it was Cole's admission that he liked her. They'd never been friends before, and that added a new dimension to their relationship. Maybe it was her growing confidence about the physical side of the relationship. She was starting to understand what was supposed to happen between a man and a woman, as well as what had gone wrong in their marriage.

Knowing full well what he would expect from her invitation, she'd asked him to her room for dinner. Amazingly enough, he'd accepted.

Elissa tried to comfort herself by remembering Millie's words of counsel.

"You don't have to do everything the first night," the older woman had said that afternoon when Elissa had confessed nervousness. "Pretend to be teenagers. Make out on the sofa. Get to second base. Leave the rest of it for another time."

Good advice, Elissa thought, dropping her hands to her sides and opening her eyes. She'd reached the point in her education where she was book smart, but ignorant in practice. Although, keeping in mind all the things she'd learned, it was easy to see what had gone wrong.

No wonder Cole had been frustrated with her. She'd lain in bed like a lump. The more she didn't respond, the more desperate he'd become to connect with her sexually.

The whole idea of an orgasm was still weird. Maybe they existed and maybe they didn't. At this point, she didn't care. Elissa simply wanted to seduce her husband. If she could get him back in her bed, and this time make him happy, they might have a second chance at their marriage. Millie had told her several times that passion allowed a marriage to ride out the rough patches. As important as that was, if Cole would trust her with his body, he just might be willing to trust her with his heart.

A knock on the door broke through her thoughts. One hand flew to her throat. Dear God, please let her get through this night without doing anything horrible. She and Cole needed a good time together, and not just in bed.

She crossed the floor and reached for the door.

Two hours later they left the table and headed to the sofa. The pleasant conversation, not to mention the wine, had gone a long way toward blurring the edges of her anxiety.

Elissa sat down first, choosing a spot halfway between the middle and the edge of the couch. Cole did the same. When they angled toward each other, their knees brushed.

"You're drunk," he teased.

"Oh, please." She leaned forward and set her wineglass on the coffee table. "This is only my second glass."

"You didn't eat anything at dinner, so you're drinking on an empty stomach."

"I had some salad." And a couple of bites of the chicken, but little else. The edges of her anxiety might be blurred, but that didn't mean she wasn't still nervous.

Cole stretched his arm along the back of the sofa and rested his fingers on her shoulder. "I know what you're thinking," he said, his dark gaze meeting hers. "You invited me to your room for dinner and I accepted. I wanted to spend some time alone with you because it's something we rarely get to do, but I'm not expecting anything to happen tonight. I'm enjoying being friends with you. It's enough." He gave her a slow, sexy smile that made her toes curl. "So relax."

Easy for him to say; nearly impossible for her to do. After all, while there was no script that said they *had* to do anything, she'd been thinking about it a lot and the idea was intriguing. Also, whether or not they even kissed, just being in the same room with Cole was enough to make her nervous.

"You just don't have a clue, do you?" she asked.

"What are you talking about?"

She waved toward him. "You. Everything about you. Look at that." She leaned over and fingered the edge of his shirt. "A plain white shirt, right? No big deal? I said casual, so you show up in this shirt and jeans. What could be simpler?"

"Elissa, what are you talking about?"

She patted the fingers still touching her shoulder. "This was supposed to comfort me, right? A little contact to ease my worries."

He nodded, obviously bewildered.

"It's been like this from the moment we first met. You intimidate me. You always have. You're so amazing. This casual little touch doesn't comfort me, Cole. It makes my skin all hot and prickly. These clothes—" She threw up her hands. "A long-sleeved shirt rolled up to the elbow is so sexy, and you don't know."

He stared at his forearm as if he'd never seen it before. "Sexy? No way."

"You're going to have to trust me on this. I'm not sure

what it is. Maybe the bare wrist and hand thing, or the muscles, or imagining what you looked like when you actually were rolling up your sleeve.'' She paused to catch her suddenly tight breath. "And the jeans. Do not get me started on them. Worn denim hugging...'' She cleared her throat. "Never mind. You get the point.''

He gazed at her solemnly. "You're crazy. Or drunk.''

She laughed. "I'm neither. I'm telling you the truth. If you being so darned good-looking wasn't bad enough, you've always known what you wanted. I can't tell you how much I used to admire that. I still do. You have drive and purpose. And confidence. I guess you're a natural leader.''

His mouth twisted. "No, I'm just better than most at faking my way through. Half the time I don't know what I'm doing with these kids. I've learned to trust my gut and pray nothing horrible happens because of a decision I've made. Besides, you used to intimidate me.''

She touched her chest. "Me? You're kidding. How?''

The fingers on her shoulder squeezed gently. She leaned into the contact, enjoying both the conversation and the man.

"You were so beautiful. Famous. At least you weren't rich. That would have been too much for me to handle.''

Elissa swallowed a sudden bubble of guilt. She refused to think about her trust fund tonight.

"I never knew what a girl like you would see in a guy like me,'' he continued. "Maybe that's why I worked so much when we were first married. I wanted to prove myself to you.''

"You had nothing to prove. I thought you were perfect already.''

He shook his head. "Not perfect. So far from that. I really messed up, Elissa, and I'm sorry. When I think about all the nights I was gone, all the times I left you while I worked on a case. After a while I figured out something was wrong between us, but I didn't know how to fix it. The more you withdrew, the more I insisted that we—" He met her gaze. "I'm sorry about that, too."

She reached up and took his fingers in hers, then lowered both their hands to the sofa cushion between them. "It was both of us."

"Maybe."

Her nerves had settled a bit. Even though it was too late to go back and change the past, it was nice to know that Cole had regrets, too. If only they'd had this conversation five years ago, when it could have done some good.

No, she thought. It wouldn't have worked then. Neither of them was grown-up enough to hear it.

"Do you miss it?" she asked. "The law firm, the city?"

"Sometimes," he admitted. "I like my work here and I love the kids, but there are days I want more of a challenge. I miss the pace of the city a little. I suppose in a perfect world I'd split my time between the two."

She linked her fingers with his and looked at their hands. They were a study in contrasts. Tanned skin to fair, large palms to small. Yet they were right together. At least, that was her fantasy. What was his? *Who* was his?

"Have there been others?" she asked, not daring to look at him.

"Job offers?"

"Women."

He leaned toward her and touched a forefinger to her chin, nudging until she raised her gaze to his. Perfect cheekbones, a bone-melting smile, eyes that promised the world. How many had tried and failed? How many had tried and succeeded?

"You're my wife," he told her. "I meant forever when I spoke the vows, and I've never gone back on my word."

She vaguely recalled she was supposed to be seducing him, but right now this seemed more important. "Why didn't you ask for a divorce?"

His expression shuttered. She couldn't have said how. No muscles made obvious movement, his mouth didn't straighten, he barely blinked. Yet he'd gone somewhere else and she hadn't been invited along.

But he didn't release her hand, and she clung to that thought, along with his fingers, as if her life depended upon holding fast.

The silence stretched until she could hear her heartbeat and the faint sound of their breathing. She searched her mind for something to say, anything that would change the subject and make things right between them again.

"I never wanted to be with anyone else," he said.

She stared at him. His words filled her mind until everything else had been pushed away.

I never wanted to be with anyone else. It wasn't a confession of love, not yet. But it was close. It was a place to start. It was the signal she'd been waiting for.

She released his hand and slid toward him. After cupping his face, she pressed her mouth against his.

This time he kissed her back without needing to be urged. This time his arms came around her, pulling her closer and keeping her safe.

She stroked his face, loving the soft skin that told her he'd taken the time to shave before coming over. She traced his ears, his jaw, the strong line of his neck, then wrapped her arms around his back and surged toward him.

They were locked together, her breasts flat against his chest, their mouths clinging and pressing and brushing in an erotic dance of discovery.

She parted her lips and he slipped inside. He'd kissed her that way before. She suspected he could do it every day for the rest of her life and she would never grow tired of the shock of his heat or the sweet shiver that rippled through her as his tongue first teased the inner skin of her lower lip before flicking delicately against hers.

There was a rightness in their embrace, a sense of homecoming. Elissa didn't know if love was like raging fire or more like a slow burn. Either could be true. Whatever the correct definition, she knew that she loved Cole, had always loved him. He was her mate, her other half, her destiny.

He raised his head and stared at her. "You always were a great kisser."

Pleasure flooded her. "Thank you. You're pretty amazing yourself. Of course, I don't have a whole lot of experience."

He frowned. "How many guys have you kissed?"

"Kissed like this, or just family kisses?"

"Real, tongue-in-your-mouth kind of kisses."

At his words, a jolt of awareness shot through her legs and burst between her thighs. Had he felt the same excitement when she'd talked about kissing yesterday? She eyed his damp mouth and wondered how long they could actually spend kissing each other. Would it ever get boring? She smiled at the thought. No doubt they would have to contend with a muscle cramp or starvation before boredom ever became a problem.

He shook her gently. "Elissa, you're not listening to me. Answer the question."

What was the question? Oh, yes, she remembered. She licked his lower lip. "Counting you?"

"Yeah."

She drew his lower lip into her mouth and sucked it. His

entire body tensed. He gripped her upper arms and set her away from him. "Will you pay attention?"

She pouted. "If I have to, although I'd rather be kissing. One."

She slipped a hand behind his head and urged him closer. He resisted. "One? You've only kissed one other guy?"

When she couldn't reach his mouth, she settled on nibbling his jaw. It was almost as nice. "No, I've only kissed you."

"Wait a minute." He straightened and stared at her. "We didn't start dating until you were almost seventeen."

"I know." She tossed her hair over her shoulders and wondered how on earth to get his attention again. She didn't want to talk, she wanted to kiss. And maybe do other stuff. Her body felt tight and hot, her breasts throbbed, and that place between her legs was driving her crazy with its tingling and clenching and aching.

She tried to kiss him again, but he held her back.

She sighed. "If we get this settled, can we go back to kissing?"

"Yes. I want you to explain to me how come you haven't kissed anyone else but me."

She rolled her eyes. "This is so incredibly dumb, but okay. We met when I was ten and, despite what you say, became friends. We saw each other when I visited the orphanage and we wrote."

"Yeah, so?"

"Oh, Cole, grow up and get a clue. I had a crush on you from the time I was twelve years old. You were seventeen and nearly a man. You knocked my socks off. I spent all my free time thinking about you, trying to get you to notice me. I mean, you did notice me, but not in a girlfriend sort of way. By the time boys started paying attention to me, I wasn't interested. I was about fifteen or sixteen, which made you twenty. You were in college. Those high school boys didn't have a chance. I went out with a couple, but there were no sparks. One date might have ended with a kiss on the cheek, but I can't remember. Now, can we go back to kissing?''

''Dear God, what did I do to deserve you?'' he growled, then buried his hands in her hair and dropped his mouth to hers.

Finally, she thought in satisfaction as her lips parted and he plunged inside. Her eyes fluttered closed as she concentrated all her attention on the sensations he invoked.

There wasn't a part of her that wasn't on fire. She remembered enjoying making out with him before, but not like this. Was it the time they'd been apart, proving the old adage of absence making the heart grow fonder?

As she squirmed to get closer, Elissa decided it wasn't that at all. After they'd married, she'd known that kissing was going to lead to other things, things that hurt and frightened her. So she hadn't been able to enjoy what was happening between them. Now, while she would confess to a lingering case of nerves, she wasn't truly afraid. Armed with information and the goal of getting Cole back in her life, she wanted to take the next step in their physical relationship.

Cole broke the kiss and trailed his mouth down her chin to her neck, then lower to the scoop neck of her cap-sleeve sundress.

She'd chosen this particular dress on purpose. Not only did the deep rose color highlight her hair and eyes, but it buttoned up the front. So if anything should happen, Cole would have easy access to her, ah…to her, well, to *her*. She'd never before chosen clothing based on the hopes of getting a man to make love to her, but it had been fun, if a little embarrassing. She was wearing her prettiest bra and pantie set, too, just in case.

"We should stop," he murmured as he nibbled on a sensitive spot below her left ear.

"Why?"

"Because I don't want things to get out of hand."

She arched her head back, giving him more room. Her breasts swelled and she leaned against him, but the pressure only increased. "Would that be so bad?" she asked.

"You don't know what you're saying."

"I have a pretty good idea."

He rested his forehead against her shoulder. "I can't do this, Elissa. I'm just not strong enough."

That got her attention. She leaned back and looked at him. "What do you mean? Strong enough to make love?"

"No." He raised his head. "I'm not strong enough to take another rejection."

Raw pain filled his dark eyes. Compassion tightened her heart, making her want to weep for him. Maybe for both of them.

"What did we do to each other?" she asked, then bit her lower lip. "It wasn't supposed to be like that. We should have enjoyed each other. I never meant for our bedroom to become a battleground."

"It's my fault. If I'd figured out how to please you—"

She pressed her fingers against his mouth. "Don't say that. I wouldn't let you. I've been doing a lot of reading lately and I can see a lot of the places where we went wrong. There are things we could have done before, to make it not hurt."

He tugged her hand away and smiled. "Foreplay. I've heard of it."

"Oh." Heat flared on her cheeks, but she ignored it and kept on talking. "Well, there's that. Foreplay. I never let you do anything. Once we started, I just wanted it over as quickly as possible. Apparently it takes some kissing and other kinds of attention for a woman to, well…''

''Become aroused?''

She cleared her throat and stared at the center of his chest. ''Yes. After becoming aroused, it can still take her a while to, um…''

''Climax?''

''Right. Assuming that's even real. My point is—''

This time he was the one to press his fingers over her mouth. ''It's real,'' he said, his smile fading. ''I should have done things differently. I should have made you see what the possibilities were. I'm sorry.''

''No apologies required,'' she said, kissing the pads of his fingers. She brushed his hair off his forehead. ''I don't want to reject you. I can't promise not to get nervous. I'm probably going to get all jumpy and maybe even clam up, but it's not rejection. It's just trying to figure out my body. I'm twenty-five years old and I don't have a clue about what goes on 'down there.' I've read a lot in the past few days. I have some ideas, and a couple of working theories. Maybe we could go into the other room and you could help me with my homework.''

She held her breath as he considered her request. Apprehension, desire, pain and a few emotions she couldn't read skittered across his face. There was, she realized, a more than even chance that he would turn down her offer. The thought made her wince. Then she remembered all the times she'd rejected him and knew that he had every right not to trust her.

''Is this homework assignment going to be graded?'' he asked lightly, rising to his feet and pulling her along with him.

Relief made her knees weak. "I've heard the teacher grades on a curve."

He put his hand on her waist, then slid it down her hip and around to her derriere. "Then you'll get an A. You've got lots of curves."

She laughed as he pulled her close. At the first touch of his mouth against hers, the humor faded. They were going to make it, she thought giddily. Cole had taken a chance on her and she was determined not to let him down.

Still kissing, they made their way into her bedroom. In a moment of boldness she'd unmade the bed, folding the comforter on the floor and pulling back the sheets. Now, as he walked her to the edge of the bed, she was glad. She didn't want anything to get in the way of them being together. She knew they weren't going to be perfect—not their first time after everything that had gone on before—but she wanted it to be right.

Cole released her long enough to close the door and turn off the light. As the darkness engulfed her, she had to swallow a shiver of apprehension.

"Could we leave the light on?" she asked.

"Sure." Light filled the room. He shifted uncomfortably. "I thought you'd be more at ease in the dark."

"I know. I would have thought so, too. But before, we always did it in the dark, and I don't want to do things the same way. Besides, one of the books said that it would help if I saw you naked."

He shoved his hands into his pockets. "Look, Elissa, we don't have to do this at all."

She crossed to him and wrapped her arms around his waist. "Yes, we do," she murmured. "I want you, Cole. I want to make love with you. I want to figure out how to apply all that I've learned so that we can both enjoy being together.'' She gave him a quick smile. ''So shut up and kiss me.''

He complied. How he complied. As his tongue stroked hers, her bones began to melt. His hands rubbed her back, then slipped lower. When he cupped the curves of her behind and squeezed, she arched against him. He moaned low in his throat, rotating his hips against hers.

Through the layers of his briefs and jeans, and through her dress and panties, she felt his hardness. Before, knowing he was aroused had always made her tense. Now she thought about what he might look like. She wanted to see him *and* touch him. Several of the books had given her ideas that she wanted to try. One had guaranteed that if she followed the technique, he would explode in her hand. She wasn't ready for any kind of explosion, but a few moans of pleasure would be nice. She'd never been able to make him do that before. They were both overdue for the experience.

But Cole seemed in no hurry to let her have her way with him. Twice she dipped below his belt to try to touch him, and both times he pulled her hands back to his waist.

''You first,'' he said, barely breaking their kiss.

Her first? ''Talk about performance pressure,'' she muttered.

He laughed. ''You're all grown up, Elissa. I like it.''

''Me, too.''

He dipped his head and pressed his mouth against the side of her neck. At the same time his hands moved to the front of her dress and began unfastening the buttons.

She held on to his shoulders, using his strength to stay upright. Her knees were still weak, but this time from anticipation, not nerves.

As he nipped at her skin, tiny electric bolts zinged through her body. Heat flared between her thighs, radiating out until all of her glowed. The back of his hand bumped her right breast. Not hard, just a small point of contact that made her gasp. She wanted his hands there, on her breasts, touching her, stroking her, doing all those things she'd read about. She wanted to feel the sensations the books talked about and she wanted to feel them with Cole.

When the last button was undone, he drew the dress down her body, slipping her arms out of the sleeves and pushing the fabric over her hips so that it pooled at her feet. Then he took her right hand in his and brought it to his mouth.

With her standing before him in nothing but a pale pink bra and a pair of panties, he licked her palm. More heat, like a tongue of fire, swept through her. The ache between her thighs intensified. Slowly, as if they had more time than any two people could need, he nibbled on each of her fingers. First he drew them into his mouth, then he tasted them from tip to base.

She hadn't thought of her hands as being especially sensitive or erotic. But if he stopped now, she would sob in protest. So when he reached for her other hand, she offered it eagerly. It didn't matter that her thighs trembled or that she couldn't catch her breath. Nothing mattered but how he made her feel.

When he'd finished loving her hands, he began a sensual assault on her arms. He traced a line from the inside of her wrist to the inside of her elbow, tasting and kissing and nibbling her into a sensual fog. He nipped at her shoulders, suckled her earlobes and traced random lines between her breasts.

Then, when she thought he was finally going to touch her throbbing nipples, he sank to his knees and pressed his mouth into her belly.

Her legs started to collapse. She had to hang on to his

shoulders to maintain her balance. Shudders racked her body. She was alive with unbelievable sensation, lost in a world she had never experienced before. Everywhere he touched was magic. Perhaps she'd never fully been alive before. Perhaps she'd passed on and this was the reward of the afterlife.

He kissed her stomach, teasing the sensitive skin, moving close to her feminine secrets and up toward her breasts, but not touching her in either place.

"Cole," she breathed, not sure what she asked for.

Yet he knew.

He stood and led her to the bed. Before lowering her to the waiting sheets, he unfastened her bra and let it fall to the floor.

Her back touched the sheet at the same moment Cole's mouth closed over her right nipple. The combination of cool cotton and moist heat made her arch toward him. She clutched his head as if to urge him to do it again, to keep doing it.

He read her mind. While his tongue mated with her erect point, he used his other hand to stroke her full curves, discovering sensitivities she hadn't dreamed existed.

Over and over he loved her breasts, alternating his hands and his mouth, making her squirm and sigh and moan.

When he raised his head, she nearly shrieked in protest, then he brought his mouth to hers and cupped her breasts with both hands.

Yes! she thought, savoring the feel of his body against hers. She shifted, then wrapped her arms around him, pulling him close. His thumbs and forefingers teased her tight buds, his lips clung to hers. She felt his arousal against her hip and nearly laughed with the joy of being with him. This was so simple, so fun. Why had she resisted so long?

She barely noticed when he drew back far enough to tug

at her panties. She was vaguely aware of kicking them off, then wiggling close to him again. But he got her full attention when he moved his hand between her thighs.

She blinked as she considered the situation. She was naked, he was not. They were sprawled across her bed. He was kissing her and had one hand on her breast and the other "down there."

"This is the most amazing homework assignment I've ever done," she said, hoping her apprehension didn't show in her voice.

Cole knew her too well. "Don't be afraid," he said.

"I'm not. I'm just—" She bit her lower lip.

"Nervous?"

She nodded.

He moved his fingers slightly. She jumped as pleasure swept over her. Her eyes widened. "Do that again," she said.

He did. The pleasure bolt returned.

"I'm impressed."

He smiled. "You're also wet as hell and it's driving me crazy."

She started to speak. He stopped her words with a brief kiss. "Wet is good. It means you're getting ready." He moved his fingers again. "I'm going to circle around and you tell me where it feels best, okay?"

"Ah, sure. It all feels really nice."

Passion flared in his eyes. "We want something a little better than nice. Close your eyes and concentrate."

She drew in a deep breath and tried to relax. He wanted her to concentrate on what he was doing. Hardly a difficult request. As his fingers moved, circling through her most secret places, she found herself parting her legs and raising her hips to urge him on.

"It's all great," she said as wave after wave of sensual excitement swept through her. "I really don't think—"

His finger brushed over something magic. Barely realizing what she was doing, she clutched his forearm. "There!"

He touched it again. Elissa had to swallow back a scream of sheer delight. She hadn't known feelings like that existed. Nothing in life had prepared her for the amazing sense of pure joy.

He continued to touch her, circling that one spot, teasing it, moving quickly, then slowly. She lost her grip on this dimension and allowed herself to float freely in a place where there was only one exquisite sensation after another. Pressure built, but she ignored it. She wanted Cole to keep doing this; she would be his slave for life.

He shifted and she parted her thighs more. One finger slipped inside her. He slid in and out, matching rhythms. She clutched at the sheets. Tension increased.

Her breath came in gasps. She couldn't focus on anything but what he was doing to her. Somewhere in her cloud of mindlessness she heard him whisper her name, heard him urge her onward. But she had no control of the journey. She could only experience the perfect pleasure, could only feel and be.

He moved faster. She became caught in a vortex. Time, space, some force she couldn't define, pulled her onward, pushing her toward the tension, toward the building pressure.

For a heartbeat she hung suspended. Then her world shattered. Not destructively, but with purpose. Like a cloud making rain, she thought. It was her last thought as the spasms took hold of her, carrying her back through the vortex, back through time, returning her to the bed and Cole's loving embrace.

Chapter Fourteen

Cole held his wife in his arms and listened to her sigh of contentment. Already the flush of arousal had faded from her skin, but he remembered seeing it. Without even closing his eyes, he could picture her as she'd looked at her moment of completion. Head back, mouth parted slightly, hands gripping at the sheets, a blushing patch sweeping across her breasts, chest and face.

"The books weren't lying," Elissa said, her voice laced with wonder. "I just sort of figured they had to be."

"I'm glad you enjoyed it." He brushed her bangs off her face and kissed her forehead.

"Enjoyed is a very weak word. I was transformed and transfixed." She laughed. "I'm too stunned to think up any more *T* words. Otherwise I would."

He touched her cheek, her neck, her shoulders, almost as if he had to reassure himself she was really here, with him, and that she'd just climaxed for the first time in her life.

"What's wrong?" she asked, gazing up at him. "You look funny. Not sad exactly, but... What is it? Did I do something I shouldn't have?"

"Never," he said, bending over her and forcing himself to smile. "I'm glad you enjoyed it. I thought it was great."

Her mouth twisted in concern. "You're not just saying that?"

"Elissa, touching you, knowing that I was making it happen, was about the best thing in my life. With my fingers inside, I could feel the contractions."

She blushed bright red, but didn't turn away. "So you know I wasn't faking it."

"Oh, yeah."

"Then why the mysterious expression?"

Her hair fanned out on the bed, a blanket of golden-blond silk. He stroked the soft curls as he considered her question. "I'm sorry for all the time we wasted. I should have tried harder."

"No!" She wrapped her arms around him and shifted, easing him onto his back, then pinned down his arms and stared into his face. "No, Cole. I won't let you ruin this with self-recriminations. The past is over. We need to let it go. Tonight we've created a miracle. Enjoy that. And while you're doing that, you can answer another question for me."

Her generosity only increased his feelings of self-loathing. He should have made it better for her. When she'd resisted being touched, he could have...

What? Forced her? Damn, why wasn't there an easy answer?

Rather than worrying about it, he looked at Elissa sprawled naked across his chest. Her hair tumbled over her shoulders and bare breasts. She looked like a pagan goddess.

"What's your question?" he asked.

"Why do you have so many clothes on?"

At her words, the need between his legs tightened painfully. His blood heated and his mouth went dry. "Hell if I know," he muttered, and reached for the buttons on his shirt.

"Uh-uh." She brushed his hands away. "I'll do it."

She was as good as her word. While he lay there, she opened his shirt and rubbed her hands up and down his chest. It was only when she repeated the actions with her mouth that he began to worry about losing control.

In a matter of minutes she tossed aside his shirt and trousers. Now she tugged at his briefs, urging him to raise his hips so she could free him of his last article of clothing.

As the material slid down, his arousal sprang free. He was large and hot and faintly embarrassed by the fact. But instead of recoiling, Elissa knelt between his thighs. She tilted her head to one side, studying his maleness.

"It's much nicer than the line drawings," she said, and rested her hands on his knees. "Does it hurt?"

"Yes, but not in the way you think. More pressure than pain."

She nodded. "Sort of an aching. That's what I felt. It's deep inside, but on the surface, too." She slid her hands up his thighs. "I want to touch you. Show me what to do."

"Just—" His muscles quivered in anticipation. When she reached the crown of hair surrounding his maleness, his breath caught in his throat. Warm, sure fingers encircled him. She began to move up and down.

"Like that," he gasped.

Her technique was faulty. She kept stopping to explore, running her fingers over the sensitive head, dropping kisses

on his upper thighs and belly, once kissing the very tip.
But he didn't correct her, or show her the quickest way to
please him. That would be for later. For now, it was enough
to have her touching him there. It was, he realized, a first
for both of them.

He opened his eyes and looked at her. There were tears
on her cheeks. Startled, he sat up. "What's wrong?"

"Nothing." She wiped her face on her shoulder. "I love
this. You're warm and silky. It's not scary at all. I could
touch you forever and I never bothered before. I never
wanted to see you naked or take you in my hands." Her
voice dropped to a whisper. "Or my mouth."

He shuddered with pleasure at the thought.

"I was a horrible wife. I don't deserve forgiveness, so
I'm not going to ask for it."

He reached down and took her hands in his. "What was
it you said to me? Don't ruin this with self-recriminations.
That applies to you, too. Come here and let me love you."

She came willingly into his arms. He kissed her mouth,
then her breasts. When her breathing had increased and her
eyes were glazed with passion, he slipped on the protection
she'd left on the nightstand, then moved to enter her.

Her tight body stretched to accommodate him. She welcomed him with a sigh, then caught his hips and pulled him
closer.

Pleasure swept over him in an uncontrollable wave. "I
can't hold back," he muttered. "Dammit, Elissa, I'm
sorry."

She smiled at him, then drew her knees closer to her
chest, urging him deeper. "Don't hold back. Give me everything right now."

"But I wanted you to have another turn."

"I will. Later." Her smile turned impish. "I was hoping

we could try that special kissing thing. You know, kissing down there?''

That image was all he needed to lose control. "Yes." He ground out the word, plunging into her twice more before passion overtook him, ripping through him with the fury of a firestorm, leaving him sated and cradled in his wife's loving arms.

Cole tossed his pencil in the air and leaned back in his chair. He wasn't getting any work done and he couldn't find it in himself to care. Not after last night.

They'd made love three more times, discovering each other, bringing each other mindless pleasure, sharing in ways he'd never thought possible. He had a feeling he was going to spend the entire day grinning like a fool.

That didn't matter, he told himself contentedly. He refused to dwell on the past or the future. What was important was the present. Elissa in his bed and his arms.

There was a danger that she would creep back into his heart, too. The sensible plan would be to back off. But he knew he wouldn't. Last night had been everything he'd ever dreamed his marriage could be. It was a miracle, for both of them.

He didn't doubt that their fundamental problems remained the same. In time, Elissa would leave him. Until then he would enjoy all that she offered and give back as much as he was able. When she left him, he would survive. He wasn't sure how, but he'd never heard of anyone dying of a broken heart. If nothing else, he would have his work. It had always been his salvation.

The phone rang, cutting through his thoughts. He picked it up. "Stephenson here."

"Mr. Stephenson, I'm Cathy with Industrial Supplies. I wanted to confirm our delivery for tomorrow. You're up in

Ojai, right?" She continued without waiting for an answer. "We'll load the truck tonight and make you the first delivery. With all the traffic, you can expect to see us between ten and eleven. Is that all right?"

"Industrial Supplies?" he repeated, then pulled open a file drawer and started flipping through purchase orders. "I don't recognize the company name. What are you delivering?"

"Let's see." He heard the woman shuffling papers. "A restaurant stove. One of our nicer ones. And a freezer unit. Let me see. Huh. That's weird. I don't have a purchase order number. It just says per Elissa Bedford. I think she paid with a personal check. I'm not sure... Oh, you're an orphanage. This is probably a donation. We get those sometimes. So is the time for the delivery okay?"

Elissa had bought them a stove and a freezer? "What? The delivery? Sure, that's fine."

"We'll see you tomorrow, Mr. Stephenson."

"Fine." He hung up the phone.

Elissa? He rose to his feet and crossed to the window. Outside several of the children played on the jungle gym. He remembered the anonymous benefactor paying for science camp. Had that all been her? Why had she done it? Where had the money come from?

He returned to his desk and picked up the phone. He had a couple of lawyer friends in Los Angeles. They would be able to give him a place to start. One way or another, he was going to get his questions answered.

Two hours later he set down the receiver. He knew about Elissa's trust fund and had confirmed she'd been the one to pay for the sports equipment. Fallon had written the check to the science camp, but he was confident Elissa had made those arrangements. He remembered her wide-eyed, innocent stare as she had sworn she hadn't been in touch with the camp director.

"Technically avoiding a lie," he said softly, knowing it was so like her.

The money from her television show had been in trust until she turned twenty-five. He wondered why she'd kept the information from him, then he grimaced. After she'd listened to him rage against his grandfather's wealth in particular and the rich in general, it was no wonder she wouldn't want to confess that she had a trust fund waiting for her. At twenty-five, he hadn't been very understanding.

But what about now? Why was she buying things for the orphanage and keeping it a secret? Was she still afraid he would judge her? Did she think he would want her money?

Neither of those sounded right. If anything, Elissa would keep quiet so he wouldn't think she was trying to buy his affection. So what did he do now? Should he confront her or just let her continue with her anonymous gift giving?

There was a light knock on his office door. "Come in," he called.

Elissa slipped inside, then turned and carefully locked the door behind her. When she faced him, she smiled, but he saw the trembling at the corners of her mouth. Despite all they'd shared last night, she wasn't sure of her welcome.

"Hi," she said, and tucked her hands behind her back. "I hope you don't mind. I thought we could, um, talk and..." She motioned to the door. "This way we don't have to worry about interruptions."

He hated the questions in her eyes, the nervous way she nibbled her bottom lip. He hadn't seen her since he'd left her bed at four in the morning. It felt like a lifetime ago.

"Come here," he said, holding out his arms. "I've missed you."

"I've missed you, too," she said, and flew to him.

He gathered her close, pulling her onto his lap and kissing her. Passion flared instantly. Their tongues mated and danced until they were both breathing hard, then he raised his head.

Her questions were gone, her mouth fully smiling. She laughed and touched his face. "You look different," she said.

"How?"

"Happier. And a little tired."

"Could it be because I didn't get any sleep last night?" A blush stole up her cheeks. "Maybe."

"You didn't get any sleep, either. How come you don't look tired at all?"

She leaned close. "Makeup," she whispered in his ear.

"Ah. You're tricking the world with your feminine wiles."

"Something like that." Her humor faded. "Are we all right, Cole?"

He cupped her face. "Elissa. Jeez, I should have known you'd want reassurance. We're more than all right. We're great. In fact, if lunch wasn't in fifteen minutes, I'd try to convince you to share a quickie right here on the desk."

She looked over his shoulder as if gauging the logistics involved. "Okay." She started unbuttoning his shirt.

"Wait." He stilled her hands. "They'll miss us if we don't show up for lunch."

"Maybe, but not enough to come looking for us."

Her mouth followed her fingers and he found it difficult to think as she trailed damp kisses down his chest.

"You'll be sore," he protested, although not with as much conviction as he would have liked. He was already hard.

"Uh-huh. We'll work around that."

"Elissa, we can't." But as he said the words, he was

tugging at the hem of her dress, trying to pull it up so he could touch her body.

They worked together to remove their clothing. When he lowered his mouth to her breasts and his fingers to her waiting warmth, he realized he didn't care about the trust fund or the gifts. Maybe he should be angry. In a way, she was keeping something from him.

Yet as he stroked her sensitive core and heard her muffled moans of pleasure he knew the information she withheld wasn't important. Not compared to how she gave to the children and to him. As her naked body trembled in his arms and she breathed his name when she reached for her completion, he knew he could not find it in his heart to expose her secret. He wanted her. Worse, he needed her. For as long as she was willing to be with him, he was willing to welcome her with open arms.

Elissa stretched her arms over her head, then rolled to look at the clock. Nearly five-thirty in the morning. She would have to leave soon, tiptoeing in the darkness, back to her own room.

"Don't go," Cole said, turning to her and tucking her naked body against his, so they lay like spoons in a drawer. One hand rested possessively on her hip.

"I have a little time," she said, absorbing the feel of him next to her.

When she'd first arrived at the orphanage, if someone had told her she and Cole would be practically living together again, she would have questioned that person's sanity. If she'd been told that not only would they be spending their nights in the same bed, but would also be making wild, passionate love to each other, she would have called for the guys in white coats.

But it was true. Since that night three weeks ago, they'd

been together constantly. Their days were spent enjoying their work and the children. Their nights were spent enjoying each other. She'd learned her body was capable of incredible pleasure, both receiving and giving. She'd learned how to reduce her wonderful husband to mindlessness with just the whisper of her fingers or her tongue. They'd explored each other, venturing on a wondrous journey from which she never wanted to return. She wanted it to go on forever.

She wanted to tell Cole she loved him.

So far she'd been holding the words back, not wanting to move too quickly. There were still problems between them. They had to deal with their past, with issues of honesty and trust. For a while she could be content sneaking around, but eventually she wanted to share her joy with the world.

"I'm glad I sent the letter," Cole said, continuing their previous conversation. "You were right to urge me to tell my grandfather that we should set up a meeting as soon as possible."

"You're so stubborn. Why did you take so long to answer him? It's been nearly a month."

"I wanted to be sure."

She felt his lips on her shoulder and smiled. She liked to think that his decision to establish a relationship with his grandfather had something to do with them. Maybe by opening up to her, he would learn to open up to other people. Or maybe she was indulging in a little wishful thinking.

"He mentioned wanting me to visit him," Cole said.

"You should go."

"Actually, I was wondering if you would like to join me."

She turned toward him and met his steady gaze. "You

want me to come with you to New York and meet your grandfather?''

He nodded. "I think the trip would be fun for both of us. I could use the moral support.''

She wrapped her arms around him and rested her cheek against his chest. "I would be honored to go with you, Cole. I think things are going to work out great with your grandfather and you won't need me at all. But I'm happy to provide whatever support I can." She glanced up at him. "Do you think we can find a hotel in New York that has mirrors on the ceiling?''

He brushed her hair off her face. "I've created a monster.''

"I know. Aren't you glad?''

"More than you'll ever know.'' His eyes darkened with emotion. "Will the bad memories be a problem? The last time you were in the city you weren't very happy.''

"Neither were you, but thanks for asking. I'll be fine. We'll make new memories. Better ones. So much has changed. I'm not the same young woman I was five years ago.''

"Some things are different," he agreed. "But not all.''

"Some things I don't want to change.'' She rose on one elbow. "Cole, it's time to stop sneaking around like this. I'm your wife. There's never been anyone else for either of us. I really care about you." She hesitated, then decided it wasn't the time to discuss the fact that she was still in love with him.

"I know you care about me, too,'' she continued. "I'm not saying we're making promises to each other. There are things to work out. But I think it's time to be open about our relationship. I would like us to tell the children and the staff that we're married and I would like us to move in together.''

He withdrew so completely that if she hadn't been naked and in his bed, she would have wondered if she'd simply imagined their time together.

He sat up and leaned against the headboard. His expression shuttered, his mouth straightened. In less than a heartbeat he'd become a stranger.

Her face stung as if he'd slapped her. Her stomach clenched tight. She'd been rejected before, but never like this. Never by him.

Is this what he'd felt all those years ago when she'd turned away from him in bed? Is this what it had felt like when she'd left him? Intellectually, she'd known that she'd hurt him, but until that moment she hadn't realized how much. But she couldn't react with compassion. Not when all she wanted to do was find her clothes and slink away.

"That's not a good idea," he said. "I don't want the children hurt or confused."

She pulled the sheet up to her shoulders and faced him. "What are you talking about? How would the children be confused? I know it's a little complicated, but if we explained it—"

He cut her off with a shake of his head. "I don't mean they would be confused by telling them we're married. They wouldn't understand when you left."

"Left? What are you talking about? I'm not going anywhere."

His dark gaze slipped past her to focus on the wall opposite the bed. "You're here for three months. That time is almost over."

His words stunned her. She had to bite her lower lip to keep from crying out. Her eyes burned, but she blinked back tears. "You can't mean that. After all of this, you can't mean you're going to send me away."

"I won't have to," he said, still not looking at her. "You'll be the one to leave, just as you left before."

"No," she told him. "No, it's not like that. I've changed."

"I don't think so."

His words carried the weight of finality. She didn't know what to say, how to convince him he was wrong. The words he'd said the first time they'd been together returned to haunt her. *Let me love you.* Not *I love you.* She understood the difference. He would commit to the physical act, which meant committing his body but not his heart.

"What has this meant to you?" she asked, motioning to the bed. "Just sex, nothing more?"

At last he looked at her. "You know it's been more than that. Our time together has been very special."

"Sure. I can tell." She shook her head. "I've been a fool. I thought this mattered. I thought *I* mattered."

She reached for her dressing gown and pulled it on. As she tightened the belt, she stood and faced him. "That's it, then."

"Elissa, don't go like this. Don't be angry."

"How can I not be? According to you, it's just a matter of time until I leave, so why not be insulted and hurt and outraged? As long as I'm going, right?"

"You don't understand."

"I understand perfectly. You don't trust me."

"I loved you once," he said slowly. "I might be able to love you again. But you're right. I can't trust you."

Her knees nearly gave way. Only by a supreme force of will was she able to remain standing. "No, you *won't* trust me."

She bent and collected her nightgown. The garment had been tossed aside in a moment of passion. Tossed aside and forgotten, like her hopes for their future.

Her whole body ached, but this time not from passion. She'd been struck down in an emotional hit-and-run. It was going to take a while to get the bleeding under control.

She straightened and walked to the door. Before returning to her room, she glanced back at him. "Here's the thing, Cole. You're not going to get rid of me this easily. Think I'm leaving all you want, but I'm not going anywhere. Somewhere, somehow, I'm going to convince you to give us a second chance. Because we both deserve it. And because we'll never love anyone else as much as we've loved each other."

Chapter Fifteen

"Stephenson," Cole said as he picked up the phone.

"Hello, Cole."

Cole put down the pen he was holding and sagged back in his chair. He didn't recognize the powerful voice that defied age, but he knew who was calling. Son of a bitch.

"Grandfather."

The old man sighed. "That doesn't sound very welcoming. Are you going to be difficult about all this?"

"Are you?"

There was a moment of silence, then a faint chuckle. "You are a Stephenson, young man. There's no doubt. I got your letter. You took your time answering me."

"Then I'd say we're close to even. You took nearly twenty-five years to get in touch with me the first time."

"I see. So you're still angry about that. About the letter I sent all those years ago telling you I didn't want to have anything to do with you."

Some of the shock was starting to wear off. Cole held the receiver in his hand, amazed that he was having this conversation with his grandfather. A man he'd never met, yet whose blood ran through his body.

"I was fifteen and you were my only living relative. You told me, in very clear, easy-to-understand language, that I was not to consider you family or ever contact you again. Angry doesn't really cover what I was feeling, Grandfather."

Some of those emotions returned. The intense pain of rejection, the betrayal of a dream of having a family of his own.

"You're going to make me apologize, aren't you?" Dermott William Stephenson asked. "Do you know who I am?"

"Yes. You're a cranky old man who destroyed a child's hope of a future. It was only when I'd proved myself to your satisfaction that you were willing to acknowledge me. It was too late then and it's too late now."

Rage fueled him and it was all he could do not to hang up the phone. Then he remembered Elissa's words, about how this man was the only relative Cole had. Couldn't he try to make it work?

Could he? After all that had happened?

"It's not too late," his grandfather said. "If it was, you wouldn't have written me back. You want me punished and I accept that. I haven't told anyone this in a long time, but I'm sorry, Cole. Sorry for a lot of things. When my son—your father—left the family firm to marry your mother, I was furious. I vowed to cut him off and I did. But that wasn't good enough. He didn't care about anything but his wife, and later, you."

The old man cleared his throat before continuing. "I would have taken him back, but he never asked."

"And you never offered," Cole guessed.

"I have my pride."

"So did my father. At least he also had his family to keep him company. Who did you have?"

"Did they teach you to hit below the belt at that orphanage of yours?"

"Actually, I learned it at law school."

"Well said." He heard the smile in the old man's voice. "What happened to your pride?" Cole asked.

"Old age has a way of changing how a man looks at things. I want to get to know you, Cole, and I'd like to think you want to get to know me, too. I'm not expecting a miracle, just some common ground and a little conversation."

In the face of that obviously sincere statement, it was difficult to hold on to his anger. "I'd like that, too."

"Good. Now tell me about yourself. You're working at that orphanage out there. In Ojai? Where the hell is that?"

Cole smiled. "North and west of Los Angeles."

"California." The old man sniffed. "I never could abide that place. Too much sunshine, too many happy people. Give me New York where people have the sense to be miserable. How many children there?"

Cole talked about the orphanage and what he was doing there. He found himself explaining about Tiffany and her mother, and little Gina's hunger for knowledge.

"I'd like to adopt that one," Dermott said. "Is she available?"

"She's not a puppy, Grandfather. You can't point to the one you like and then take her home. There are strict procedures to be followed."

"Humph. You're saying you wouldn't let me have the girl."

Cole shook his head. "Let's say I'd want to get to know you first."

"Figures. You're softhearted, boy. Actually, it's not a bad quality, but if you tell anyone I said that, I'll deny it. You still married?"

The question caught Cole off guard. "Yes. Elissa's with me."

"Pretty girl."

"How would you know?"

"We were at the same party once. Some big charity affair, years ago. When you were still in the city. I came because I knew you were going to be there. I wanted to see how you'd turned out."

The image of a lonely old man slipping into a party to catch a glimpse of his only grandson made Cole sad. They'd both wasted so much time. And for what?

"You should have introduced yourself."

"So you could snub me in public? No, thank you. You wouldn't have been interested in me then. You were still angry. So, do I have any great-grandchildren?"

"No. Elissa and I haven't had children yet."

"Five years is a long time, boy. What are you waiting for? With a looker like that, they're going to be pretty babies. I'd like to see a couple of great-grandchildren before I die. Not that I'm pressuring you."

"I understand."

The old man continued talking, but Cole barely heard him. He was too caught up in the thought of having children with Elissa. He knew he'd made it sound as if they had been together all this time. This first phone call wasn't the place to discuss his marital problems. It was unlikely he and his wife were going to work things out, yet if they did, he would love to have children with her. His grandfather was right—they would have pretty babies. Because they would be blessed with their mother's giving heart, they would be pretty where it mattered—on the inside.

"How's the first week of next month for your visit?" Dermott asked. "I've cut back on my hours, so I can be flexible. I thought you and your wife could stay here, instead of at some hotel. It's big enough, so you'll have privacy."

The gruffly issued invitation touched Cole in a way something more elegant or practiced couldn't. "We'd like that. The first week of next month is fine." He glanced at his calendar. "How about if we arrive the third?"

"Fine. We have lots to talk about, including why you're wasting yourself at that orphanage."

"It's not a waste, Grandfather. Children are our future."

"Yes, yes, I've heard the politicians talk, too. The concept has merit, but there are dozens of others who could run the place as well as you, maybe better. You're good at your job there, but you were brilliant in the law. Don't bother telling me you don't miss it, because I know you do. Oh, maybe you can go a couple of months without thinking about it, but then it hits you hard and you find yourself wishing you were back. I know, because I tried to leave the law once, too. Damn fool mistake."

"I can't be bought, old man."

His grandfather laughed. "I know. A shame, if you ask me. Buying people saves time. But we'll work it out the old-fashioned way. Man to man." There was a pause. "I'm looking forward to seeing you, Cole. I wish we'd done this years ago."

Some time during their conversation, the anger had disappeared, leaving behind only regret. "Me, too."

"Well, then." Dermott cleared his throat. "I'll call you next week some time to confirm your travel plans. Maybe we could go to the theater. I'm sure we can find something we'd all like to see. Maybe even take in a football game. You like football, don't you?"

"Yes, Grandfather. Very much."

"Good. I'll talk to you soon."

The old man hung up.

Cole set down his receiver. Conflicting emotions battled for dominance. When the fighting stopped, he was left feeling sad about all that the two of them had missed. At least it wasn't too late. At least they were going to get a second chance.

He rose to his feet and crossed to the window. Elissa stood in the center of a group of children. She'd bought a book on how to make balloon animals and was in the process of teaching them, as well as herself. Even with the window closed he could hear their laughter.

The sound beckoned him and he left his office. As he came around the side of the building, Elissa saw him. She smiled broadly, then the smile faded.

He hated that. Ever since she'd told him they should let the children know they were married and he'd refused, they'd been cautious around each other. No, he told himself, knowing it was useless to lie. It wasn't that he'd refused to tell the children, it was that he'd admitted he wasn't willing to trust her to stay.

That hadn't changed. He'd expected her to be gone that day. Every day since had had him wondering if today would be the day she left. Yet she continued to stay—and to share his bed. Alone at night, naked in each other's arms, only then did her eyes darken with something other than hurt. He loved her over and over again, hoping the passion between them would be enough to keep her with him. His grandfather had talked about not expecting a miracle, yet Cole prayed for one daily. He prayed that Elissa would stay; he prayed for the courage to believe in her. He knew his prayers would go unanswered.

"What's going on?" she asked as she met him on the lawn. She'd left the balloons and the instruction book with the kids.

Cole shoved his hands into his pockets to keep from touching her. She wore a simple dress, minimal makeup and her hair loose around her shoulders. Autumn was well on its way, yet just looking at her, he believed they could hold on to summer forever.

"My grandfather called me."

"Oh, Cole, you must be thrilled." She clapped her hands together. "Tell me everything. How was it?"

He recounted the telephone conversation.

"Was he what you expected?" she asked.

"Sort of. A little gruff, very opinionated and used to getting his way."

"An older version of you?" She arched her eyebrows.

He smiled. "Maybe. In about forty years. Despite everything, I liked him. I tried to stay mad, but I couldn't."

She briefly touched his upper arm. "I'm so glad. This is great. So, are you going to see him?"

His gut clenched. "I thought we'd agreed to go to New York together. Have you changed your mind?"

Her expression tightened. "No, but I assumed you had. If you don't trust me to stick around and be part of your future, how can you trust me with your family?"

"It's not like that, Elissa."

"Then what is it like?" she asked. "Explain this to me. You can love me with your body, but not with your heart? I'm here, right now. I want to be with you forever. I want to give our marriage a second chance. But I can't do it alone. You have to meet me halfway."

Familiar frustration filled him. "You think I don't want

that?'' He glanced over her head and saw the kids watching them. Taking her arm, he led her around the building to a bench under a tree. When she sat down, he settled next to her.

"You don't trust me," she said quietly.

He couldn't answer.

She folded her arms over her chest and looked at him. "I love you. I never stopped loving you. But that's not enough, is it?"

He hadn't thought he would hear the words again and didn't know how he'd thirsted for them until they eased the need inside. She loved him. She still loved him.

Yet she'd left him.

"Your silence speaks volumes," she said sadly. "I'm beginning to think I've set myself up with an impossible task. For the rest of our lives you're going to be waiting for me to walk out the door. All I can do is be here and hope that one day you'll trust me. It's not a fun way to live, Cole. We could be so happy together, if only you would believe in me again."

"I want to," he said, his voice hoarse with emotion. "Dear God, if you only knew how much. But you don't know what it was like when you were gone." The empty apartment, the gaping hole in his chest, the nightmare that became his life.

"You're right," she said. "I don't know what it was like. You don't know what it was like being ignored and overlooked. You don't know what it was like waiting for you to come home, only to get a phone call saying you were working late. You don't know what it was like when you forgot to call." She grimaced. "I'm not saying what I felt compares with what you went through, but we both had pain."

She ducked her head. "You don't know what it was like

to leave, to go back to Los Angeles and wait. You don't know what it was like to realize my husband didn't care about me enough to come after me."

"What the hell are you talking about? If you'd loved me, you wouldn't have left me."

"Maybe," she said, raising her chin and meeting his gaze. "I'm not saying I'm proud of what I did. I was young. I wanted to get your attention. I thought if you loved me, you would come after me."

"You left me," he repeated.

"Yes, and you let me go."

They sat less than a foot apart on that bench, yet he felt the distance stretch until there was a chasm between them that neither could cross.

"I want so much for us," she said. "I want us to be happy together, to enjoy life. I love you. I want to be with you forever. How long are you going to punish me for your parents daring to die and leave you alone, for your grandfather acting so inconsiderately, for my own young and foolish behavior? It's taken you twenty years to forgive your grandfather. Do I have to wait that long, too?"

"I don't know."

She shook her head. "There aren't any words, are there? There's nothing I can say to convince you?"

She loved him. That should be enough, but it wasn't. He wouldn't trust her again. He wouldn't take the risk. This time her leaving would destroy him.

"Cole?" she asked, her voice thick with tears.

"No," he said simply. "There's nothing you can say."

The door to his office banged open. Millie swept into the room, then slammed the door shut behind her.

"You're angry," he said, noting the color in her cheeks and the way her eyes flashed at him.

"And they say men aren't perceptive," she said sarcastically. "Although in your case, it happens to be true."

"We aren't going to discuss my personal life."

She stalked to the chair in front of his desk and sank down. "Yes, we are. Not as employer and employee, but as friends. Or aren't you willing to admit we're friends?"

He leaned back in his chair. "You've been more like family than just a friend."

"Good. Think of me as your mother. I might not be able to turn you over my knee and spank you, but I can still box your ears. I just might do that, if you push me too far."

"You're not going to say anything I haven't already said to myself."

"Fine. You can listen to it again and maybe this time you'll be willing to hear." She crossed her legs as if settling in for the long haul. "What are you doing? Why are you acting like such a fool?"

He didn't pretend to misunderstand. Every day Elissa slipped further and further away from him. It was like watching a tree die leaf by leaf. He could mourn the process, but he couldn't stop it.

"She's going to leave anyway," he said. "We might as well get it over with."

She raised her hands in the air. "Lord, save us from male logic." She focused her gaze on him. "Explain that to me. You love this woman, you want her in your life, yet with every action, you push her away."

"It's not that simple. I haven't been pushing her away."

"You haven't been talking to her. You go out of your way to ignore her."

His silence was tacit agreement. What Millie didn't know was that each night he stole into Elissa's room. He half expected her to reject him, but she never did. Silently she opened her arms and welcomed him with her body and her heart. She never let him leave without telling him she loved him. He never stopped believing it was only temporary.

"I've had it with you," Millie said, glaring at him. "Here's the deal. You've hidden away long enough. You needed time to lick your wounds and that's what the orphanage has provided. You're healed by now and if you're not, you need to get over it. Get back in the real world, Cole. Go home, where you belong."

He hated the fact that she echoed his grandfather's words. That he didn't belong in the orphanage. "You don't know what you're talking about. This is my world."

"No, it's not. It's a resting place. You've done a great job and we all appreciate that. Now go back to your practice full-time."

"What about the orphanage?"

"There will be other directors. We'll find the right one. Someone who sees this as his or her life's work. Not a refuge. Take your wife and go."

The idea was appealing. He would have sold his soul to make it all come true. "It's not that simple."

"Because you want to make it complicated," Millie said. "Listen to me. You're acting like a child. Grow up. Take responsibility for your actions and your relationships. If you let Elissa out of your life this time, you're never going to get her back. Worse, you're never going to get over her. You've been given a second chance. Don't blow it."

She stood, walked around the desk and leaned over to kiss his cheek. "You're a wonderful man, Cole. You deserve to be happy. Don't let fear and male pride stand in the way of that."

Elissa slowly replaced the receiver. She'd lived through several earthquakes and was familiar with the sensation of having the ground shift beneath her feet. But no six-pointer had prepared her for this.

Tears flowed down her cheeks. She couldn't wipe them away fast enough. An ache grew in her chest until it was hard to breathe. It wasn't fair. What had he done to deserve this?

It took a couple of minutes to bring her tears under control. When she thought she could talk without breaking down, she went in search of Cole. She had to be the one to tell him.

She glanced at her watch. It was close to twelve-thirty. He was probably still in the dining room. She made her way there and found him in conversation with a couple of the college staff members. She hovered by the side door.

When Cole looked up and saw her, he quickly excused himself and walked to her side.

"What's wrong?" he asked, taking her hands in his. "You've had some bad news. I can see it on your face. What is it?"

She squeezed his fingers tightly, wishing there was something she could say. But the past few weeks had taught her words were an inadequate way to express her feelings.

"I'm sorry," she said, feeling the tears well up again. She blinked them back. "So very sorry. I wish there was something I could do." She sucked in a breath. "There was a phone call from your grandfather's attorney. Dermott had a heart attack and died this morning. It was very quick. He didn't suffer."

"No." He jerked away from her and turned to the window. His body tensed with emotion. "Dammit, no. He's not dead. Not yet. We were going to meet each other. We were going to get a second chance."

"I'm sorry," she murmured, moving behind him and

wrapping her arms around his waist. He was stiff, as if holding himself apart from the pain.

"Don't be," he said, pulling away and heading for the door. "It doesn't matter. Nothing matters anymore. Nothing ever did."

He disappeared outside. She gave in to the tears then, letting them fall unchecked. The world around her blurred, but that didn't matter. As Cole had said, nothing mattered. Foolishly she'd thought he would need her to help him get through his pain. She thought she could be there for him. But he didn't need her. Not her love, her friendship, not even her money.

He hadn't stuck around to hear the rest of what the attorney had to say. Cole was the sole heir to his grandfather's considerable fortune. At one time, she'd thought she could make a difference at the orphanage. What a joke. Now he would earn more in interest in a couple of months than the amount of money she had in her entire trust fund.

He didn't need anything from her, except maybe sex. No doubt there were dozens of women eager to have him in their bed, so even the sex was replaceable.

All she'd ever wanted to do was love him. But loving him had never been enough.

Chapter Sixteen

Cole stood in his office, not knowing what to do. His flight to New York didn't leave until the morning. He could pack in about ten minutes, so there was no need to start that now. An odd restlessness took hold of him, making him pace to his desk, then to the window. Once there, he stared out at the grounds.

It was late afternoon and most of the children were outside playing. He could see their smiles, hear their laughter. The happy sound did little to ease his hurt or his anger.

Why had his grandfather died before they could meet? What kind of trick was it to get him to believe, only to rip it all away again? His chest ached with a painful hollowness. To have been so close.

If only he'd answered the letter sooner. If only he'd flown to New York right away. If only he'd known how much he was going to miss an old man he'd never even met.

An old man who'd left him a financial empire.

The attorney had made that clear. Except for a few bequests left to charities, everything belonged to Cole. The empire required a leader, someone who could guide it and help it grow. If Cole wanted, the attorney could recommend several financial planners, although Dermott had hoped Cole would run it himself.

The money was the least of it, Cole had told the attorney. Right now he couldn't think about that. Yet as he watched the children, he realized he now had the resources to do everything he wanted. Paint, get a new roof, hire more staff, maybe build a few more dorms and take in more children.

He turned from the window. He would think about that later. Right now he needed...something.

He tried to shake off the restless feeling, but couldn't. What was wrong with him? He'd felt sadness before; he should be used to it.

He began to pace, then knew he needed more. He needed Elissa.

Without stopping to think about how they'd parted not three hours before, he headed for her room. The hallway door was partially open. He tapped as he entered, but there was no response. He heard movement in the bedroom and crossed the floor.

As he paused in the doorway, he started to speak. But before he could say anything, his gaze fell on the suitcase lying open on her bed.

Coming on the heels of the tragic news of his grandfather's death, this new revelation cut through him like a finely honed steel blade. He prepared himself for the liquid warmth of blood pouring out of his chest and gut. Most of his brain shut down with shock, but the small part functioning formed a violent protest.

No! Dear God, she couldn't be leaving him. Not now.

Not yet. He wasn't ready for her to abandon him. He couldn't deal with it, wouldn't survive. He needed time. He needed her.

He tried to back out of the room, but his body refused to cooperate. Instead of walking away, he found himself trapped, waiting for her to turn and see him there.

It didn't take long. She opened a dresser drawer and removed a nightgown. On her return trip to the suitcase, she spotted him. Her sad expression didn't change, nor did she stop what she was doing. She placed the nightgown on top of the other clothes, then straightened.

"How are you doing?"

He stared at her, unable to answer the question. How dare she even ask? How did she think he was doing?

"Cole?" She approached him. "You look awful. I know you're upset about your grandfather, but are you feeling all right, physically? Is something else wrong?"

His body went numb. Was he even breathing? Did it matter? Without Elissa he had no world, no life.

Her green eyes clouded with confusion, then her mouth opened. "Oh, no." She took a step back, shuddering as if she'd just seen the devil himself. "No."

She returned to the suitcase and pushed the nightgown onto the bed, then drew out a dark garment. She held it up. "Do you see this? Damn you, Cole, do you see? It's a black dress. My *only* black dress. I wasn't leaving you, I was packing for New York. I thought…"

Her voice trailed off. She turned away, but not before he saw tears trickle down her cheek.

As he registered the fact, her words sank in. Not leaving? Going with him to New York?

"Elissa?"

She crushed the dress in her hands. "Oh, what's the point? You'll never believe me, never trust me. I'm a fool to try again. I should have learned it all the first time. You're just waiting for me to go, aren't you? Why didn't I see that before? You're not interested in a second chance, not really.''

She wore her hair loose, and she pushed a few wayward curls off her face. Her mouth quivered, then straightened. She tossed the dress back into the suitcase and swept the nightgown in after it.

"Fine," she said, her voice thick with tears. "You win. I'll go away. You won't have to worry about me again.''

He watched as she ran to the dresser and began pulling things out, then stuffing them into her suitcase. Her actions were frantic.

He couldn't believe what was happening. The scene was surreal and he found himself unable to speak or even to think clearly. He knew there was something he had to tell her, some important words that would make her understand. But the agony stole them, leaving him empty and gasping, simply trying to hold on.

She was leaving and there was nothing he could do to make her stay.

He clenched his hands in a feeble effort to fight off the waves of pain. The darkness in his soul expanded until he knew the blackness would swallow him whole. It would be a waking kind of death. Alive, yet not alive. Here, but always wanting to be somewhere else—always wanting to be with her.

Didn't she know he needed her more than his next breath?

Elissa bit her lower lip. "It's sort of humiliating to admit it, but I thought you might need me this time.''

"I do," he said, managing to speak past the tightness in his throat.

"For what?" she asked. "I was the one sending the gifts.

I paid for the jungle gym and the science camp. Oh, and the new stove and freezer. There was a trust fund set up with our earnings from the TV show. I didn't tell you when we were first married because I thought you would think less of me.'' She gave a harsh laugh. ''As if that were possible. Anyway, the money was released on our twenty-fifth birthday. That's when I decided to come here. I thought if I helped out at the orphanage, you might like me better. Silly, huh?''

''No,'' he whispered. ''Not at all.''

''I wasn't trying to trick you. I would have told you the truth eventually. I think I secretly wanted you to find out on your own and then to admire me. Like I said, pretty dumb.''

He leaned against the door frame and crossed his arms over his chest. It was that or go to her, and he couldn't allow himself that comfort. ''I knew,'' he said. ''I found out a few weeks ago.''

She looked surprised. ''You never said anything. Weren't you angry?''

''No. I thought it was nice.''

She nodded. ''Nice. Good, but not good enough, right?''

That wasn't what he'd meant. Why couldn't he find the right words? It just hurt so badly. How could she leave him? Hadn't she promised to love him forever?

What had he done wrong?

''Now you can do everything you want with the orphanage. When I talked to the lawyer, he mentioned your inheritance. Congratulations. You can fix up this place, and then go live in New York. You're great with the kids, Cole, but your heart is in the city. You'll be happier back there. It's your world.''

His world was with her. Why hadn't he seen that before?

She turned and walked into the small bathroom. A few

minutes later she came out carrying two zip-up makeup bags. She placed them in the suitcase, then glanced around the room. There was nothing of hers left. She closed the case and locked it, then brushed away the last of her tears.

The hell of it was, the right thing was to let her go. She would be happier without him. He'd always known that.

She crossed to him and stared at him. A tremor rippled through her. "I will always love you, Cole. No matter what." She swallowed. "When I get back to L.A. I'm going to find an attorney. I want a divorce. That way you never have to worry about seeing me again."

Tears returned to her green eyes. She swiped at them with the back of her hand. "I wish you the best. Try to be happy." Then she took her suitcase and left.

He stood alone in the silence of the room. He couldn't think, he couldn't feel, he could only breathe in and out and wait for the darkness to overtake him.

Later, when the sound of her car had faded and the first tendrils of hopelessness began to wrap around his soul, he found the right words.

"I love you, Elissa," he said aloud. "Please don't leave me."

But it was too late; she was already gone.

Elissa picked up the phone and dialed the familiar number. After two rings, her sister picked up. "Hello?"

"Hi, Fallon, it's me."

"Oh, no. You're crying. What's wrong?"

Elissa smiled, despite the ache in her heart. "Here I've sipped hot tea, splashed my face with water and tried to think happy thoughts, all before calling you. How can you know I've been crying?"

"Because I know and love you. What's going on?"

Elissa hunched deeper into the corner of her sofa. The

apartment that had been her home for nearly three years was now cold and unfamiliar. She couldn't sleep, couldn't find a comfortable position. It was as if the very fabric of her world had been ripped apart and she was left dangling in the wind.

"I'm back in Los Angeles," she said.

"What?"

Elissa quickly filled her in, sparing no details, including Cole's determination to believe that she would leave him.

"I love him," Elissa said as the tears began again. "But it's hopeless. He'll never trust me. There I was, packing to go with him to New York and he assumed I was walking out on him. What kind of hideous person does that make me? Bad enough that he thinks I would leave, but on the day he hears about his grandfather? He must think I'm sub-human. N-now—" Her voice cracked. "Now he's got that inheritance and he doesn't even need my money." She sniffed. "Hold on. I have to get a tissue."

As she set the phone down and crossed to the box on the kitchen table, she had the oddest sense of déjà vu. As if this scene had played itself out before.

She realized it had. When she'd left Cole five years ago. History repeating itself. When would she be free of that trap?

"Did you really think Cole would ever be interested in you for your money?" Fallon asked when Elissa said she was back.

"No, but I thought it might help."

"That's crazy. Cole wouldn't care. If anything, it would annoy him."

"I know. That's why I didn't tell him before. But when I told him yesterday, he said he already knew and it didn't matter. He said my giving stuff to the orphanage was n-nice." Her voice cracked as new tears rushed down her cheeks. "Men in love don't say words like nice. He doesn't love me. I don't think he ever did. It's hopeless."

"Hush. You're going to be fine." Fallon made soothing noises.

"Now I have to figure out what to do with my life. I'm so confused."

"I know. It's okay."

Elissa sniffed. Something wasn't right. Fallon always had something to say about everything.

"What are you thinking?" Elissa asked.

"That's not important. Right now you need to focus on getting through one day at a time. You don't have to make a decision about your future right now."

Elissa frowned. "Fallon, I really want to know what you think about the situation. I value your opinion and your advice."

"You sure?"

Something in Fallon's tone told Elissa she was going to regret it, but she said, "Yes," anyway.

There was a pause on the line, then a rapid burst of conversation.

"Grow up," Fallon said. "There you are crying in your apartment because Cole is in New York at his grandfather's funeral. Poor little Elissa. Cole doesn't trust you. Cole doesn't love you. Why should he? Look at yourself. You're upset, claiming he's not in your life, but *you're the one who left.*" She spoke slowly, emphasizing the last five words.

"This is what you always do," she continued. "You have this bizarre notion that the only way you matter is by acting in a certain way or performing a task. When we were growing up you always had to be the perfect one. For a long time I thought you did it to show Kayla and me up.

But that wasn't it at all. You did it because you thought if you didn't, our parents wouldn't love you."

Fallon drew in a breath. "Honey, we all love you for *you*. Nothing else. It's not what you say or what you do. It's who you are. I'm not saying you can get over this in a few minutes, but I think if you're aware of it you'll deal with it more easily."

Elissa was glad she was sitting down. Fallon's assessment of her character had her reeling, maybe because it was so accurate. Still, it was humiliating to have her most private flaws discussed publicly. "But I—"

"Not yet," Fallon said. "I'm not finished. Cole invited you to meet his grandfather, he came to you after he'd recovered from the shock of hearing the man had died. He probably wanted you to go with him to the funeral, but when he saw you packing, he jumped to conclusions. After the past you two shared, do you blame him? If he doesn't trust you, he's obviously a very smart man. Instead of standing your ground and insisting you go with him to New York, you left. By walking out, you just proved him right. About everything, little sister."

Elissa sat feeling stunned. Her tears had stopped and her mouth was hanging open. She closed it, then asked, "Are you done now?"

"No, but I'll let you talk."

"I'm not sure where to start defending myself."

"Don't bother. You were a hundred percent in the wrong."

It was as if her words clicked on a light in her brain. Elissa sat up straight and gasped. "Oh, no," she whispered.

Images from her time at the orphanage flashed through her mind. Memories from the past, incidents, conversations.

"I did it again," she said, wondering why she hadn't figured it out for herself. "I left him yesterday just like I did five years ago. I wanted him to prove he cared by making me stay. I wanted him to make me feel special and important.''

"Doesn't he do that anyway?" Fallon asked.

"All the time." Elissa clutched the receiver more tightly. "Every moment he's with me I know I'm so lucky. All his touches, all his actions. He cares about me. If it's not love, it's very close. If I'd stayed..."

She dropped her head to her knees. "What have I done?"

"You've made a mistake. It's done some damage, but it's not fatal."

"I told him I wanted a divorce."

"That was so stupid, Elissa," Fallon snapped, then sighed. "Sorry. I know you need me to be supportive. I lost it for a second. Go to him and tell him you realize you were acting like a child, trying to get his attention. He deserves the honesty, if nothing else."

"What if he won't give me another chance?"

"Beg. Camp out on his doorstep if you have to. Move back into the orphanage and campaign to win him back. Send a notarized letter promising you'll never leave again, no matter what. Prove to him you've learned your lesson."

"Thanks, Fallon. I appreciate the advice."

"No problem. Call me if you need anything else, or just to talk."

"I will. I've got to do some thinking now, so I'm going to go."

They said their goodbyes and hung up.

Elissa covered her face with her hands. She'd been a fool. In her childish quest for attention, she'd thrown everything away. Risked it all. And for what?

Would Cole be willing to give her another chance? If she were in his position, would she trust herself? She didn't think so. Still, she had to try. Somehow, she would figure out a way to convince him.

Cole waited for the elevator doors to open, then stepped out into the thickly carpeted hotel corridor. The funeral was over, as was the reading of the will. He had another appointment with the attorney tomorrow, to go over the details. Right now he was too tired to think. All he wanted to do was fall into his bed and sleep.

Yet lately sleep wouldn't come. As soon as he shut out the lights, all he would do was remember Elissa and miss her. He figured the wound would stop bleeding in time. Maybe in a hundred years or so. Maybe when he was dead.

In addition to all his financial wealth, his grandfather had left him a great apartment. The penthouse, of course. Maybe he would consider staying in New York. There was plenty of work to do. If he could keep busy enough, he might trick himself into forgetting.

Or he could do the smart thing and go after her. The long flight had given him time to think. Elissa had been packing to come with him; *she'd* been willing to stand by him. His assumption that she was leaving—more proof that he refused to trust her—had driven her away. If he was alone now, he could only blame himself.

He had to find a way to get her back. She had loved him once; surely he could convince her to love him again. At one time he wouldn't have taken the chance or risked trusting her. His grandfather's death had taught him differently. Time was precious. He and his wife had been given a second chance, unless they were both stubborn enough and foolish enough to throw it away.

He was determined to prevent that from happening again. They'd already lost so many years, because he wasn't willing to put it all on the line. Funny how he could risk everything for a deal, but in matters of the heart he played it safe. Caution had nearly cost him the person who mattered most.

As he reached his door, he heard someone call his name. He glanced up. The floor concierge walked toward him.

"Mr. Stephenson, I need to speak to you for a moment. I've done something and if it's wrong, I need to correct it right away." The man was in his late twenties, well dressed in a tailored suit and expensive shoes. His hands twisted together nervously.

"What's the problem?" Cole asked.

"Your wife is here. She asked me to let her into your room, and I did. As I said, if that's a problem, I'll be happy to remove her."

Elissa? Here?

He fumbled with the key and realized his hands were shaking. "You did fine," he said, jamming in the plastic key. At last the green light flashed and there was a click as the mechanism unlocked. "Just fine."

"Thank you, sir. If there's anything—"

Cole stepped inside and closed the door, cutting off the other man's words.

He'd left in the afternoon and now it was after 8:00 p.m., so he would have expected the suite his grandfather's attorney had reserved for him to be in darkness. Instead, soft light glowed from the sitting room and spilled onto the carpet from the bedroom beyond.

He saw proof of Elissa's presence. Her purse on the table by the door. A pair of pumps next to the sofa. A bottle of his favorite white wine chilling on ice. Relief so sweet he could taste it swept through him. He didn't care why she'd come back. If there were conditions, he would meet all of them. He loved her and he never wanted to lose her again.

He sensed movement and turned toward the balcony

Curtains fluttered in front of open doors that beckoned him. He walked across the floor and stepped out into the moonlit darkness.

She stood at the railing, facing the park. Instead of one of her usual summer dresses, she wore a tailored black suit. The style flattered her figure, drawing attention to her slim waist and long legs. She'd piled her hair on top of her head, leaving her neck bare. His arms ached to hold her; his mouth wanted to touch the delicate skin at her nape.

She stiffened slightly as if she'd sensed his presence. Slowly she turned toward him. Without saying anything, she crossed to him and hugged him close.

For that moment, as she offered and he accepted comfort, there was no need for words. They communicated with touch, her body telling him of her sorrow on his behalf and of her willingness to be what he needed. At least for now.

"Are you all right?" she asked.

"I'm not sure. Numb."

"I'm so sorry about your grandfather," she said. "I wish you could have met him."

"Me, too. We talked on the phone, but I wanted more. I wanted to meet him and look him in the eye."

The heat of her body reminded him of their last parting. "Elissa, I—"

"No." She cut him off with a shake of her head. "I'm sorry, but I have to go first. There's a lot I have to tell you and I don't want to forget it."

She disentangled herself and returned to the balcony railing. "I don't remember the city being this pretty," she said.

"That's because the view from our apartment wasn't this nice."

"Maybe. I prefer to think it's because I've changed." She shrugged. "Not that I expect you to believe that. After the way I behaved a couple of days ago, I don't deserve anything from you. All my promises of love and commitment. All the times I said I wasn't leaving and at the first test, I bolt. Some lessons are hard to learn.''

"You don't have to tell me this."

"Yes, I do. When we were first married, I was terrified of you. Not that you would hurt me in any way, but that you would be disappointed by me."

"But I loved you."

"I know that now, but then I wasn't so sure. I never had much confidence. As the middle of my sisters, I was always the peacemaker. I had a role. I believed that I had value because of what I did or what I could give. That never really changed. When I married you, there didn't seem to be anything I could give you. You were always working late, so I couldn't cook. The sex was a problem, so I wasn't offering much there. In the end, rather than face my own shortcomings, it was easier to believe you didn't care about me. So I left, fully expecting you to come after me. But you didn't."

"I thought you didn't love me anymore. I wasn't going to force you to stay with me."

"I know that now. At the time all I could see was another rejection. I lived with that for years, until the inheritance gave me the false confidence to try again. This time I was going to be Lady Bountiful, giving to all in need."

He thought of all she'd given. Not in money, but in time and caring. "The children adore you."

"And I love them. But it's not about the money or gifts, is it? They don't know it was me and they still care. I think that's when I started to get it. That's when I started to realize that I had value on my own. But I was still afraid."

She turned toward him. The light from the hotel room spilled onto the balcony, illuminating her features. Her smile was sad. "I think I would have been able to hang in there if you hadn't inherited all that money. Once you had that, I realized you didn't need me. Again. The past overwhelmed me and I ran, as I had before.''

He crossed to her and took her hands. "This time I was coming after you."

She squeezed his fingers. "I'm glad it didn't come to that. I finally get it, Cole. It's not about the money or who comes after whom. It's about loving myself enough to believe someone else would bother. I'm not sure I'm a hundred percent on that, but I'm working on the problem.''

She drew in a deep breath and raised her gaze to him. "I know you have no reason to believe me, but I'm going to say it again. I love you with all my heart. I swear, I'm never going to leave you, no matter how many inheritances you have, or how much money, or where you have to live. If necessary, I'll camp on your doorstep, I'll hide in the back seat of your car. Maybe I'll even get a job at your office and be in the way all the time.''

His heart flared hot enough to burn away the darkness in his soul. Light poured in. Light and love.

He drew her to him and touched her cheek. "That won't be necessary.''

"I'm almost afraid to ask, but why?''

He smiled. "Because I love you and I want to be with you for the rest of both our lives. I want to grow old with you. I want to have children and watch them grow. I want to build a home next to the orphanage and divide our time between Ojai and New York. I want you. It was wrong of me to assume you were leaving, and I apologize. Please forgive me and stay with me as my lover, my wife, my other half.''

Wonder filled her green eyes. "I don't understand. You love me?''

"Yes.''

"You believe that I love you?"

He laughed. "Yes. Why is this so hard to understand?"

"It just is. Does this mean..." She paused. "Do you trust me?" she whispered.

"With my heart and soul." He bent his head and kissed her.

Their lips clung together in a moment so perfect it defied description.

When they separated, he held her close. "I don't promise not to get weird from time to time," he said. "Old habits are hard to break."

"I'll just slap you until you snap out of it."

"That'll work." He cupped her face. "Are you sure?"

"More than anything."

"Then I have something for you." He hesitated, suddenly embarrassed by the gesture. Maybe it had been a mistake.

"What?"

He reached into his trouser pocket and pulled out the plain gold band he'd slipped on her finger when they'd first been married. "Five years ago you left this behind," he said. "I've kept it, hoping one day you'd want it back."

"Oh, Cole." She took the ring and put it on. "Thank you for saving it. And for believing in me, and for loving me and just everything."

They kissed again. He was content. Whatever the future might hold, both Elissa and the eternal symbol of their love were back where they belonged.

* * * * *

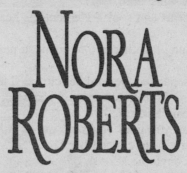

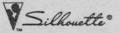